LUNA
STRONGHOLD

BOOK TWO OF THE SYNAXIS CHRONICLES

An Epic Science Fiction Thriller by

Robert David MacNeil

DEDICATION

This book is dedicated to my amazing wife Linda, for her patience and continual encouragement, and for believing this book should be written.

To my friends and family who read the draft version and offered so many great suggestions.

To Lisa and Susan who painstakingly edited the manuscript, correcting my many errors.

And also to Keith, whose gift of "second sight" prompted the writing of this book.

Published by Robert David MacNeil

ISBN-13: 978-1518805431
ISBN-10: 1518805434

Visit me on the web at ionaportal.com
Email me at RobertDavidMacNeil@Gmail.com
Or follow me on Twitter at @RDavidMacNeil

TABLE OF CONTENTS

SECTION FOUR: DESCENT INTO HELL

EPILOGUE

NOTES

ABOUT THE AUTHOR

"There is no question that there is an unseen world. The problem is, how far is it from Midtown and how late is it open?" – Woody Allen (*Without Feathers,* p. 11.)

"There are more things in heaven and earth, Horatio, than are dreamt of in your philosophy." – William Shakespeare (*"Hamlet"*, Act 1 scene 5)

* * *

With a few minor exceptions, all geographical descriptions in this book are accurate. The only major departure from geographical accuracy in this book is the description of Oban and the Isles Airport, which in real life has a runway 600 feet short of the landing requirement for a Gulfstream G280.

All historical references in this book are accurate.

All present-day characters in this book are fictional, and are not intended to represent any persons, living or dead.

The SYNAXIS, of course, is real.

MAIN CHARACTERS

Lys Johnston – Lys (rhymes with bliss) has the ability to open portals to other worlds. Her gift has already saved the human race once, but her hardest task still lies ahead.

Patrick O'Neil – A member of the Iona Synaxis. Just when his shattered life was finally coming together, the woman he loves volunteers for a suicide mission to hell.

Roger Johnston – Lys Johnston's brother. Roger is a medical doctor and can't believe the wild stories Lys told him about an alien race called the Irin. Then he meets one.

Alexander Carrington – A wealthy survivalist who plots with the Archons to destroy the human race.

Grat Dalton – A psychopath employed by Carrington.

Jamie Fletcher – The executive assistant to Alexander Carrington. Jamie has an IQ of 185 and a photographic memory, but those gifts may cost Jamie her life.

Michael and Erin Fletcher – Michael is an angelologist. Erin heads up the Iona synaxis.

Derek and Piper Holmes – Founders of the first synaxis, they now travel the world planting new ones in an attempt to thwart the Archon invasion.

Eliel (An *Irin* warrior) – Eliel appears to be an attractive 21 year-old woman, but she's visited our world for thousands of years and walked the streets of ancient Babylon and Rome.

Kareina (An *Archon* Commander) – Kareina has been sent to the Earth-realm to prepare the way for the Archon invasion.

Hewett (the Toad) – The head slave of Abadon

PROLOGUE

The New Mexico Facility

THE FOUR CORNERS REGION
OF NEW MEXICO

The old Chevy truck shuddered and jounced along the dusty washboard-rutted track illuminated only by the feeble light of its dirt-shrouded headlamps. Weary from the long day, the driver clenched the wheel firmly, staring numbly at the road ahead.

For Ignacio Vincente Cortez, the day had begun before dawn at an abandoned farmstead in the desert northeast of El Paso. He'd arrived at the designated time to find a 1953 Chevy two-ton farm truck parked in a tumble-down barn behind a faded and weather-beaten mobile home. It was fueled, with keys in the ignition.

Entering the barn, Ignacio walked to the rear of the battered truck and glanced at its cargo. The old truck's high wooden-box sides were straining under a load of over-ripe cow manure, already buzzing with flies.

"*Mierda*," he muttered in disgust. "Another manure truck!" Batting the swarm of flies from his face, he shook his head and quickly climbed into the cab. Someone less experienced might have questioned why

1

anyone would pay good money to transport a load of bovine excrement more than four hundred miles through the hot New Mexico desert, but Ignacio knew better than to ask questions. He drove for these people regularly and had no doubt that the truck's odiferous cargo concealed something far more valuable than manure.

For most of his adult life, Ignacio had supported his family through back-breaking menial labor and odd jobs. But five years ago, a wealthy client he'd done work for on several occasions approached him with an offer to do some "driving." For each delivery he made, he'd earn more money than he could get for a month of manual labor. It meant being away from home a lot, but with an ill-tempered, corpulent wife and four screaming kids to feed, he'd accepted the job without question.

Ignacio had been selected because of his reputation for reliability, but also for his ability to appear nonthreatening. A middle-aged Hispanic male with oily black hair, he was heavy-jowled with an unshaven face, a beer belly, and a smell that rivaled the manure now drawing flies in the back of the truck. Few would have chosen to give him a second look, and fewer still would have suspected him to be a courier for a major Mexican drug cartel.

Driving for the cartel was the easiest money he'd ever made, and a manure truck, unpleasant as it was, meant a valuable cargo. Nobody ever searched a manure truck. He might even get a bonus.

While the drives were long and boring, the

payments had always been good. But Ignacio would have refused the job this time had he known what was hidden beneath the manure, and the horrific death his cargo could bring to millions of people.

Following carefully rehearsed instructions, Ignacio rolled through El Paso just as the sun was rising. Staying well below the speed limit, he followed I-25 to Albuquerque, then continued north on Route 44 to Farmington, located in New Mexico's northwestern corner. At the outskirts of Farmington, Ignacio pulled off at a roadside café and wolfed down six greasy tacos and a bottle of *Dos Equis Ambar.*

Continuing through Farmington, he turned north on State Route 170, snaking through a sandy forest of piñon pines and juniper trees. As the aging truck lumbered into high desert, the scrub forest gave way to a sun-baked expanse of bare rock, sagebrush, and dusty sand as fine as talcum.

North of the town of La Plata, Ignacio slowed and turned left onto an abandoned oilfield access road. Passing through a maze of abandoned roads and capped wellheads, the hard pack gravel gave way to rutted sand.

Through the long afternoon, the truck followed the track westward, its big tires thudding over rocks and through gullies, winding along sandstone ledges and around steep canyons.

This was Four Corners country—the only place in America where four states meet, and one of the wildest, most inaccessible regions in the nation.

Wispy clouds scudded across a deep cobalt sky. Toward evening, the winds increased, whipping up dust devils that slid spectrally across the horizon to the south.

After a westward trek of more than thirty miles, Ignacio angled north into the mouth of a broad canyon where the road ran along an arroyo shut in between towering red mesa walls.

As darkness descended, prairie dogs and ring-tailed cats flitted occasionally across the road ahead.

Glancing at the odometer, Ignacio took a deep breath. After 436 miles, his journey was nearly complete.

The sun had already set as the old truck pulled up to a chain-link fence topped by a double coil of razor wire. The fence stretched entirely across the canyon, broken by a single gate. In the dimly lit gatehouse, two guards clad in black coveralls stood alertly, watching his approach.

He'd been expected.

An efficient guard examined his papers and quizzed him for five minutes before opening the gate and waving him through.

Ahead, the canyon narrowed abruptly and angled to the left, then widened into a steep-walled valley. Less than twenty-five miles to the northwest, the ancient Anasazi peoples had once built cliff dwellings into the walls of a similar canyon. Here, however, no structures were visible, yet the place was clearly not uninhabited. Five helipads were spaced around the valley floor. Two were occupied by luxurious American Eurocopter AStars, and one by a massive 234LR Chinook transport. A maze of paved roads led from the helipads to three sets of steel blast doors set into the side of the mountain.

The floor of the canyon was brilliantly lit by quartz-halogen lamps affixed to the canyon walls.

One set of steel doors was standing open, and before it, nine men stood watching the truck approach.

The men awaiting the shipment wore identical, nondescript black jumpsuits... all except their leader. The man in charge was dressed as a Texas cowboy in tight Levi denims, a plaid shirt, and well-worn alligator boots. Even before the truck pulled to a stop, the cowboy was barking instructions to his crew.

Ignacio eyed the cowboy with a sense of foreboding. The man was solidly-built with thick black hair and a face as worn and leathery as his boots. His thin, colorless lips were drawn tight in a grimace as he peered at Ignacio with the cold, emotionless eyes of a psychopath.

As Ignacio brought the truck to a halt, the men donned protective masks and went to work, using shovels and rakes to clear the manure from the truck, exposing a set of stainless steel canisters.

Ignacio stood to one side and watched with interest as the canisters were uncovered, still not suspecting the true nature of his cargo. It didn't look like a typical drug shipment. He counted twenty identical stainless steel canisters, each measuring 24 inches by 16 inches by 8 inches. The canisters rested directly on the truck's steel deck, supported by its heavily reinforced frame.

With the canisters exposed, one of the men used a high pressure hose to blast away the remains of the manure, then directed Ignacio to pull the truck away from the manure pile.

Following the man's instructions, he pulled the truck up to the waiting doorway and watched with mounting curiosity as the crew manhandled the first of the heavy canisters out of the truck and onto a waiting cart, carefully wiping it clean of any residual manure.

A balding, middle-aged Anglo in a white lab coat had emerged from the underground fortress. He wordlessly opened the canister and examined its contents, carefully "sniffing" its interior with some kind of electronic probe. After a few moments, the technician nodded to the cowboy, and allowed the crew to wheel the cart through the blast doors into the interior of the mountain. The man repeated the process with each canister until all twenty had been examined, then accompanied the last canister into the tunnel.

Ignacio would never know that the nondescript cargo he'd delivered to this remote canyon held the potential to bring hellish death to millions. For within each of the sixty-pound canisters was one modified Soviet RA-120—a miniature nuclear device developed by the Russians in the last days of the Soviet Union. Each one contained a single critical mass of plutonium with a yield of 4.5 kilotons, about one-third the explosive power of the Hiroshima bomb.

The RA-120 was part of a class of Special Atomic Demolition Munitions, known in the intelligence community as SADMs. Designed to be transported and detonated by a single individual, they'd been nicknamed "suitcase" nukes.

In the chaos following the dissolution of the Soviet Union, more than 100 of these devices remained unaccounted for. They'd been clandestinely snatched up by a far-sighted Russian oligarch and hidden away in a cavern in the Urals, knowing that at the right time they could be sold to the highest bidder.

And an American bidder had finally made him an offer he couldn't refuse. Secreted across the old Soviet border, they'd been refitted in an underground lab in Tunisia, then trekked overland to Mali where they were loaded onto an aging 727—an unmarked plane used by a Mexican drug cartel for its lucrative trans-Atlantic trade. Arriving at a remote landing strip in Central America, the cartel had easily smuggled the canisters across the Arizona border.

Ignacio watched the unloading without comment.

When the last of the canisters disappeared into the mountain, the cowboy approached him, eyeing him with disgust. Without a word, Ignacio extended a filthy clipboard. The cowboy received it, slid a pen from his pocket, and quickly scrawled his name on the receipt.

Retrieving the clipboard, Ignacio glanced at the

cowboy's signature. The letters were written erratically with a strange backward tilt, but the signature was legible enough. It read Grat Dalton. He studied the name for a moment, then turned wearily toward the truck to begin the long drive back to El Paso. Before he reached the cab, however, the cowboy called to him.

"DRIVER…" He barked. "Wait a minute!"

Ignacio turned and eyed the cowboy with trepidation. Grat flashed him a toothy grin. "Here… let me give you a little something extra for your effort."

Grat extended his left hand to reveal a thick roll of bills.

Ignacio's eyes lit up, greed instantly replacing apprehension.

"Gracias, Señor," he stammered in surprise, and turned to approach the cowboy. In his mind, Ignacio was already picturing what the extra money would buy him a few nights later in the brothels of Ciudad Juarez.

With the driver's eyes fixed on the wad of bills in his left hand, Grat slid his right hand down to unsheathe a 16-inch Bowie knife from the side of his right boot, taking care to conceal it behind his back.

The unsuspecting driver approached, extending his hand to receive his reward. But instead of placing the roll of bills in Ignacio's hand, Grat suddenly clenched the money tightly in his fist and batted Ignacio's hand away.

Like a ravenous wolf leaping on its prey, Grat lunged forward, reaching his clenched fist around the startled driver's back. He pulled him close, their faces almost touching. Ignacio frantically backpedaled, trying to pull away, but to no avail. Grat brought his right hand around, and jerked it forcefully upward, thrusting the knife into the driver's abdomen and angling it up under his ribs. In one smooth motion, the razor-sharp blade ripped through layers of flesh and fat, piercing Ignacio's diaphragm and penetrating his heart. Death was almost instantaneous.

As the driver's mouth dropped open and his uncomprehending eyes begin to glaze, Grat maintained his grip, pushing the knife still deeper—watching with sadistic pleasure as the last remnants of life drained from Ignacio's body. Finally, Grat jerked the knife free and wiped it clean on Ignacio's shirt as his lifeless form crumpled to the ground.

Turning to his assistants, Grat kicked the body roughly, "Get rid of this," he said coldly, "but keep the truck. We'll use it again."

His task completed, the cowboy flipped open an ancient, grime-encrusted cell phone and pressed a key for a pre-programmed number.

The voice at the other end answered on the second ring with a curt, "Yes."

RAVEN'S NEST, IN THE MOUNTAINS NEAR BOULDER, COLORADO

Alexander Carrington was the only surviving son of California newspaper magnate William P. Carrington.

In the years since his father's tragic death, Alexander had leveraged the family's fortune into serious money by producing some of Hollywood's bloodiest—and most successful—slasher flicks. Then, while still in his forties, he'd multiplied his millions many times over through shrewd investments in the cable TV and video-game industries.

Now in his early 50's, Carrington used his well-deserved reputation for decadence as a cover for his ultimate goal, the single-minded pursuit of raw political power.

His sprawling, high-tech mansion, Raven's Nest, was blasted deep into the side of a granite mountain, a forty-minute drive out of Boulder, Colorado.

Carrington's dark bloodshot eyes surveyed the view before him. His private office featured a wall of floor-to-ceiling armored plate glass windows, affording him a panoramic view of the Colorado Rockies, with the city of Boulder just visible in the distance. While those privileged to visit Raven's Nest often commented on the breathtaking view, few realized that a simple code tapped into the household computer would activate four-inch-thick steel blast doors that could slide into place in less than twenty seconds, transforming the lavish mansion into a fortress-like survivalist stronghold—protecting its inhabitants from the very holocaust Carrington was preparing to unleash.

His cell phone rang. Carrington picked up the latest model iPhone, flicking the slide with a smooth motion to answer it. "Yes."

"Mr. Carrington, this is Grat Dalton at the New Mexico facility. The shipment has arrived. It's been examined and secured."

"Has the driver been silenced?"

"Yes, sir."

Carrington's lips drew taut in a satisfied smile.

He glanced at the woman seated across from him. She brushed a strand of long black hair from her eyes and returned his smile. Though she appeared to be in her early twenties, the woman had been his trusted advisor from the start of his 30-year career. He attributed much of his success to her sage counsel.

"Excellent, Grat," he said curtly. "Kareina's with me now. I'll let her know the plan is coming together. You know what to do." Without waiting for a reply, he mashed the lock button to end the call.

"And now it begins." Kareina's face hardened. "Our years of preparation are about to pay off. The opening of the Iona Portal was a setback, but our plans are too well established to be thwarted. In less than three months, the Earth-realm will be ours."

SECTION ONE:
THE IONA SYNAXIS

Chapter One: Columba

THE ISLAND OF IONA, A.D. 587

Leaning heavily on his staff, the old man lurched his way up the steep slope of *Sithean Mor*—the Hill of the Angels. *I've been to the top of this hill more times than I'd care to count,* he thought. *It's strange to think that this will be my last time to climb it.*

Attaining the summit of the grass-covered mound, he raised his hands into the air, the signal for a meeting with the watchers. A few minutes later, he saw in the air overhead what at first appeared to be a great, white-winged bird soaring toward him.

With wings extended, the Irin warrior known as Araton slowed his descent and landed beside the aged saint, quickly folding his wings back into an unseen dimension.

"I'm glad to see you, my friend," the old man grinned. "I've come to tell you that I've completed my assignment. The golden plates you provided are inscribed, sealed and placed in the vault, and it is buried in exactly the place you specified." He breathed a deep sigh of relief. "My work is now complete."

"You have done well, Columba." Araton said, placing his hand on the old man's shoulder. "All these years you have done very well."

Columba looked around him, surveying the beauty of his beloved Iona. "I've lived on this island 34 years, nearly half of my life. I can scarcely remember my home back in Ireland.

"Life on Iona has been difficult at times. Our first year here we nearly starved," the old man shook his head as he remembered. "There've been attacks by the Archons, times of sickness and hardship, not to mention the bitter winter weather, but we made it through. And my diligence has been more than rewarded. The monastery is flourishing. The portal is stable, teams are being sent out, and new centers are springing up all over Scotland.

"But I'm tired, Araton. I'm ready to rest."

"And a well-deserved rest it will be," the messenger said. "The Archon plans have been thwarted. You have saved your world from terrible destruction."

They walked together back to the monastery and climbed the gentle slope to Columba's cell, a simple hut of uncut native stone with a beehive-shaped thatched roof, cradled between the massive stone slabs on *Cnoc Nan Carnan.*

Pausing at the door of his cell, Columba looked out across the monastery one last time. Columba's cell was situated on a rise of land overlooking the rest of the monastery. From this vantage point he could see it all.

The place was not what the word "monastery" would come to describe in later centuries. In Columba's day, a monastery was just a community—a cluster of thatched huts, surrounded by a stone and earthen embankment. Celtic 'monks' were allowed to marry and bear children. They tended fields, raised livestock, practiced crafts, and worshipped God. But most importantly, they wrote—copying and recopying the priceless ancient manuscripts by hand, often with lavish decoration.

Iona was a place of learning. Like most of the other monks on the island, Columba was fluent in Greek, Hebrew, Latin, and Gaelic. In the darkest of the dark ages, in a time when many of Europe's kings and priests were illiterate, the monks of Iona would purchase slaves, educate them, set them free, and send them out by twelves throughout Europe to start schools and plant new monasteries. As Thomas Cahill wrote, the Irish really did save Western civilization, and they did it, for the most part, from the little Scottish island of Iona.

In the seclusion of Columba's cell, the two talked late into the night. The flickering flame of the lone oil lamp lent the rock-walled chamber a cozy feel despite the evening chill. They talked of things to come, and what would take place in the last times.

"I'm thankful I will not live to see those days," Columba said, then after a long pause, finally added, "I feel my time has come."

"You have sensed correctly that this is your last day, Columba. You have finished your course. A great reward awaits you."

As midnight approached, Columba reclined his frail body on the six-foot stone slab that served as his bed.

Peacefully, and with great contentment, Columba of the *Uí Néills* closed his eyes and breathed his last.

It was later recorded that at midnight, an immense pillar of fire appeared over the eastern tip of Iona, illuminating the earth like the summer sun at noon, as thousands of shining *Irin* poured through the portal to honor the passing of their friend.

The Island of Iona

IONA

Mrs. Maclean's B&B

Valium

Cnoc nan Carnan

Iona Abbey

Dun I

St. Columba Hotel

Sound of Iona

Baile Mor

Fionnphort

Ferry Route

Machair Cottage

The Bay at the Back of the Ocean

Cnoc Angel

Mull

Chapter Two: Lysandra

THE ISLAND OF IONA, PRESENT DAY

Despite being in excellent physical shape, Lysandra Leigh Johnston was panting by the time she reached the top of *Dun I*, the highest point on Iona. It was a crisp, clear, spring day, and the first sunny day in more than a week. As Lys had set out for her morning walk, she'd found herself surrounded by scenes of transcendent beauty.

Winter was finally over. During the past week, the grass in the fields had transitioned from brownish stubble to luxuriant green. Clusters of multicolored wildflowers were splattered across the landscape. Baby lambs frolicked on fresh grass, framed by the rugged, heather-clad hills that rose to the north and south.

It was one of the clearest days Lys could remember on Iona, and she hadn't wanted to miss the view from *Dun I*. *Dun I*, Gaelic for "Hill of Iona," was known for its stunning panoramic views and had long been one of her favorite places on the island. Her long, ash-blonde hair feathered softly in the breeze as her steel-blue eyes scanned the horizon.

To the north, Lys could see the Isle of Staffa, famous for the volcanic caves that inspired Mendelssohn to write the "Fingal's Cave Overture." Beyond Staffa was the Isle of Skye, at least 50 miles distant. To the east was the Isle of Mull, with the new volcanic cone of Ben More towering above the landscape. In the southwest she could just make out the coast of Ireland. Lys had heard that Ireland could be seen from Iona on clear days, but this was her first time to actually see it.

At her feet, of course, lay the island of Iona, which had been her home for the past year.

From a distance, Iona appeared to be nothing more than a storm-swept sliver of land, three-miles long and one-mile wide. Located off the western coast of Scotland, the place was rocky, rugged, and almost treeless, boasting less than 130 permanent residents.

For such an unassuming little island, Iona had an incredible history. At one time, it was known all over Europe. Kings of many lands sent their sons to study on Iona, and kings from Scotland, Ireland, Norway, and even France, chose to be buried here because they believed it was close to heaven.

Iona was what the Celts called "a thin place," where the seen and unseen realms almost touch. Years earlier, a well-known writer said that the veil separating our world from the invisible dimension seemed as thin as tissue paper on Iona.

Lys smiled. That quote was no longer accurate. With the opening of the Iona Portal, the tissue paper had been torn in two. On Iona, two parallel dimensions were now connected. The *Irin*, a benevolent alien race from the parallel world of Basilea, now interacted freely with humans, and the whole atmosphere of the island had changed. Stepping off the ferry onto Iona now was like stepping into another world. The sense of peace and well-being was so tangible; Lys had seen more than a few first-time visitors moved to tears as they encountered the power of the place.

The Caledonian MacBrane ferry was just now approaching from Mull, plowing a watery furrow on its passage to Iona. Tourists crowded the deck, eager to set foot on the ancient isle. In spite of its remote location, Iona attracted an incredible number of visitors—more than 130,000 every year.

The vast majority were day-trippers. Most of those on the ferry would have left Oban that morning and taken the Calmac ferry to Craignure on Mull's eastern shore. Loaded onto their tour busses, they would have made the ninety-minute journey across Mull to Fionnphort, where they boarded this small ferry for the crossing to Iona.

Finally arriving on Iona, the pilgrims would be allowed just two hours to explore the island and buy their postcards and souvenirs before boarding the ferry for the return trip. Lys always felt sorry for them. *Many of them have come from the other side of the world to be here, and all they get is two hours on Iona.*

Lys couldn't believe she'd lived on Iona for over a year.

After the opening of the Iona portal, the Irin had

explained that for the portal to remain open, a synaxis had to be established on Iona.

Synaxis is the word the Irin use to describe a group of humans who form a special relationship with the Irin. In a synaxis, a portion of the Irin life-force is transferred to the humans and many long-dormant powers begin to awaken. Some discover that they have gifts of healing. Some have the "second sight" and are able to sense events before they happen. Some are singers, able to change matter and direct energy through the sound of their voice. Others can see beyond their own dimension.

Two years earlier, Lys had been part of the first synaxis, formed by the Irin in Dallas, Texas, in an attempt to avert the Archon invasion. Their first assignment had been to reopen the Iona portal.

In light of the need for a synaxis on Iona, two members of the original synaxis, Michael Fletcher and Erin Vanderberg, had immediately volunteered to relocate to the island. Their friends from Mull, Angus Maclean, Catherine Campbell, and Malcolm MacKinnon agreed to join also, so the Iona synaxis began that winter.

Lys moved to Iona in the spring to help reinforce the portal, with Patrick O'Neil, another member of the original synaxis, arriving two weeks later. The Irin also brought into the synaxis an older woman native to Iona and a married couple from Mull, bringing the synaxis to ten, a *minyan*, as their friend Marty Shapiro called it.

Keeping the portal at full strength required the synaxis to meet at least weekly. Rain or shine, they gathered between the massive stone slabs atop *Cnoc Nan Carnan.* Lys would use her gift as singer, releasing a sound that reverberated between the dimensions, strengthening the tenuous wormhole from the Earth-realm to Basilea. They'd later discovered that Catherine Campbell had the singer gift also, though not as strong as Lys, but Lys was working with her to help her develop it.

Erin Vanderberg—now Erin Fletcher—was in the process of building a permanent residence, dubbed "Iona House," on the island. The site was located on the island's northeastern shore, beside the white sand beach of *Traigh Ban.* It commanded a stunning view of the Sound of Iona with the island of Mull in the distance. When completed, Iona House would provide accommo-dations for the entire synaxis.

After months of planning, construction was now well underway.

While Iona House was being built, the synaxis members had rented space in guesthouses around the island. Lys and Catherine Campbell chose Machair Cottage, a delightful bed and breakfast on the western shore of Iona, overlooking the beach known to the locals as the Bay at the Back of the Ocean.

The guesthouse was a perfect match for Lys and Catherine. It offered two cozy guestrooms, a lounge with a big window looking out over the Atlantic, and featured a well-equipped guest kitchen provided for their use. Lys and Catherine had rented the guest rooms for the entire year.

Lys had spent many days in front of the huge picture window in the guest lounge. The bay looked like something from a Caribbean travel brochure: a broad, crescent-shaped beach with the whitest sand she'd ever seen. Before her lay 2,000 miles of open ocean, stretching westward to the shores of Labrador. With a view like that, it's no wonder Lys had taken up sketching, and finally found time to catch up on her writing. Lys had also taken a part-time job, working in the office at the St. Columba hotel four hours a day. She found it a good way to get to know more of the locals, and feel a part of the community.

The only town on the island, Baile Mòr, known locally as "the village," was just a fifteen minute walk from the guesthouse. Richard and Maggie, who ran the guesthouse, also operated the island's taxi service, so getting to and from the town in bad weather was never an issue.

Michael, Erin, and Patrick had taken accommodations at Mrs. Maclean's Bed and Breakfast, a larger, purpose-built guesthouse on the island's eastern shore. It was located just down the road from the site of Iona House, which was convenient for Patrick, since he was supervising the construction work.

Lys had quickly acclimated to life on the island. She found she couldn't go past the Spar shop without buying one of their giant fruit scones. She'd learned to get there early, since the scones are a favorite of the islanders and often sell out before lunchtime.

Lys discovered that the Heritage Tearoom is the best place for tea, cake, and conversation. She often took her tea and cake on a table in their garden, graciously sharing her treat with friendly robins and blackbirds, while visiting with the locals.

Time was different on Iona. The island is small enough to explore quickly, leaving plenty of time for people and conversation.

This is how we were meant to live, she thought, *surrounded by unspoiled beauty and without the continual pressure of time. You get to know people more deeply here. Back in the States there was never enough time for people.*

Lys loved to watch the islanders' children play. They were different somehow. The word that came to mind was carefree. Sitting in the tearoom garden, she mentioned the observation to Mrs. McGowan, one of her new acquaintances. Mrs. McGowan explained that children on Iona are carefree because they grow up without fear. They'd never been warned not to talk to strangers. There was no crime on the island. There was an unspoiled innocence about them.

Lys loved the sound of the Abbey bell and the cries of the herring gulls. She loved the salty tang of the sea air. She'd loved watching the seasons change.

She had arrived on the island in the early spring. The place had been alive with wildflowers. Lambs were being birthed and Iona seemed full of new life. Walking into town one day, she'd laughed out loud to see a group of lambs playing king of the hill on some rocks in a nearby field.

Spring soon gave way to summer. Summer was tourist season. During the day, the village was packed with pilgrims visiting the historic sites and searching for souvenirs in the gift shops. It got so crowded on some days that reservations were required at the hotel restaurants. But even in the summer, when the last ferry of the day departed for Mull, Iona settled again into its quiet routine. The days were long, and the skies often clear and sunny.

The Irin presence on the island was now continual. It was the only place on earth Lys had seen any of the Irin actually relax. One evening in late summer, Lys had been walking to the village when suddenly Eliel was walking beside her.

To a casual observer, Eliel had the appearance of an attractive young brunette with haunting silver-grey eyes. But Eliel was an *Irin*, more than 20,000 years old. She had walked the streets of ancient Rome and Babylon, and when not hidden from view, her most distinctive feature was a pair of beautiful, white feathered wings.

Stopping at the Martyr's Bay Pub, Lys ordered a pint of Velvet, her favorite Scottish ale, while Eliel drank her usual Guinness Draught, a rich, dark beer from Ireland. Lys and Eliel sipped their drinks, ordered a second, and talked casually about their lives 'till late into the night. As the pub was about to close, Eliel bid farewell and simply faded from view, sliding into the concealment of the shadow realm.

When autumn came, it felt like Iona was battening down for a long siege. Leaves were falling, guests departing and hotels closing. A brisk north wind moaned around the Machair Cottage gables and a beaded curtain of raindrops clung to the window, with occasional droplets slithering down the glass.

One stormy October Saturday, Lys was walking through the village and saw Mrs. McKendrick closing down her shop for winter. It seemed sad to see the tourist shops closing, but she knew the islanders were looking forward to having Iona to themselves. "The island is ready for the end of the season," Mrs McKendrick said. "It's like hibernation. It's important, but we'll be ready for summer too."

Winter meant weeks of constant rain mixed with windblown snow. When winter storms blew in with sleet and gale-force winds whistling around the house, Lys spent most of her free time in the guesthouse, making only the necessary expeditions to the Spar shop for supplies.

The biggest winter threat to island lifestyle came when the gale-force winds shut down the ferry service, cutting the island off from the outside world, sometimes for days at a time.

Lys had just been returning from a shopping expedition to Oban when the first storm of the season blew in. High south-easterly winds whipped through the channel separating Iona and Mull.

Fortunately for Lys, the ferry crew decided to risk one last crossing before shutting down for the duration. It was a spectacularly crazy run, with mountainous swells 12-feet high. A crashing wave soaked Lys up to her waist as she made a mad dash from the lurching ferry to the concrete ramp. She discovered later that a man had been swept into the sea making a similar attempt the previous winter.

The pub closed for the month of January, and reopened in early February with limited hours. Toward winter's end, the Argyll Hotel restaurant held an Indian theme buffet that drew a good crowd, despite it being a cold, stormy evening.

The storms finally passed, and in late March Iona enjoyed several weeks of amazing weather. The air was crisp, cold, and clean.

The night skies were awesome, and filled with stars. Looking overhead was like staring into infinity. The Milky Way was clearer and more distinct than Lys had ever seen it. On some nights, nature put on a special light-show—the *aurora borealis*, and the skies above Iona became a kaleidoscope of light.

Winter finally ended. The island was gradually returning to life—the snowdrops began blooming in front of Machair Cottage and daffodils in some of the more sheltered gardens.

The hotels, shops and pub were open full time and

the island again was filling with visitors.

After a full year, the beauty of Iona was still not lost on Lys. She would often stop in the middle of the road to drink it in. *Am I really here?*

Chapter Three:
Lys and Patrick

THE ISLAND OF IONA, PRESENT DAY

The most significant development in the past year for Lys was her deepening relationship with Patrick O'Neil.

A few weeks after she arrived, Lys had been walking north along the eastern shore of the island. Just past the Abbey, the village gave way to open countryside. Granite boulders were scattered across the terrain and sheep grazed contentedly on the green, terraced slopes.

She was just passing Mrs. Maclean's Bed and Breakfast when Patrick came out the door. He glanced around, as though checking the morning weather, then, seeing Lys, waved a friendly greeting.

Flashing him a warm smile, she called, "Hey, Patrick, want to go for a walk?"

"Where are you going?"

"Up to the north end. I love the view from the beach there."

"Let me run back inside and get my shoes. I'll be with you in a minute."

Patrick had just arrived on the island a few days earlier, though he knew Iona well from previous visits.

Patrick and Lys had both been members of the original synaxis in Dallas but had never spent much time together.

A few seconds later Patrick returned, bounding down the stairs and across the lawn.

He was only slightly taller than Lys and well-built, with reddish brown hair that usually looked at least two-weeks overdue for a haircut. Lys had always found him attractive.

Enjoying the beautiful spring morning, they walked together to the north beach, where they sat on the sand to watch the waves. The day was perfect, one Lys knew she'd long remember. As they talked, the sea rolled back and forth among the ancient stone formations, tapping out a cobblestone melody on the rocky beach. A seal surfaced offshore like a fuzzy periscope. Iona Sound sparkled to the east. Lys and Patrick were amazed at how comfortable it felt to be together. Conversation was easy.

"We've known each other for almost two years," Lys ventured at last, brushing a wisp of windblown hair from her eyes, "but I don't really know much about you. Tell me about yourself."

"My life has been a wild ride." Patrick responded with a laugh. "My dad was in the military, so I moved around a lot as a kid: Hawaii, Germany, even Japan. I finished high school in Cocoa Beach, Florida, where I lived as a beach bum for a year before I decided it was time to do something with my life. I enrolled in the University of South Florida in Tampa and majored in finance, but still spent every free moment at the beach.

"When I graduated from college, I spent ten days on an adventure tour backpacking the Gobi Desert in Mongolia. Then I married the girl of my dreams and somehow landed a great job with an investment firm in Dallas.

"After a few years on the job, I ended up with a corner office in one of the tallest buildings in in the city. I had it all—a nice house, beautiful wife, and two great kids. It was the American dream.

"But then my wife had an affair with her boss and decided she'd rather be married to him. I came home one day to discover that she'd served me with divorce papers. My dream became a nightmare. The divorce proceedings dragged on for a year. My wife had the better lawyer, and in the end got the house, the kids, and everything else important to me.

"All through the trauma of the divorce, I kept having this crazy, recurring dream. I was sitting on a green hill topped with huge rock slabs. The countryside was rugged and with few trees and I could see the ocean in the distance. What made the biggest impression was the green. The landscape was a shade of green I'd never seen in Texas. I assumed it was my ancestral homeland, Ireland.

"There was a Presence with me on that hill. I don't know any other way to describe it. Every night as I approached the top of the hill, the Presence enveloped me with an overwhelming sense of peace and well-being. Nothing else mattered as long as I was in that Presence. I always awoke from the dream feeling strengthened and refreshed.

"Month after month I had the same dream every night.

"When the divorce was finalized, the dreams stopped, but I couldn't get that hill out of my mind. I had to find it. So after six months of pointless activity, I walked away from my job, cashed in what was left of my investments, and bought a ticket to Ireland.

"I followed the trail of my namesake, Patrick, the patron saint of Ireland. I think I visited every hill Patrick ever set foot on. I walked the Hill of Slemish where he tended sheep as a teenager, and the Hill of Slane where he defied the High King of Tara. I finished the trip on Cathedral Hill in Downpatrick, standing over Patrick's grave.

"Ireland was an incredible place, but I left without ever finding my hill.

"But there was still one more place I wanted to see. When I was a kid, my Irish grandmother loved to regale me with stories of the old country. One of her favorite stories was about Iona. She said our ancestors left Ireland and for almost two hundred years lived on this island. She described Iona as a mystical place. 'An isle of lights and faeries' she used to call it.

"So when I left Ireland, I knew I had to see Iona. I met Michael on the way here, and on our first morning on the island he took me on a walking tour, and we ended up just down the road at *Cnoc Nan Carnan.*

"It was one of the most amazing moments of my life, and totally surreal.   As we climbed to the top of the hill and stood between the huge rock slabs, I knew I was returning to a place I had visited many times before. I had found the Hill.

"A few weeks later I was in the synaxis meeting in Dallas where I met you."

"That's quite a story, Patrick," Lys said thought-fully, "I'm sorry your ex-wife put you through so much hell."

"I'm over the trauma now, but it definitely wasn't fun.

"But now it's your turn," he smiled. "I've always wanted to get to know you. Tell me about your life."

"Well," Lys began, "I grew up in Dallas, but went to college at the University of Colorado at Boulder, where my brother Roger had gone. I'd visited him there a few times while he was in college and fell in love with Colorado. I decided I wanted to live there.

"When I graduated, I got a job as the receptionist for the biggest law firm on the Front Range. It wasn't the career I'd planned for, but in a tight job market, and a degree in art, I was just thankful to have a job. It helped that my dad was a good friend of one of the firm's partners.

"Surprisingly, being a receptionist at a busy law firm was a good fit. I've always been a people person and a problem solver. I really enjoyed working there.

"About the time you were going through your

divorce I was having a nightmare of my own. I met a man, fell in love, and thought we were headed toward marriage, but as time went by he became abusive, first verbally, then physically. I tried to end the relationship but he refused. He stalked me for months, making terrible threats. I finally had to file a restraining order against him, but I still lived in fear for almost a year. I haven't been in a relationship since.

"Then about two years ago, Kareina started stopping by the office around break time. She looked normal enough, and claimed to work in another office, just down the hall. She told me she'd just moved to Colorado and didn't have any friends and that I looked like a friendly face.

"I felt sorry for her and tried to befriend her. A few weeks later, she invited me to go with her to a party at a big underground mansion Alexander Carrington built up in the mountains. I'd heard bad things about Carrington and his parties, but I was curious. Since Kareina didn't have a car, I knew I'd be driving, so I figured I could leave whenever I wanted.

"Huge mistake!" Lys laughed. "It was the party from hell. I felt like I was in the middle of a Roman orgy. We finally got out, but on the way home, Kareina's two subordinates ran me off the road and nearly killed me. When I finally got out of the hospital, I went back home to Dallas to recover, and that's when I met you at the synaxis."

"Sounds like we've both been through hell."

Patrick laughed.

After hours talking on the beach, Lys and Patrick walked down the road to the Saint Columba Hotel for lunch. Patrick ordered grilled goat cheese with black olives and sun-dried tomatoes on barley bread. Lys had the same. They swapped stories of their lives and sipped fine wine most of the afternoon.

That had been the first of many days together. Patrick showed her the sights of the island: the beach where Columba first landed, the old marble quarry, the hill of the angels, and the blowhole where strong Atlantic swells were channeled through fissures in the rock, exploding skyward in a dramatic imitation of Old Faithful.

As the months passed, they got to know the Iona tourists never see, and grew to love its inhabitants: the farmers, boatmen, bed and breakfast owners, and shopkeepers.

Lys and Patrick were becoming part of the community, and both recognized the feelings that were growing between them. But having both been badly burned in past relationships, they'd agreed to take things slowly.

But as their second year on the island began, they both looked forward with anticipation to what the future might hold.

Neither of them could have foreseen that within one month, Lys would be thrust into a hell more real and more terrifying than she could ever have imagined, and that the tranquil little island of Iona would once again play a critical role in the survival of the human race.

Chapter Four: Venison Stew

MACHAIR COTTAGE, ISLAND OF IONA

Patrick answered his cell phone on the third ring.

"Hey, Lys. What's up?"

"Hello, Patrick. I'm calling to make you an offer you can't refuse. Catherine and I would like to invite you and the Fletchers for dinner tonight!"

"Sure! What's the occasion?"

"Catherine went hunting on Mull with Malcom and Angus a few weeks back and bagged a red deer, so she's making her world-famous spicy venison stew."

"Yum!" Patrick said with genuine enthusiasm. "That's one of my favorites—a Highland classic. You know I wouldn't miss it."

Catherine and her friends, Malcolm and Angus, had grown up on Mull and often went hunting there together. They jokingly called themselves the Fionnphort Gun Club. Catherine had a well-deserved reputation as one of the best shooters in the Highlands, and was known as an excellent chef as well.

"I'll check with Michael and Erin," Patrick continued, "but I'm sure they'll go for it too."

"By the way," Lys interjected, "can you pick up a

half-dozen eggs from Cnoc Oran on the way? I forgot to get them earlier. It's my turn to fix breakfast for Catherine and me in the morning, and I'm dying for some Scotch eggs!"

Lys saw the big white Hummer pull into the drive, right on schedule at 6:00 p.m. Every time she saw it, it brought back vivid memories of their wild ride across Mull in the midst of an erupting volcano.

Following the battle for the Iona Portal, Erin had tracked down the owner of their borrowed Hummer and purchased it. It was now the official vehicle of the Iona synaxis.

Lys was waiting at the door when Patrick, Michael and Erin came up the walk. She greeted Patrick with a warm embrace and a quick peck on the cheek. Michael and Erin got the embrace, minus the kiss.

Lys escorted them to the guest lounge and took drink orders, recommending either a nice French Syrah or an Italian Sangiovese to pair with the venison. Erin chose the Sangiovese, which was her favorite wine, while both Michael and Patrick went with the Syrah. Lys retreated to the kitchen and returned a moment later to distribute the drinks.

Leaning back in his chair to sip his wine, Michael, as usual, bore the look of an absent-minded professor, complete with an untrimmed beard, horn-rimmed glasses, and rumpled clothes. He'd been told more than once that he had all the style of an unmade bed.

His wife, Erin, by contrast, though casually dressed, exuded an aura of beauty—her silken, chestnut-brown hair flowing in rich cascades over her shoulders. Erin's late husband had left her a considerable fortune, as well as his private jet, both of which she now devoted to the synaxis.

The table was set, and Catherine was putting the finishing touches on a bountiful Scottish feast, stubbornly refusing any offers of assistance.

Waiting for the preparations to be complete, their attention was drawn to the big picture window, where a spectacular sunset was in progress over the Atlantic.

Catherine set the last dish on the table with a flourish and proudly announced, "Dinnah is served!" She was doing her best to imitate the accent of a proper English butler, but her Scottish brogue still showed through. They all laughed as they eagerly moved to the table.

Catherine stood at the head of the table while the others took their seats, obviously enjoying the anticipation on their faces as they surveyed her culinary handiwork.

Catherine had the healthy look of a woman who spent much of her life outdoors. She was dressed in her usual outfit, tight jeans and a man's plaid flannel shirt, worn with the shirttail out. Her relaxed attire only served to accentuate her natural femininity. She was tall and well proportioned, with long raven tresses framing a face both gentle and strong.

As was the custom, they all passed their plates to Catherine, who served generous portions to everyone before serving herself.

They all ate in silence for several minutes, enjoying the savory stew.

Lys finally broke the silence. "Have you realized that Patrick and I have been on Iona for a full year now?"

Michael and Erin glanced at each other and smiled.

"We were just talking about that this morning," Erin said. "I think you got here about the time we returned from our honeymoon."

"Time flies when you're having fun," said Patrick, looking at Lys. "It's been an incredible year. I feel like Iona is the home I've searched for all my life."

"I can't believe how the island has changed since you opened the portal, Lys." Michael said. "I'd been to Iona several times before the portal opened, and it was always an amazing place, but now it blows me away.

"Last year Araton took Erin and me to Basilea to activate Erin's gift as a *sent-one*. It was a wonderful experience to be in a universe where there is no Archon influence. It felt like we were literally in heaven.

"But living on Iona now, I feel almost the same thing.

"It's not just the presence of the Irin," he continued. "It's the absence of the Archons. The Irin presence here has become so strong no Archon would dare approach the island. So Iona now is almost a place without evil. You might call it Heaven on earth."

"I know what you mean," Lys said. "I wish the whole world could be like this."

"If we succeed in driving out the Archons," Michael rejoined, "it very well may be!"

Catherine poured them each a refill on their wine, and turned to Patrick.

"How's the work on Iona House coming?"

"It has the usual complications," Patrick said. "It's a definite hassle having to ship in all the materials from Oban. You can't even buy a box of nails on Iona!

"But amazingly, we're still on schedule. Phase one should be finished in about two months, and we'll be ready to move in."

"Phase one?"

"Yes, Araton came by a few weeks ago and asked us to add an addition on the north side of the house, providing two extra guest rooms, so we've drawn up plans for a second phase. We should start excavation for that as soon as I get back from the States."

"You're going home?" Michael asked.

"Yes, I have a few matters to attend to, and my daughter is having a birthday party next week, so I promised I'd come."

"That's wonderful!" Erin exclaimed. "Michael and I are going back to the states ourselves. We leave next Monday, and we'll be there for two weeks. Would you like to fly with us? A corporate jet is so much more comfortable than flying commercial."

"I appreciate the offer, but I already have my tickets, and I can only stay a few days. But maybe we can get together with some of the others while we're there."

"A synaxis reunion!" Michael beamed. "Now that would be fun."

"Lys," Erin said, "Why don't you come too? Catherine is strong enough with her gift that she can tend the portal while you're gone, and you're welcome to fly with us. It would be so good to get the first synaxis together again."

"I'd like that." Lys said. "I hate to be away from Iona, but it would be great to see the old group. I'd also love to see my folks. I missed not being with them at Christmas.

"Catherine, would you mind maintaining the portal yourself for a few weeks if I go?"

"Not a problem," Catherine smiled reassuringly, "I'm always ready for a bit of a challenge. Go and see your family. I promise not to let the world fall apart while you're gone."

"I should also fly up to Boulder to see my brother." Lys added. "I visited with Roger on Skype last night and I think he's still going through a hard time."

SECTION TWO: THE PLOT

Chapter Five:
Jamie Thatcher

RAVEN'S NEST, IN THE MOUNTAINS
NEAR BOULDER, COLORADO

Jamie Thatcher exited the private elevator from her apartment and strode purposefully into the Carrington Corporation executive office suite on the top level of the Raven's Nest complex.

At 34, Jamie was the administrative assistant to media mogul Alexander Carrington, widely considered to be one of the most powerful men in the nation. Her office fronted his, at the very end of the hall, her desk barring the path to Carrington like winged cherubim guarding the throne of some ancient despot.

Entering her office, Jamie paused to admire the panorama of the Colorado Rockies visible through the floor to ceiling armored plate glass windows that made up the east wall of her office. Jamie never tired of the beauty of Colorado. Far to the east, the sun was just climbing through layers of early morning mist into the broad sky of the eastern Colorado plains.

Jamie was the kind of woman who instantly captured a man's attention, and held it. Her sleek ebony hair, inherited from her Japanese grandmother, was worn long and straight, complimenting a sleeveless black dress cut low between her breasts and ending well above her knees. A casual visitor might have assumed Jamie was just another of Carrington's sex symbols, but that impression shattered when they saw her eyes. Alert and piercing, Jamie's eyes revealed her as far more than a pretty face. She was intelligent. Beyond intelligent. Jamie was a genius with an officially recorded IQ of 185. She'd spoken in full sentences at 7 months and taught herself to read by age four. In college, she could skim through the textbook an hour before the exam and still get the highest score in the class. She had an eidetic memory, and could recall with complete accuracy anything she'd ever read.

Her few acquaintances described Jamie as hardened, efficient, and totally focused. She socialized rarely, hadn't dated in years, and had little interest in trying. When Carrington first hired her she'd had a brief stint as his mistress, but Jamie quickly decided she liked him better as a boss than as a lover.

But she was totally committed to Carrington. Jamie was, in fact, the only human being Carrington fully trusted. Though Carrington made the decisions for his far-flung enterprises, Jamie was the one with the skill to make it work.

Jamie effortlessly slid her body into a custom-made desk chair, fitted precisely to her form. In place of a traditional desk, she faced what appeared to be a highly polished two-inch thick slab of black granite supported by a chrome steel base. The slab was slightly inclined toward her and was uncluttered by papers, phones, or intercom—just an unbroken surface of black stone, five feet wide and three feet across.

Sensing her presence, the ebony surface came to life. Shining icons of every shape and color now floated in the darkness before her. What appeared to be a slab of granite was, in fact, a surface computer of her own design. Using a series of multi-touch gestures, Jamie could interact with the dozens of tiles, icons, and virtual objects, giving her complete access to Carrington's far-flung network.

While Jamie ran the daily operations of Carrington Enterprises, her true passion was Raven's Nest. Raven's Nest was more than Carrington's home. It was a 92,000-square-foot underground complex with fifteen bedrooms, four private apartments, a ballroom, movie theater, art gallery, beauty salon, and on the upper level, the executive offices of Carrington Enterprises. The estate grounds also featured several guest houses, a pool, five helipads, and parking for 40 cars. Jamie helped design most of the Nest's electronic systems, and knew every inch of its sprawling structure.

Jamie tapped an icon and a keyboard appeared on

the surface in front of her. Rounded keys rose like black bubbles from the slab's surface. Glowing letters and symbols appeared on each one. As the keyboard formed, a note pad appeared, floating in the darkness just above it. Jamie's nimble fingers danced out a quick email, then tapped another icon to send it scurrying off through cyberspace. The virtual keyboard disappeared, raised keys melting back into the surface.

The door to Carrington's private elevator slid open and Alexander Carrington stepped out.

"Good morning, Mr. Carrington," Jamie said without looking up.

"'Morning, Jamie." Carrington muttered. He paused for a moment, admiring Jamie's slender form before he spoke again. "I missed you at the party Friday night."

"You know I never come to your parties, Alexander," she replied, glancing at him with a knowing smile. "You just want to get me drunk so you can have wild, perverted sex with me."

"Would that be so bad?" he objected.

"I've told you before, Alex. You can have my brain or my body, but not both. I won't work for my lover."

"You know I crave your bod, Jamie," he pouted, only half in jest, "but I can't survive without your brain."

"There you go, then." She grinned and returned to her work. They both enjoyed the playful banter, but Carrington sometimes genuinely regretted that it never led anywhere.

"By the way," he added, "Kareina should be here at ten, and Grat Dalton's coming at 10:15. Please show them in as soon as they arrive."

He pulled the door shut behind him and glanced around his office with satisfaction. His office was huge, thirty-five feet long by thirty feet wide, almost the exact dimensions of the oval office in the White House.

It was designed to be both efficient and impressive. The east wall, thirty-five feet long and fifteen feet high, consisted of floor-to-ceiling armored plate glass windows, offering a stunning panorama of the Colorado Rockies and the plains of eastern Colorado. First-time guests never failed to be awestruck by the view.

The west wall featured a black marble fireplace flanked by two armchairs. The fireplace featured a holographic projection of a roaring fire that looked so real, newly arrived guests sometimes tried to warm their hands in front of it on cold winter days. On either side of the fireplace, the west wall was bedecked with priceless works of art by a variety of the old masters. Carrington didn't personally care for them, but they were good investments, and visitors always seemed to be impressed.

On the north wall beside the door to Jamie's office was a frequently used wet bar, stocked with only the finest cognacs, wines, and spirits from every part of the world.

In the very center of the office, two overstuffed leather sofas faced each other across a mahogany coffee table stocked each day with the latest editions of the Wall Street Journal and the New York Times. The conversation area provided a comfortable location for both casual visits and high-level conferences.

South of the conversation area, a massive mahogany double-pedestal desk stood facing the entrance. The desk looked like a command center, which is what it was designed to be. It was the place from which Carrington hoped to shape the destiny of the world. The only objects on the desk were a notepad and an open laptop computer, which was located to the right of center so Carrington had an unobstructed view of the door. A keypad and touch-screen computer were built into the surface of the desk.

On the south wall, behind the desk, stood a polished, mahogany credenza. The wall above the credenza was adorned with tastefully framed photographs of Carrington with kings, presidents, and Hollywood luminaries. Resting on the surface of the credenza were five gold-plated trophies—awards for some of Carrington's most successful motion pictures.

The first four trophies were Saturn awards, presented by the Academy of Science Fiction, Fantasy & Horror Films. The Saturn trophies were visually stunning—gold-plated representations of the planet Saturn connected by a pylon to a heavy, gold-plated base.

The final trophy in the row, his most recent, was

the most treasured of all his possessions—something no amount of money could buy.

It was a simple, fourteen-inch tall, nine-pound statue depicting a knight holding a crusader sword. The knight had been beautifully rendered in an Art Deco style and was made of gold-plated britannium on a black metal base. It was the motion picture industry's most coveted prize: an Oscar.

While Carrington's movies had met with great commercial success, they hadn't always earned him the respect of traditional Hollywood. So it was a matter of great personal pride when, two years earlier, his name was called at the Academy Awards ceremony. The theater had erupted with thundering applause as Alexander Carrington walked forward to receive his first Oscar.

Of course, his involvement in the film industry was just a stepping stone. His success in that realm, along with his achievements in television, video games, and the Internet, merely served to open doors for Carrington to the political power he craved.

Carrington's office was now the center of a worldwide empire. He was a kingmaker with international influence, a twenty-first century version of the media mogul.

Media moguls had first emerged in the 19th century with the development of mass circulation newspapers. By controlling the flow of information, a handful of men found they could exercise almost unlimited power in a modern democracy, influencing public opinion and determining the outcome of elections.

In the 20th century the influence of these men expanded into radio, television, and film studios. Rupert Murdoch, for example, used his vast media power to support such politicians as Margaret Thatcher, George W. Bush, and Nicolas Sarkozy. Silvio Berlusconi used his almost total control of commercial television in Italy to make himself Prime Minister.

But Alexander Carrington had gone beyond any of them. Expanding from film and television to the Internet and video games, Carrington found he could literally control the direction of an entire culture. Many saw him as the driving force behind Hollywood's subculture of violence, glorifying death, vampires and zombies.

Not content to be a kingmaker in the political realm, Carrington's goal was to supervise the rise and fall of nations. To do that, he had attracted a number of unsavory allies, from Mexican drug lords to Mideast terrorist groups. He was also a survivalist, with his own private army.

Carrington walked leisurely to his desk and sat down. He felt he'd been prepping for today's meeting all his life. Everything he'd done to this point had just been laying the groundwork. Today he would take it all to a new level.

Chapter Six: The Meeting

RAVEN'S NEST, IN THE MOUNTAINS NEAR BOULDER, COLORADO

Jamie glanced after Carrington as he shut the door to his office. She couldn't shake the thought of Carrington's parties.

Attended by well-known leaders in government and industry, his parties were notorious for their debauchery. Many attendees commented that, for sheer hedonism, parties at Raven's Nest made the Playboy Mansion, or even the fabled orgies of Rome, seem tame. Jamie had only attended one Carrington party, and still cringed at the thought of it.

At that party, five young women, costumed as medieval peasant wenches, served trays loaded with flutes of Dom Perignon Champagne to a group of influential senators and congressmen.   Carrington had invited the group for a private showing of his latest film, and to discuss several matters of pending legislation. As an added twist to the evening, Carrington had instructed the girls to remove an item of clothing every time they returned to the kitchen for more champagne.

Of course, when the guests noticed the progressive undressing of the serving girls, the demand for Champagne dramatically increased. By the end of the party, the serving girls were totally naked, and the guests were totally bombed. At that point, a photographer was brought in, taking photographs of key national leaders with naked women in a variety of compromising poses.

Thanks to the addition of the date-rape drug, Rohypnol, to the final round of Champagne, the senators and congressmen woke in their rooms the next morning feeling groggy, but with no memory of the party's outcome. Carrington had Jamie file the photos for future use.

Carrington had only used those photographs on a few occasions, but at key moments in his career they provided the leverage he needed to get a bill passed.

Jamie had few moral qualms about working for Carrington, but she wasn't proud of it either.

The hardest part for her, emotionally, was with the way Carrington treated "the furniture."

Carrington didn't list the serving girls at the party as employees. On the books they were listed as furniture. They were a standard fixture of Raven's Nest and served in a variety of capacities.

Their primary job was to lounge around the mansion in revealing attire, bolstering Carrington's debauched reputation. They also provided entertainment at Carrington's parties and performed certain other services for special guests. Contrary to rumors,

Carrington himself never slept with any of them.

The furniture at Raven's Nest was changed yearly. At the present time, Carrington's furniture went by the names Rustie, Randie, Taylor, Elise, and Nicole. Culled by his operatives from shady strip clubs and red light districts, the girls were chosen for physical beauty and lack of close family connections. Those who met the qualifications were lured to Raven's Nest with the promise of a life of luxury for one year, on the condition of complete anonymity. They were allowed no outside communication, and never used their real names. In exchange for their services, they were promised an end-of-year bonus of $100,000 cash.

Poor kids. They didn't realize that, having seen the inner workings of his empire, Carrington would never let them go free. At the end of their year, instead of being set free with one hundred-thousand in cash, they were drugged, bound, and flown on a Carrington jet to a Middle Eastern nation, where they were handed over to a shadowy character known as the *sheik* for his private harem. None were ever heard from again.

At 10 AM sharp, Kareina Procel entered Jamie's office, and passed through to Carrington's without a word. After twelve years with Carrington, Jamie still didn't understand his relationship with Kareina. She still appeared to be in her early twenties, though she'd been with Carrington far longer than Jamie. Kareina's official title was creative assistant, but when Jamie heard Kareina and Carrington interact, she was never sure which one was really in charge. Kareina had no set hours and drew no salary, but always seemed to be there when Carrington needed her.

At 10:09, another icon glowed on Jamie's desk. Tapping it with her index finger, Jamie watched a video window appear in the middle of the slab. The window was digitally foreshortened, lending the impression that she was peering through the slab's surface at a computer monitor facing her just below. The picture revealed a sleek black helicopter landing on one of the rooftop helipads. The computer had already identified it: Grat Dalton arriving from the New Mexico facility for his 10:15 AM appointment with Carrington. She watched Dalton exit the copter. The helipad attendant checked his ID and clipped a top-security access tab to his shirt. As long as he wore that tab, the computer would compare it with his facial scan and the signal from the company ID in his wallet, granting him unfettered access to the entire complex.

Grat Dalton was the newest member of Carington's entourage. Rumored to be a direct descendant of Gratton Hanley Dalton, of the infamous Dalton gang, he gave Jamie the creeps. Hired at Kareina's request, he held the title of Special Projects Director.

Jamie considered the man a psychopath.

At about 10:16 Grat ambled into her office and was directed to go in for his meeting with Carrington.

Twenty minutes later, the intercom icon glowed and Carrington invited Jamie to join them in his office also. Carrington was seated at his big mahogany desk, looking like an absolute monarch seated on his throne.

Comfortable armchairs had been arranged across the desk for Grat and Kareina, and a third chair had been brought in for Jamie. Carrington motioned for her to sit.

"Jamie, Grat has brought me an SD card with some very important data. Before I put it in the safe, I want to be sure we have a backup. As usual, Jamie, that's you."

He slid the card into a slot on his laptop, and pulled up the file on the screen. "Take a look at this, Jamie. Take as long as you need."

Jamie scanned the page. It was a list of 20 numbers, each 17 digits long. She read thru the list, then glanced up at Carrington.

"You have them?"

"Yes, sir."

Grat was scowling in disbelief. "You mean she'll really remember all 20 numbers?

"Absolutely. Let's have a demonstration." He spun his laptop around facing Grat.

"Jamie can repeat for you any of those numbers on the screen, forwards or backwards. Go ahead and ask her to repeat one."

Grat looked up at Jamie and said, "Give me all seventeen digits of the fourth number from the bottom of the list."

Jamie glared at him, but at a nod from Carrington, she said, "021 713 4997 0765 432."

Grat's mouth dropped open. "I'll be *damned!*"

"And she'll remember those numbers tomorrow, the next day, and twenty years from now."

"Jamie, our friend Grat only needs the first number right now. Would you write it down for him?"

Jamie took a slip of paper from the pad on Carrington's desk, and wrote down the first of the seventeen-digit numbers, sliding it across the desk to Grat as Carrington returned the SD card to its envelope and secured it in his wall safe.

"Is that all, Mr. Carrington?"

"Yes, Jamie, thank you."

As Jamie left the office, Grat and Kareina stood also, their meeting evidently over.

Kareina moved to follow Jamie from the office, but Carrington called to her. "By the way, Kareina, whatever happened to that girl, Lys Johnston, you brought to one of my parties a while back? I had a very pleasant dream about her last night, and I'd still like to get her in bed."

"I'm afraid that won't be possible," Kareina muttered in disgust. "Lys has joined the enemy's camp."

Jamie had just finished tapping out a quick email to her sister, Becky, in Dallas when Grat Dalton left Carrington's office and strode to the exit without a word. The look of grim determination on his face sent chills down her spine.

Chapter Seven: Lys's Dream

FLAGSTAFF MOUNTAIN ROAD, BOULDER, COLORADO, 1:35 AM

Like the blazing eyes of a hell-spawned banshee, the speeding BMW's green xenon headlamps flared angrily in Lys Johnston's rearview mirror. "They're after us again..." she said, trying in vain to control the tremor in her voice, "...faster this time!"

Acting instinctively, she slammed the accelerator, letting a wave of inertia push her torso deep into the seatback. The soft, leather-trimmed upholstery enfolded her body, cocooning her in a protective embrace; but the increased speed brought no illusion of safety—she knew her Corolla could not outrun the BMW. Her pursuers' low-slung coupe was effortlessly carving a path through the dark, twisting curves, relentlessly devouring the pavement as it approached.

Coming out of the straightaway, she squealed through a tight S-curve, barely keeping four wheels on the road. Her fading hope rekindled as the pursuing lights winked out of sight behind a massive granite outcrop. But that hope was instantly crushed when the BMW re-appeared around the bend moments later, closer than before. The sudden burst of acceleration had temporarily increased her lead, but the men were now playing catch-up and overtaking her rapidly.

A flood of cold, unreasoning fear crept up her spine. "They're almost on top of us," she said, glancing nervously at Kareina. "This has gone on way too long!"

Gritting her teeth in frustration, Lys looked for a place of refuge, searching the road ahead as it wound through a dense forest of Douglas fir... *a convenience store... a bar...some roadside café... any place with lights and people!* She saw nothing but cold, desolate pavement fading into darkness.

With no escape in sight, she fixed her gaze on her pursuers as they inexorably closed the gap.

In some deep recess of her brain, Lys knew she was dreaming, reliving the horror of that night, almost two years ago, when she'd first encountered the alien race known as the Archons. Against her better judgment, Lys had agreed to go to a god-awful party at Alexandar Carrington's with her new friend, Kareina Procell. She was on her way home when the BMW appeared. Lys knew now who the men were and why they wanted to kill her. She also knew Kareina's true identity, and shuddered at the thought. Realizing that it was a dream did not lessen the terror.

Lys had just entered a set of treacherous hairpin turns where the road zigzagged down the mountain to Boulder.

Entering the first curve, she slid her foot onto the brake, taking the turn much faster than she intended. Her tires squealed, but the BMW was still riding her tail.

She punched the accelerator but the next curve was already in sight. Warning signs flashed past. She tried to take it at 50, tires screaming in protest. Too fast! Hammering the brake, she froze as the Corolla broke into a skid, almost slamming the guardrail before she regained control.

Lys could feel her heart pounding. Adrenaline was flooding her bloodstream. Her breathing deepened, her palms went cold, and her hands were beginning to tremble. She gripped the wheel with whitened knuckles, struggling to control her rising panic. As the road ahead straightened, she jammed the accelerator to the floor.

The BMW had coasted through the last switchback, but now charged ahead, engine thundering.

Approaching the next curve, the BMW pulled up beside her. The mountain here loomed close on the left with a sheer drop-off to the right.

Another cluster of warning signs swept past. The maximum speed limit for the turn was 30 but the men were pacing her—she didn't dare let them pull in front. She started into the curve at 50, barely keeping control.

She chanced another look at the BMW. The man in the passenger seat was leering at her, not three feet away, and the look on his face made her blood run cold.

Lys was no stranger to the longing gaze of men. With an easy smile, carefully-toned body, and light, ash-blonde hair tumbled loosely across her shoulders, Lys had often held a starring role in some man's romantic fantasy. But she sensed nothing amorous in this man's leer. What she saw in his face was a terrifying look of bone-chilling brutality. She shuddered involuntarily—a tremor of revulsion snaking through her core.

Their eyes met for an instant and the man's lips went taut, baring crooked teeth in a vicious grin... the gape of a wolf about to rip the flesh of its cornered prey.

In a moment of chilling recognition, Lys saw what the men were after. With gut-wrenching certainty, her mind embraced the truth she'd been struggling for the last thirty minutes to reject. For Lys now knew, beyond all doubt, that the men in the black BMW were planning to kill her.

Her gaze fixed resolutely on the rapidly-tightening curve ahead. *A thrill killing...* the thought came numbly to her mind ... *and I'm to be the thrill...* Resisting a wave of nausea, her mind raced, striving frantically to form a plan of escape. But it was not to be.

At the tightest part of the curve, as her tires shrieked, struggling to maintain their hold on the road, the men swerved abruptly to the right. With a resounding concussion and the sound of shattering glass, the BMW slammed the Corolla hard, lifting its front end from the pavement and driving it into the guardrail. There was an agonizing scream of ripping steel, a crash as the guardrail gave way, and a long moment of silence as the Corolla sailed through the air.

The welcoming lights of Boulder spread wide

before her. Lys seemed to float for a moment in mid-air. Then, by the glare of her one remaining headlight, she saw the ground rising to meet her...

Lys awoke from the dream drenched in sweat, her body trembling.

It had been three months since she'd last had the dream, but the terror of the event was never completely gone. She remembered awakening in the hospital, with her brother, Roger, at her side.

Surviving the crash had been a miracle, but the horror had only just begun. After the wreck, the mysterious Kareina, who'd been with her in the car, was nowhere to be found. Roger tried to convince her that Kareina was just a figment of her imagination, but Lys knew better.

Then came another attempt on her life. Someone fired a high powered rifle at her hospital window, just missing her, but hitting Roger in the chest. He'd been in ICU for three weeks, barely pulling through.

But the attacks continued. She'd been kidnapped, bound, and thrown into the icy waters of a Scottish loch. She'd survived an erupting volcano and vicious hordes of bat-winged Archons. Finally, Kareina had appeared again and tried to thrust an obsidian knife into her neck.

I guess you aren't paranoid if they really are trying to kill you!

Lys knew why she'd had the dream. Today was the day of the synaxis reunion. She looked forward to seeing everyone again, but it did bring back memories—both good and bad.

She glanced at the alarm clock. 6:00 AM. *No use trying to get back to sleep.*

Chapter Eight: Reunion

FRISCO, TEXAS (A SUBURB OF DALLAS)

Lys drove up to Derek and Piper Holmes' residence a little before seven that night and experienced a serious case of *deja-vu*. She vividly remembered her first visit to the place.

The first time she'd come, Lys was still suffering the debilitating effects of the accident in Colorado. Her face was battered and bruised, and three damaged disks in her back made every movement painful.

At that gathering, she'd met her first Irin, the young woman named Eliel, and through her had been instantaneously healed of her injuries. Through Eliel, Lys also learned that she had a very special gift.

Eliel revealed that Lys was a "singer." …that something in her life-force could produce a sound that resonated between the dimensions, giving her the power to open portals to other worlds.

That night Lys became a member of the synaxis, a small group of humans who had joined with the Irin for the defense of the world. Eliel had explained that their first task was to open a portal on the Scottish island of Iona, forming a gateway to her home dimension of

Basilea. The purpose of the portal was to allow a free flow of Irin into the Earth-realm, providing the strength in numbers to overcome the Archon advance.

With the aid of those Irin, several members of the original synaxis now led their own synaxis groups, some in remote corners of the earth.

Comparing their schedules a few weeks earlier, they'd realized that the nine original members of the Dallas synaxis would all be back in the Dallas area for a brief period. They'd decided to schedule a reunion.

Eliel had promised to attend also, and wanted to fill everyone in on the latest developments in the battle against the Archons.

Derek and Piper Holmes met Lys at the door with a warm embrace. She truly felt they were family now, closer even than her natural family.

Derek—usually just called Holmes—was tall and ruggedly handsome with piercing green eyes and black hair tousled casually. He'd always been athletic, and at 43, was diligent to work out an hour a day to keep in shape.

Piper was 38 and attractive, with an infectious smile and sandy-blonde hair worn in a casual style. Before their marriage, Piper's full name had been Virginia Ann Piper, but everyone just called her Piper. When she married Holmes, she thought of a using the hyphenated, "Piper-Holmes" but decided it seemed awkward. She finally decided on Virginia Ann Holmes for a legal name, but still introduced herself as Piper.

Holmes and Piper had led the original synaxis, and now spent most of their time assisting the Irin in planting new synaxis groups in various locations.

Holmes and Piper quickly learned that the Irin had been in contact with people all over the world. They were now in the process of bringing scattered individuals together into new synaxis groups.

The synaxis groups worldwide now numbered more than 90, with more being added every month. And they were springing up in surprising places.

There was a synaxis made up entirely of Eskimos in a little Inuit village called Kotzebue, located above the Arctic Circle in Northwest Alaska.

There were native Hawaiians at Kailua-Kona, a Spanish speaking group in Ushuaia—the southernmost city in Argentina, Mongolians living in primitive *gers* just outside of Ulaanbaatar, Ashanti tribesmen in Ghana, Ethiopian Jews in Jerusalem's old city, and a group of Maoris on the southern island of New Zealand.

Michael Fletcher had noticed that a surprisingly high percentage of the new groups were made up of native peoples, and had already developed a theory. His idea was that our western culture is based on a rationalistic mentality—we think it's necessary to understand something before we accept its reality, which makes us tend to discount anything supranormal. But native peoples don't have that problem. They're much more open to accept what they don't yet understand.

Holmes and Piper appreciated all the frequent-flyer miles they had racked up with their new lifestyle, but were truly thankful to finally have a few weeks at home.

Entering the house, Lys crossed the expansive flagstone entry and entered the great room where the gathering would be held.

The great room looked like it had come out of some medieval castle. Its furnishings were massive, and in a Mediterranean style, with a great deal of rich leather and wrought-iron. Great wooden beams supported the ceiling high above them. A balcony overlooked the room on three sides, while directly ahead, on the fourth side, a massive rock wall was highlighted by an equally massive walk-in stone fireplace. A well-stocked wet bar occupied the southwest corner.

Piper fixed a drink for Lys and they were soon deep in conversation, sharing the things that had transpired in their lives since the last time they'd been together.

One by one, the other synaxis members arrived. In addition to Michael, Erin, and Patrick, there was Ron Lewis, a large, barrel-chested man with a close-cropped beard. Ron was now leading a synaxis in Toronto, Canada.

There was Reetha Shire, a young black woman who had just planted a new synaxis in Southern California, and Marty Shapiro, a medical doctor with wiry hair, a neatly trimmed mustache, and mischievous smile. He now led a synaxis in Wellington, New Zealand.

There were lots of hugs and even more conversation as Holmes and Piper kept drinks flowing.

About an hour later, Eliel arrived. She didn't come to the door; she just appeared in the room.

As the group welcomed her, Eliel folded her wings back into a dimension where they couldn't be seen, and took a seat in front of the fireplace.

After a few minutes of casual conversation, she began. "I wanted to meet with you here this evening because we are again in a perilous situation. The Archons are continuing to move forward with their plan to invade your world. They've used their mental powers to conceal the details from us, but we believe they are almost ready to implement it.

"The opening of the Iona Portal allowed us to greatly reinforce our presence in your world. Iona is now established as an Irin stronghold, which gives us a fighting chance to defeat the Archons, but I need to warn you that the outcome is still not assured."

"Is there anything we can do to help?" Piper asked.

"Yes, you can all help greatly. First, I'd like all of you to keep your schedules flexible for the next few weeks, and be prepared to travel. That means, keep a bag packed. You may need to leave on very short notice.

"And Erin, if you could have the Vanderberg jet

on call, that could facilitate matters tremendously."

Erin smiled. "Since my marriage to Michael, we're calling it the *Fletcher* jet. Rex Vanderberg tried to kill me more than once, so I've erased his name from everything I own. But I'm *always* happy to make the jet, and its crew, available for synaxis use at any time. You saved my life, and you are my top priority. Just let me know when you need it."

Eliel paused a moment and glanced at Lys. "One more thing we feel strongly about, Lys. It's time for you to recruit your brother Roger for the synaxis. We believe he has a crucial part to play in what is about to happen."

Chapter Nine:
Roger Johnston

BOULDER, COLORADO, 7:20 PM

Lys pulled the rental car up to the curb in front of her brother's house.

Roger Johnston was seven years older than his half-sister Lys, but they'd been close since they were kids.

Roger had graduated from the University of Colorado at Boulder, went through Yale medical school in Connecticut, served his residency at Massachusetts General in Boston, and was now a surgeon at Brentwood Memorial Hospital in Boulder. Almost five years ago he had a whirlwind romance with a cute nurse at the hospital. Two weeks later they'd flown to Vegas and married. Their marriage had seemed happy enough, but when the initial infatuation wore off, Roger always seemed somehow unsettled.

Then, three years ago, his wife and infant daughter were killed when a drunk driving a pickup truck ran a stop sign, T-boning their car just a block from home. Roger was home at the time and actually heard the collision. He'd never recovered. He sold their dream home and bought a beautiful replacement, but it always seemed sterile. It looked like something from a decorator's magazine. Everything was in the right place, but it had no soul.

Since his wife's death, Roger had poured himself into his work, totally neglecting any semblance of a personal life. His only social relationship had been with Lys, and that was now almost nonexistent.

For the past year Lys had been out of the country helping to establish the synaxis on Iona. Though they emailed often and Skyped occasionally, Roger and Lys hadn't actually seen each other for many months.

Roger met her at the door. "Roger, it's so good to see you," Lys smiled broadly as they embraced.

"It's good to finally get you back from Scotland!"

"It's good to be back, even if it's just a brief visit. Scotland is beautiful, but I'll always love Colorado. And I've missed my big brother!"

Roger, looked up, noticing the two people coming up the walk behind Lys.

"Roger, I've brought some friends I'd like you to meet. This is Patrick O'Neil, and this young woman is Eliel. They're both part of the synaxis group I've told you about.'"

Glancing at Patrick and Eliel, Roger's face sobered. "No offence to any of you, but Lys, let me make something clear up front. I'm happy to meet your friends, but I don't want to hear any more about that cult you're in. You're my sister and I love you dearly, but all that talk about angels and demons is too much."

Roger graciously invited them in and fixed drinks.

"Roger, I think you've misunderstood about the synaxis." Lys said as she took a sip of her wine. "It's not a religious thing. The Irin and Archons are alien races from universes parallel to ours. They've been locked in warfare for thousands of years, and our world is the battleground.

"I do sometimes call the Irin angels, because that's what they look like. They're what our whole concept of 'angel' was based on. They're guardians, sent to help us defend our world against the Archons."

Roger cut her off, "Look, sis, I'm glad you've found something you're excited about. If it works for you and gives your life some meaning, I'm all for it. It's just not for me."

Lys was determined not to let it rest, "Roger, you saw how I was healed of my injuries. Can you explain that medically?"

"You did have an unusually quick recovery, but there's a lot that happens medically I can't explain. Every doctor has seen examples of apparent miracles.

"When I was at Massachusetts General, a man was brought in who'd been in a motorcycle accident. He'd been broadsided by an SUV and his cycle flipped into the air and landed on top of him. It broke almost every bone in his body. When we looked at the X-rays we knew he couldn't live more than a few hours.

"His wife was already filling out the forms for the

disposition of his body when the man regained consciousness and tried to get out of bed. More X-rays were taken, and bones that had been shattered in the first set of X-rays were now whole. One week later he was released from the hospital.

"We have no way of explaining something like that. But just because the human body has recuperative powers we don't yet understand, doesn't mean I have to believe in angels... or aliens for that matter."

Lys saw an opportunity to press her point. "Roger, did you ever consider the possibility that something else was at work in cases like that? The Archons and Irin have been moving among us for thousands of years. They're more involved in our lives than we've ever imagined."

"So you think one of your angel friends healed that man? Sorry sis, I just can't buy that."

"But think about all the things I told you about in my emails," Lys persisted. "...the things that happened to me in Scotland: the eruption of Ben More, the battle over Iona, the opening of the portal. How do you explain those?"

"You happened to be in Scotland when a volcano erupted. I saw the reports about it in the news and I'm sure it was impressive. I'm sure it caused some strange phenomena in the sky. But frankly, a lot of what you wrote I just can't accept."

Lys looked at Roger for a long moment. "So what would it take to make you believe?"

"For starters," he laughed, "why don't you introduce me to one of your angels?"

"Roger..." Lys paused, glancing at Eliel and back to Roger, then said quietly, "I already have."

Seeing the perplexed look on Roger's face, she added, "My friend Eliel here is one of the Irin."

At that, Eliel stood up, smiling demurely. As she stood before Roger, two great feathered wings unfolded from a hidden dimension. Without effort she rose six inches into the air, and her whole body began to glow with a brilliant white light.

"What the...." Roger said. He sat dumbfounded, speechless, mouth hanging open, staring at Eliel, struggling to process mentally what he was seeing.

After several minutes of uncomfortable silence, he extended one hand cautiously in Eliel's direction, as though wanting to touch her to see if she was real, then hesitated and quickly pulled his hand back, unsure what was appropriate.

Eliel couldn't help but smile.

Roger looked at Lys, then back to Eliel. Finally, he seemed to come to a decision, "Well... o-kay." He said tentatively, "I guess seeing is believing. I can't argue with what my eyes see, but this is really hard to get my mind around. I hope you give me a little while to assimilate all this."

Eliel again concealed her wings, planted her feet firmly on the floor, and allowed the glow of her life-force to fade, once again appearing to be a normal young woman.

Roger sat in silence for several minutes more, then glanced at Lys. "I'm sorry I doubted you, sis. But you have to admit, it did sound pretty strange. I guess I should tell you that you've made yourself a convert."

Then looking to Eliel, he said, "So, please tell me more about who you are and this battle that Lys has been writing me about."

Eliel sat down opposite Roger. "Roger, it's okay to feel uncomfortable. You should have seen how Lys reacted the first time she met me!

"Believe me, I know this is a major paradigm shift. And yes, it is okay to touch me." She extended her hand and placed it lightly on Roger's for a moment. "I am real."

"To help you get acclimated, let me give you a little background. As Lys has probably told you, your world is not as you've imagined. Your universe is one of a whole series of parallel universes occupying the same physical space, but each universe exists in a different dimension. You might think of them as stacked up, like layers on a cake. Unfortunately your world is sandwiched between two warring realms. My realm is called Basilea and my people are the Irin.

"The other realm is called Hades and its inhabitants call themselves Archons.

"Both of these races have visited your world since ancient times. Your mythology is full of encounters with us. But the Irin and the Archons come here for vastly different reasons. The Archons' goal is to enslave the human race and seize your world for their own. The Irin have been sent to prevent that."

"What are the Archons like?"

"Archons are cold, malevolent creatures with no hint of empathy or compassion. When they come into your world, they usually operate invisibly from the shadow realm on the edge of your dimension. From that place of concealment, they've instigated wars, caused plagues and brought about many natural disasters. They also target individuals.

"Archons have an intrinsic hatred of the human race, and they're sadists at heart. They get pleasure by inflicting pain and suffering. They sometimes seem to make a game of it—tormenting victims for decades, prolonging agony to the point of madness. Your legends sometimes call them devils or demons and those legends portray them accurately. Archons are even similar in appearance to the demons painted by your medieval artists. When they're not using their telepathic powers to disguise their appearance, Archons are scaly, reptilian creatures with bat-like leather wings."

Eliel paused a moment, looking at Roger with great intensity. "I've come to tell you all this because your world is at a precarious place. The Archons are no longer content to operate from the shadow realm. They're about to implement a plan to invade your world in force. If this Archon invasion can't be turned back, the human race, as you know it, will be destroyed. Your world will be devastated, and those of you who remain will be enslaved and tortured.

"We believe the next few months will determine the outcome, and we feel that you have an important part to play. We'd like to invite you to join us."

Chapter Ten: Dealey Plaza

DOWNTOWN DALLAS, EAST OF THE TRIPLE UNDERPASS

It was a sunny Friday afternoon in late April. Hordes of office workers had already begun exiting downtown Dallas via Dealey Plaza, winding along Houston and Elm Streets to access Interstate 35E for the long commute to the suburbs.

Dealey Plaza was the birthplace of Dallas, and the location of the first structure built in the city, a house that had also served as a general store, courthouse, post office, and fraternal lodge.

The present Dealey Plaza Park was constructed by the Works Progress Administration in 1940. It was designed to be a quiet urban oasis, a touch of tranquility in the midst of a rapidly growing city. The park might have retained that peaceful identity had it not been for the events of November 22, 1963, when President John F. Kennedy was assassinated as his motorcade was passing through it.

JFK's assassination was one of the most visually horrific events of the television age. Like the 9-11 attacks and the Challenger space shuttle disaster, those who were alive when it happened remember exactly what they were doing when they heard the news.

Visitors from all over the world still flock to Dealey Plaza every day, rain or shine. They walk around on the grassy knoll re-enacting the events of that day in their minds, trying to visualize how it could have happened.

On this particular spring day, tourists were posing for photos with the former Texas School Book Depository building in the background.

Others stood at the edge of Elm Street, pointing at the white "X" in the middle of the street marking the spot where the fatal shot ended Kennedy's life. (Earlier in the day, one idiot actually risked his life dodging Elm Street traffic, holding his cell phone high to take a selfie where Camelot ended.)

Nearby, a Japanese woman stood, puzzling over the odd wording of the memorial plaque positioned near the edge of Elm Street. It read, "Dealey Plaza has been designated a National Historic Landmark. This site possesses national significance in commemorating the history of the United States of America." The woman thought to herself, *why couldn't they just say what happened here?*

Another tourist had climbed up on the pedestal where Abraham Zapruder made his famous film. He was holding his hands as though grasping an old style movie camera, trying to visualize Kennedy's motorcade going by.

Scenes like these are common at Dealey Plaza, but on this day something happened that was not common—a scene so bizarre it caught the attention of every person on the grassy knoll and instantly diverted their attention from the Kennedy tragedy. For amidst the line of gleaming BMWs and luxury SUVs making their way from downtown Dallas toward the interstate, there lumbered an old Chevy farm truck, piled high with a fresh load of cow manure. It was buzzing with flies. The truck had come south on Houston Street and turned west onto Elm, following the route of Kennedy's motorcade.

Just as the old truck came to the "X" marking the spot of Kennedy's death, it shuddered, chugged, and died, clouds of smoke billowing from under the hood. As it lurched to a stop, the driver angled it across all three lanes of traffic. Within minutes, traffic in downtown Dallas came to a standstill, horns blaring.

A man dressed in faded cowboy attire jumped from the cab of the truck, opened the hood, and stood watching the smoke stream from the engine. Then, to everyone's surprise, he turned and walked away.

The Unlikely Hero

Jake O'Malley never pictured himself as a hero, and few who knew him would have guessed him one either. Known even among friends as a foul-mouthed, hard-drinking womanizer, Jake's goals in life didn't go far beyond getting falling-down drunk on the weekends and finding semi-attractive females willing to indulge his animal lusts.

But this Friday afternoon, Jake would unwittingly lay down his life to save tens of thousands of people he'd never met.

Jake was the owner of Jake's Heavy Haulers, a tow truck business that specialized in moving and removing large vehicles. Eighteen wheelers and motorhomes were his specialty.

Earlier in the afternoon, he'd gotten a call about an eighteen wheeler broken down on Industrial Boulevard, just north of downtown Dallas. He'd driven *Betsy*, his newest hauler, from his base in South Dallas all the way to Industrial Boulevard, only to find that the driver had finally gotten his rig started and left.

Cursing aloud, Jake turned around in disgust. He headed south on I-35E, and was just coming up on the Commerce Street exit when the dispatcher came on the horn with news of the broken down manure truck.

Jake made a hard right and followed the exit through the triple underpass, thudded over the median to Elm Street, and backed up to the manure truck, not more than seven minutes after the truck's driver had abandoned it.

Jake quickly hitched up the truck, and to a round of cheering applause from the bystanders, headed off for the city's new impound lot in the community of Wilmer, just south of Dallas.

Alexander Carrington had estimated that during rush hour, it would take close to an hour to get a big wrecker into downtown Dallas, giving Grat Dalton plenty of time to escape. Following Carrington's instructions, Grat had set the timer for an hour, assured that the device would go off while the truck still sat in Dealey Plaza and with surrounding streets clogged with hundreds of angry commuters.

But thanks to Jake O'Malley, when the bomb finally detonated, it was long gone from downtown. Jake towed the truck south on I-35E, then east on the 635 Loop, and finally south on I-45 to the Wilmer-Hutchins exit. The last thing Jake remembered was pulling the manure-laden farm truck into the city impound lot.

The nuke's initial fireball—hotter than the interior of the sun—instantly vaporized Jake O'Malley and everything else within a five-hundred foot radius. It unleashed a shockwave radiating outward at close to the speed of sound, carrying enough thermal radiation to cause third-degree burns and leveling all structures within a half-mile of the explosion.

In Dealey Plaza, the blast, coupled with the resulting fires, would have taken out half of downtown Dallas, resulting in tens of thousands of deaths. But detonating in a sparsely settled area, the explosion resulted in less than four hundred deaths. Prevailing northwesterly winds carried the radiation away from the city.

SkyCam Seven

She'd been keeping the manure truck in view for the last ten minutes. The big tow truck had exited the interstate and was headed toward the impound yard. *Perfect!*

Becky Thatcher's left hand eased the collective lever down as her right hand pushed the cyclic forward. The result was an immediate change in the thwop-thwop sound of the main rotors as the blade angles subtly shifted. The helicopter zoomed in low giving Becky the perfect shot, just in time for her last report of the day.

Becky loved being a helicopter pilot. A copter's graceful ability to slide through the air in any direction, then hover motionless in midair, gave her a sense of freedom like nothing else in life. It was a love that ran in her family. Her dad had flown choppers in the military, loved it, and made sure both of his daughters learned to fly as well. Though Becky and her older sister Jamie were both skilled chopper pilots, Jamie's career path had taken a different direction. But Becky Thatcher could think of nothing she'd rather do than fly.

The steadycam was ready... *there's the green light from the studio.*

Becky performed her usual mental countdown bringing her up to airtime, *3... 2 ... 1...*

"This is Becky Thatcher," she began in her perkiest television announcer voice, nearly shouting to be heard above the roar of the rotors, "with SkyCam 7, Dallas/Fort Worth's premiere traffic copter. Folks, I'm just about to wrap up for the day.

"I want to end today's report with a follow-up on what was certainly the most bizarre traffic story of the year. If you missed the earlier reports, a farm truck loaded with cow manure was abandoned at Dealey Plaza around 4:15 PM today, blocking all three lanes of traffic on Elm Street and threatening to snarl traffic throughout downtown Dallas. Fortunately, a tow truck was on the scene within minutes and hauled the thing away. But there's still no word on who the truck belongs to or why it was there.

"So here's one last shot of it. I'm going to try to get closer so you can see it clearly. If you recognize this truck, please call the Dallas police. The wrecker is just now hauling the manure truck into the city impound lot."

Chapter Eleven: Revelation

ROGER JOHNSTON'S HOME, BOULDER COLORADO

The message had been posted in social media, and distributed to every news source. Within hours, nearly everyone in America had read its sobering threat.

"To America, Great Satan and leader of the crusader alliance. You bear full responsibility for the Zionist-crusader war against Islam. You have shed rivers of blood in our lands so we have ignited a volcano of rage in yours. You mourn the losses of 9-11 and the destruction in Dallas. But what you have seen in New York and Texas are only the beginnings of your suffering. If you continue your policy of aggression against Muslims, you will see horrors beyond your imagining. Our message to you is clear: meet our ten demands immediately or more destruction will follow."

The message was signed, "Crimson Jihad."

At 1:00 AM Saturday morning, the Fletcher jet

touched down at Boulder Municipal Airport. By 2:00 AM, the members of the original synaxis were meeting with Eliel at Roger Johnston's home.

"But what do the Archons hope to gain?" Roger asked. "If their goal is the total destruction of our world, a suitcase nuke is pitiful. I mean, any nuke is frightening, but as nukes go, this was not all that powerful. What was it, about a third the power of the Hiroshima bomb? It could wipe out a small area of one city, but it won't bring civilization to an end."

"You're absolutely right," Eliel agreed, "But their real weapon is not the bomb. It's fear.

"Right now, people are in shock, and waiting to see how the government responds. They still believe there might be a negotiated solution.

"But there is no solution. There can't be. Crimson Jihad's press release called for America to meet its 10 demands. But no demands were ever issued. And there's no one to negotiate with. Crimson Jihad doesn't even exist. It's the name of a fictitious terrorist group from an old Arnold Schwarzenegger movie! There's no way your government can respond to this threat. They don't even know who detonated the bomb.

"So within a few weeks, more bombs start going off. We've learned that the man behind this bomb is a wealthy survivalist named Alexander Carrington. He lives right here, in the mountains outside of Boulder. Carrington is in league with the Archons, and just happens to have nineteen more suitcase nukes squirreled away in a cavern in northwestern New Mexico.

"Imagine what will happen if nukes start going off in random cities, all across the country, a few days apart. Within days, people are fleeing every city.

"In September of 2005, when Hurricane Rita threatened the Texas coast, more than a million people tried to evacuate Houston. It was chaos—highways were gridlocked in every direction for hundreds of miles. Thousands of cars ran out of gas, others overheated. People were left stranded along the highway and more than a hundred died.

"Now picture that same thing happening in every city in your country, all at the same time.

"Your government appears helpless. Crimson Jihad issues statements charging that the government is refusing to meet their demands. There are riots. Government facilities are overrun by crowds demanding action.

"But there are already operatives in place with a plan. In 2004, the US military war college began offering a course called "Perspectives on Islam and Islamic Radicalism." The course taught that the only effective way to fight terrorism is to engage in total war against Islam, which includes the destruction of the holy cities of Mecca and Medina.

"While the course was repudiated and is no longer taught, the thinking behind it has not gone away. With no other way of responding, military leaders will see hitting Islam as the only way to strike back. We estimate that before bomb number six explodes, your government will have nuked Mecca and Medina into radioactive rubble.

"Far from stopping the destruction, it will ignite worldwide chaos. You saw the response when a cartoonist drew a picture of Muhammad. Imagine what would happen in the Muslim world if American nukes take out their holy sites.

"And we're not just talking about riots in the Middle East. Remember, Muslim immigrants from North Africa have over-run much of Europe. Close to a third of the youth in France are Muslim, with Germany and England not far behind. Europe will burn.

"We're looking at the total collapse of Western civilization within weeks. The world will be plunged into a new Dark Age and billions will die of disease and starvation.

"The collapse will be so total that the Archons can easily move in and seize control. They may actually be welcomed. And the human race will be enslaved to the forces of Hades."

When Eliel finished, every member of the synaxis sat in stunned silence, looking at each other and back to Eliel.

"Isn't there anything we can do to prevent this?" Holmes asked.

"We have only one hope. Carrington has an assistant who has access to his entire facility. This assistant has memorized the detonation codes for the bombs. She's been a staunch supporter of Carrington, but her sister was killed in yesterday's attack, and she's shaken. Her name is Jamie Thatcher."

"Jamie?" Roger's eyes widened in unbelief.

"Yes, you dated her for two years back in college, and she still thinks of you as her lost love. We think it may be possible for you to enlist her help."

Chapter Twelve: The Path

BOULDER CREEK PATH,
BOULDER COLORADO

Boulder Creek flows out of the mountains west of Boulder, down through the center of the city, skirting the University of Colorado campus, and continuing into the rural plains on the east. In dry seasons, the creek becomes a mere trickle, but in the spring, when water from the snow melt rushes down the canyon, it becomes a living river gushing through the rocks and cascading over mini-waterfalls.

Running alongside the creek is Boulder Creek Path, a 5.5 mile greenbelt and walkway through the heart of Boulder. The Path passes beneath the streets of the city, allowing downtown workers to enjoy a quiet stroll beside a rushing mountain stream, mere steps from their offices.

For many, the Path forms an intrinsic element of the Boulder lifestyle. It is used by all. Athletic locals, known as "Pathletes," use the Path as a workout venue; jogging, cycling, or riding scooters and skateboards. College students take it to and from the UC campus, moms with strollers see the Path as a pleasant escape from the pressures of childcare, and the elderly come on sunny days, pushing their walkers and enjoying the tranquil scenery. All intermingle, and all have their own reasons for coming.

For Jamie Thatcher, the Path had always been her place to rest, unwind, and be restored.

On this beautiful Saturday morning, Jamie drove Flagstaff Mountain Road from Raven's Nest down to the base of the mountain and parked her car at the Eben G. Fine Park on the western edge of the city. From the park she began a meandering stroll, heading east on the Path, savoring the crisp mountain air and the delight of a sunny Colorado spring day.

The Path was a great place for people watching, but crowds were light today. A lot of people were at home, glued to the television screens, hungry for any news on the Dallas tragedy.

Yet even in a time of crisis, people still came to the Path.

A few brave souls were tubing or kayaking through the icy rapids.

Others were fishing in the deeper holes for trout. Jamie laughed to herself. *Fly fishing in an icy mountain stream—in the center of downtown Boulder!*

She passed play areas for kids... a big sandbox and a playground.

Couples from the nearby University of Colorado were lounging on rocks or stretched out on blankets, sunbathing beside the ice water creek.

People with books and e-readers were camped out on the benches, sandwiches in hand and open cans of Coke on the bench beside them, taking a lunch-hour break from downtown shops to read and enjoy the day.

Jamie had been walking for close to an hour when she came to Scott Carpenter Park. The Park had been named for a resident of Boulder who also happened to be the second American astronaut to orbit the earth. Appropriately, the children's playground featured a large rocket ship.

Being at the Park brought back memories.

The happiest years of Jamie's life had been her last two years of college. She'd been in love with the one true love of her life, Roger Johnston. During the two years they'd dated, she and Roger had often come to this very spot.

They would head out from the UC campus on pleasant Saturday or Sunday afternoons, walking Boulder Creek Path hand-in-hand to Scott Carpenter Park. When they got here, they'd spread a blanket on the grassy hillside and spend the afternoon talking, reading, and sharing their dreams, enjoying the crisp Colorado air with the majestic "Flatirons" rock formation in the distance.

She'd always assumed they'd get married, but as graduation day approached, Jamie got her acceptance letter from the Computer Science Graduate Program at Stanford. Located in the heart of California's Silicon Valley, Stanford was the top ranked computer science school in the world. It was a no-brainer for Jamie.

Meanwhile, Roger was accepted into Yale Medical School in Connecticut, an opportunity he knew he could not pass up. They'd talked for hours, trying to find a way to keep the relationship going, but could see no way to make it work.

She hadn't seen Roger for years, but still felt a bond with him. She'd heard he'd moved back to Colorado, and hoped his life was happy. All she had of Roger now were memories.

This park had been their place. She still came here when she needed to think. Sometimes she imagined she'd see Roger here one day.

But today she was just numb.

Jamie entered the Park, found a shady bench at the edge of the woods and sat down.

She sat for a long time, not thinking, just staring off into the distance.

Usually, walking along the creek, Jamie would feel her stress and tension melting away. That had not happened today. Becky's death hung over her. It seemed unreal, like a dream you are thankful to wake up from.

But it was not a nightmare. Becky was dead. Jamie had stayed up late into the night, playing and replaying the last video feed from Skycam 7, trying to figure out some way Becky could have survived, but each time the answer was the same. Her little sister had been instantly vaporized by the blast. There would not even be a trace left of her body.

Tears began to flow down her normally hard exterior.

Jamie thought about their weekly Skype chat. Every Saturday night she and Becky had a regularly scheduled online visit to catch up on the events of the week. They'd each pour a glass of their favorite wine, lean back on a comfortable chair in front their laptop, and spend an hour in relaxed conversation, feeling connected again in spite of the distance between them. That would not happen tonight... or ever again. She felt sick.

Trying to get her mind off her sorrows, Jamie looked around at the park. It was beautiful. The Flatirons in the distance were as majestic as ever. Even on this day of tragedy, many people were out enjoying the pleasures of Boulder. Little kids were playing on the playground and climbing up the rocket ship.

She heard footsteps coming up behind her. Whoever it was stopped, but did not speak. She finally turned and looked up.

Roger Johnston stood there, smiling warmly. "Hi, Jamie."

Jamie's mouth fell open in unbelief. "This can't be real. I must be imagining this! I was just thinking about you."

"I've been thinking about you too, Thatcher. Mind if I sit down?"

"Please!"

Roger eased himself down beside her, careful to leave a comfortable amount of space between them.

"I was watching the news and heard about Becky. I'm so sorry. When I heard what happened, I thought I might find you here today."

"How many years has it been?" she asked.

"It's been much too long. I've missed you, Jamie. But this isn't just a social visit." Roger paused, torn between his desire to be with Jamie, and the knowledge of what he must say to her. Finally, he spoke. "I have something to tell you, and then I need to leave. You need some time alone right now to think.

"Jamie, I found out some things last night; don't ask me how."

He paused a long time, then looked into her eyes and spoke with dead seriousness.

"Your boss Carrington was behind the Dallas bomb. And he has 19 more cached in a man-made cavern in New Mexico. He's planning to do terrible things that will kill millions of people. I believe the man is insane."

Not giving her a chance to reply, he continued. "I'm not asking you to believe me, but I know you have access to everything he does. Check and see for yourself. If you find out I'm right, I'm here to help. I'll be here in this park next Saturday at the same time."

They sat looking at each other for what seemed like an eternity. Jamie was in shock, and could find no words to say.

Then Roger stood and walked away.

As Jamie watched him leave, her mind surged with conflicting emotions. She hadn't seen Roger for years and the sight of him aroused long buried feelings. She longed to call him back, to spend the day with him, to have intimate talks and be close like they'd been so long ago.

But Roger hadn't come for that. He'd come to tell her who killed Becky.

Shock gave way to anger. Why had Roger intruded on her mourning to bring ridiculous accusations against Carrington!

But as she replayed Roger's words in her mind, the anger gave way to confusion.

Jamie knew Carrington had a facility in New Mexico. She'd been there a few times to set up the network, but not recently. It was the special projects site, now headed by Grat Dalton.

Then came the horror of realization.

Roger had said there were twenty bombs, and the Dallas bomb was just the first.

Grat had given her a list of twenty numbers on a chip, each seventeen digits long. He had taken one number with him when he left.

Detonation codes?

Her mind wanted to dismiss the thought as ridiculous, but she had to know for sure.

Gaining access to the New Mexico facility would not be a problem. Jamie had Carrington's highest level security clearance, which gave her full access to all of his facilities.

But how to do it without raising suspicions? Ideally, it should be a time when both Carrington and Dalton were out of the picture.

Her brain instantly culled the relevant information from her eidetic memory:

1. Carrington's schedule: Carrington was presently in California, meeting with the director of his latest picture. He was scheduled to return on Monday.

2. Grat Dalton's schedule: Dalton should be at the New Mexico facility all week, but rumors were that he got drunk every Saturday night and slept 'till noon on Sundays.

3. Her timing: The New Mexico facility was 290 air-miles from Boulder, a distance her Eurocopter AStar 350 could cover in less than two hours. She could make the round trip, have two hours to search the facility, and be back in Raven's Nest in less than six hours.

A plan formed in her mind.

Sunday morning at 5:00 am, Jamie Thatcher took her private elevator to the helipad deck, and walked with resolute determination to pad 3.

Chapter Thirteen: Nicole

SCOTT CARPENTER PARK, BOULDER COLORADO

The next Saturday afternoon, Roger was waiting in the Park

Jamie walked directly to the bench, sat down next to him, and for several minutes said nothing, quietly staring into the distance. Finally she scooted her body closer to Roger so their shoulders and hips touched, as if needing some form of physical contact. Then she spoke.

"You were right."

She let the weight of those words sink in for several minutes, then continued, "I flew to New Mexico last Sunday morning. I told the guard on duty I was there to check out a glitch in the network. I have top security clearance, same as Carrington, so the computer gave me access to the entire complex.

"I searched the facility and found them in a vault near the back of the complex.

"There were nineteen stainless steel canisters, all lined up, one for each of the remaining detonation codes."

She paused, staring lifelessly across the park.

Finally she continued. "There was also an empty space where one more bomb had been."

Tears began trickling down her cheeks. She bit her lip, trying to constrain her rage.

"The bastard!" she finally blurted. "He killed my sister!"

Images of Becky flooded her mind. She and Becky playing silly games as kids, opening presents on Christmas mornings, family vacations at the beach in Hawaii. Overwhelmed by irreplaceable loss, Jamie began to sob.

Roger tentatively put his arm around her. Jamie leaned into the embrace, welcoming the comfort.

"Jamie, you've got to get away from there. It's not safe for you. I have some friends who can help. Come with me and I'll take you someplace where you'll be safe."

"I'd like that," she said thoughtfully, "But there's something I must do at Raven's Nest before I leave. Can you pick me up there tonight around nine?"

"Yes, but be careful. If Carrington finds out you're planning to leave, your life could be in danger."

"There's an emergency exit at the base of the mountain. It's well concealed and not guarded. I'll draw you a map to show you how to get there." She took out a slip of paper and quickly jotted some directions. "I'll see you tonight."

RAVEN'S NEST, IN THE MOUNTAINS NEAR BOULDER COLORADO

Jamie re-entered the Raven's Nest complex and stopped by her office to check the network. Everything was normal.

She was about to leave when the intercom beeped from Carrington's private residence. "Jamie, I just got a message from the sheik. He wants more furniture. He said the last item we sent wasn't very durable and he needs a replacement. Who's next on our list?"

"Nicole is next in line to leave, but she's still got two months left on her contract."

"Get her prepped. Tell her she's looking a little pudgy lately and I've decided to let her go early. Tell her to pack her things and assure her we'll pro-rate her remuneration based on her time here.

"Have her come to my office at nine p.m. to get her check. We'll ship her out tonight."

Jamie tapped out a simple text message to Nicole. "Carrington says you've put on too much weight and has decided to let you go. Your remuneration will be pro-rated based on the time you've been here. Be at his office tonight at 9 to pick up your check. He'll arrange to fly you out."

Jamie's hands were shaking by the time the

message was sent. She knew her time had come. Before she could do what she intended however, she had to give the computer a few last minute instructions. She hit the icon to pull up the virtual keyboard and quickly tapped in some codes.

Leaving her desk for the last time, she walked into Carrington's private office, opened the wall safe and withdrew the tiny SD card from its envelope, pondering what to do with it. She had to keep Carrington from gaining access to the codes whether she made it out of the Nest alive or not. That meant destroying the SD card. And she had to do it now. She glanced around Carrington's office, and saw a way.

Jamie stepped out of the private elevator to her apartment, feeling a rising sense of panic. She knew she might have only minutes before she was found out, but there were things she wanted to take when she left. She pulled a small overnight bag from her closet and began packing carefully selected items.

There was a loud pounding on her door.

Jamie froze. Had she been discovered already?

The pounding came again.

Opening the door, Jamie was relieved to see only Nicole, who was clearly distraught.

Nicole was just the kind of girl Carrington's guests expected to find lounging around Raven's Nest: a pretty face concealed by way too much makeup, platinum blonde hair worn in a short bob, and a figure that had doubtless been artificially endowed. She was wearing one of the outfits Carrington personally selected for the girls who serve as Raven's Nest furniture—in this case, a negligee made from a single layer of a black diaphanous fabric so sheer it left very little to the imagination.

Before the door was fully opened, Nicole blurted, "Jamie, I got your text. I... I don't understand! What's happened?" She looked like she was about to cry. "I haven't gained weight. Honest! Look at me! I weigh every day; I exercise; I eat almost nothing. I'm hungry all the time! I keep all the rules and I've done everything Carrington has asked! Why is he firing me?"

Jamie couldn't keep up the charade. She looked at Nicole sternly. "It's all a lie, Nicole. It's always been a lie. That's the kind of man Carrington is. He never intended to give you any money. If you meet him in his office tonight, you'll end up drugged, bound, and flown on a Carrington jet to the Middle East where you'll be added to the harem of a terrorist mastermind Carrington calls the sheik. That's where Carrington's used furniture always goes, and none of the girls are ever heard from again."

Nicole looked like she'd been punched in the face. She was shaken, but somehow she didn't doubt the truth of Jamie's words. Struggling to recover, she stammered, "What should I do?"

"I'm leaving Raven's Nest tonight, and you should too. You can come with me if you'd like."

"That door across the hall is the hatch to a system

of access tunnels. Go through that door and follow the tunnel straight ahead for 100 yards. It twists and turns, and there are a lot of side passages, but stay on the main corridor. It dead-ends at an elevator. Take the elevator all the way to the bottom level. It leads to an emergency exit at the base of the mountain. Wait for me just inside that door.

"I still have a few things to pack. I'll meet you at the exit door in fifteen minutes. A friend will be waiting outside with a car."

Nicole slipped the hatch open and peered nervously down the darkened corridor. On the other side of the door, Raven's Nest was a different world. No longer the luxury mansion, the walls of the tunnel were unfinished, rough-cut granite. The floor was bare concrete. Beyond the first thirty feet, the corridor lay in total darkness. And it was cold.

The maze of access tunnels ran throughout the entire Raven's Nest complex, providing essential services, power, and computer network access to every room. Heating and AC ducts were bolted to the ceiling, while water and sewer lines, tangles of electrical wiring, and bundles of fiber-optic cable were affixed to the walls. Every twenty to thirty feet, side corridors branched off. Some were nearly as big as the main corridor; others were accessible only by crawling. The hum of distant machinery filled the air.

Seeing Nicole's hesitation, Jamie explained, "A system of motion detectors activates the lights, sector by sector as you pass through the corridor. You can always see at least thirty feet in either direction. Just keep walking."

Feeling the rush of cold air from the tunnel, Nicole glanced down at her own nearly naked body. She felt an inexplicable wave of shame. "I better put some clothes on before I go out. I'll grab something quick, then wait for you at the exit."

Nicole sprinted down the hall toward the dormitory assigned to Carrington's furniture, her bare feet slapping the marble floor as she ran.

Chapter Fourteen: Discovery

RAVEN'S NEST, IN THE MOUNTAINS NEAR BOULDER COLORADO

Carrington was meeting with Grat Dalton and Kareina in his private residence.

Carrington and Kareina sat on a plush leather sofa, sipping snifters of Remy Martin Louis XIII Rare Cask Cognac, poured from a crystal decanter on the coffee table. Seated across from them on an identical sofa, Grat Dalton held a longneck Shiner, which he was chugging straight from the bottle.

"Pardon me for sayin', Mr. Carrington," Grat drawled, leaning back on the couch and holding his beer in front of him, "but you've got yourself one damn mess here. You give this girl full access to everything you do. She knows more about your business than you do. Then you kill her little sister. I think you've got serious problems."

"I agree." Kareina interjected. "Jamie's loyalty has been seriously compromised."

"Look, she doesn't even know I had anything to do with that bomb."

"You don't think she's figured it out?" Kareina countered, "I see it in her face. She knows you killed her sister. She's capable of anything now."

Then she added, "Are you sure the detonation codes are secure?"

"Not to fear." Carrington assured her. "The codes are in my safe, and while Jamie does have the combination, I've set the computer to alert me anytime the safe is opened. I also put a tracking program on Jamie, so I can tell at a glance where Jamie is anywhere in the complex. It will alert me any time she enters my office."

Seeing the skepticism on Kareina's face, Carrington called out, "Computer! Tracking! Display the current location of Jamie Thatcher."

A schematic of Raven's Nest appeared on an 80-inch screen mounted on the far wall, but the computer's response stunned him. "No location available for Jamie Thatcher. Tracking program has been deactivated."

A chill went down his spine. He tried another question. "Has anyone tried to open my safe?"

"Security monitoring for your office has been disabled."

Without a word, the three slammed down their drinks and darted for the elevator.

As the elevator opened into Jamie's office, Kareina glanced at Carrington, "She's after the codes. She may already have them."

They proceeded into Carrington's office, where

he quickly opened the wall safe. The envelope with the SD card was gone.

Touching a button on the control pad, Carrington barked, "Security lockdown. No one leaves or enters Raven's Nest without my approval. This is an all security alert. Find Jamie Thatcher and bring her to my office."

He tapped the code for the helipad attendant.

"Yes sir?"

"Have you see any sign of Jamie?"

"No sir, she's not been up here."

He checked the other security stations, but no one reported seeing her.

"She must be using the access tunnels that lead to the bottom of the mountain. Jamie designed that whole system." He tapped the monitor screen on his desk. "The emergency exit has not been opened. She hasn't left the complex yet."

Carrington paused, glancing around his office. Something else was wrong.

One of the awards was missing from his credenza. The Academy Award statuette.

Then he saw it. On the floor behind the desk was what remained of his Oscar. It was no longer beautiful.

Oscar's head was badly dented and bent to one side. It had been repeatedly slammed against the floor with such force that the slab of marble beneath it had cracked.

Seeing his ruined Oscar, Carrington reached down

to pick it up, then drew his hand back. He couldn't bear to touch it.

He cursed aloud and began pacing back and forth, enraged that Jamie would dare destroy his Oscar. What made him even angrier, however, was the sudden realization that he could never again trust Jamie Thatcher with anything. Turning to Grat, he hissed two words, *"Kill her!* And bring me that SD card!"

"Mr. Carrington," Grat smiled broadly, "Jamie Thatcher is a bug lookin' for a windshield. I guarantee she'll be dead within the hour." Grat strode out of the room, reaching down to grasp the Bowie knife sheathed in his right boot.

Kareina, meanwhile, rifled through the contents of the safe, checking to be sure the SD card was really gone. Satisfied with her search, she walked over to examine the once-beautiful statuette. As she picked it up, she noticed bits of debris on the black marble floor beneath it.

She crouched down to examine them, brushing a wisp of long black hair from her face as she did. The floor beneath where the Oscar had been was littered with tiny shards of colored plastic, bits of shiny wire, and the remains of a silicon memory chip, now smashed to powder.

Kareina gasped. The debris beneath the ruined Oscar was the remnants of the missing SD card. Jamie had used Carrington's Academy Award to pound the SD card to oblivion.

"Carrington!" she barked.

Carrington walked to her side, saw the scattered debris, and instantly knew what had happened. He knelt down and nudged the silicon dust with his index finger. There was no way any data could be recovered. In an explosion of blind fury, he threw back his head and let out a bellow of rage.

Kareina looked at him sharply, "Where's Grat?"

"I sent him to kill Jamie."

"You *fool!*" Kareina exploded in rage. "We can't kill her! With the SD card destroyed, the only copy of the detonation code list is locked in her brain. We need her alive."

A look of horror came across his face as he realized the truth of her words. All their plans depended on that list of codes, and he had just sent Grat to destroy the one remaining copy.

Kareina hissed, "Call him back!"

Carrington got on the intercom. "Attention Grat Dalton. Return to my office immediately."

Silence.

"Grat Dalton, this is Carrington. Call my office now!"

They waited, but there was no reply.

"It's no use," Carrington said. "He must have already entered the access tunnels. There's no intercom system in there."

"Use your phone."

"That won't work either. The access tunnels are deep in the granite mountain, there's no cell phone signal.

There's no way to contact him."

Kareina stared at Carrington with unmitigated fury, then screamed, *"Find one!"*

SECTION THREE: SEEKING REFUGE

Chapter Fifteen: Escape from Raven's Nest

RAVEN'S NEST, IN THE MOUNTAINS NEAR BOULDER COLORADO

Jamie gathered a few items in a small overnight bag, then left her apartment and entered the access tunnel. Something wasn't right.

After the first thirty feet, the tunnel should have been in total darkness, but far up ahead she saw a glow coming from one of the side tunnels. Someone in that tunnel had activated a motion detector.

"Nicole?" Jamie called tentatively, her voice echoing down the corridor.

No answer.

"Is anyone there?" she called again.

Still deathly silence.

Jamie proceeded into the corridor, remaining alert to possible danger.

As she walked, the lighting system followed her. Every twenty feet or so a new light came to life as one behind her switched off. The lights were all fairly dim, providing just enough illumination to pass through the corridor.

Even though she had personally designed the system, it felt a little disconcerting. Apart from the dim glow from the side tunnel far ahead, she walked in a pool of light in the midst of total darkness.

She'd gone about sixty feet when a newly activated light revealed something on the floor—a puddle of dark liquid near the entrance to one of the side tunnels. *Was the Nest leaking?*

She knelt down and cautiously extended her index finger. The liquid was warm. Holding her finger closer to the light she saw that it was also red. She gasped involuntarily, wiping the blood from her finger on the wall beside her.

Half knowing what she'd find, she peered down the narrow side tunnel. A body lay crumpled on the concrete floor. Taking a few steps closer confirmed her suspicions. It was Nicole. Her throat had been slashed from ear to ear, nearly decapitating her. *Grat Dalton has been here! I've been found out.*

She knew instinctively what had happened. Nicole had been hurrying down the corridor, anxious to get to the elevator. Grat was waiting in the side tunnel. He would have grabbed Nicole as she went by and slashed her throat with one smooth motion.

Jamie reached out her hand to touch Nicole's forehead. It was still warm. *She's only been dead a few minutes.* She thought of the dim light she'd seen coming from the side tunnel up ahead. *Grat is still here. He's between me and the elevator.*

A shudder passed through her body. She returned to the main corridor, trembling, unsure what to do.

Then another light blinked on fifty feet ahead as Grat Dalton stepped back into the main corridor.

"Sorry about the girl, Jamie," he drawled. "I didn't mean to hurt her. Really, I didn't. I thought that was you comin' down the hall.

"No matter. There's still time for you. You know you're trapped, Jamie. If you go back inside the Nest, you're dead. Security is sweeping the complex and they will find you. They've all been alerted, and Carrington has ordered your death. All I'm asking for is that SD card. Give it to me, and you're free to leave."

He began strolling casually in her direction.

He doesn't know the SD card is destroyed. He'll kill me with no hesitation.

Jamie's mind was racing. *I know every inch of this tunnel system. Dalton doesn't. I could find my way through this place in the dark.*

At the corner of the side corridor she found a small network access panel. She flipped it open and tapped the code to kill the power to the access tunnel lighting.

The corridor went black.

"Nice move, Jamie." Grat laughed. "I'll enjoy hunting you in the dark!"

Jamie fled down the side tunnel.

Jamie's plan was simple. If she could coax Grat to follow her into the maze of access tunnels, she might be able to double back to the main corridor by another route.

She visualized the schematic of the tunnel system. There was a way.

The service tunnel to the theater lay just ahead. Crammed with AC ducts and wiring, Jamie knew it led to a small access hatch to the right of the theater's screen. From the projection booth at the rear of the theater she could enter another tunnel that would lead her back to the main corridor.

But it was taking a chance. Once in the theater, if tracking had been reactivated, the computer would recognize her presence immediately.

She'd have to chance it.

The corridor had narrowed. Just ahead, she knew the tunnel to the theater branched to the left, but it was only waist high. Moving forward in total darkness, she slid her hand along the wall. There!

She had to be sure Grat was still following her. "You'll never catch me, Dalton! I designed this tunnel system. I know it by heart."

The answer came back immediately. "I'm right behind you, babe!" Dalton was much closer than she'd imagined.

On hands and knees, Jamie scrambled through the narrow tunnel leading to the theater. It ended at a steel access hatch.

Opening the hatch, Jamie found herself in Carrington's private theater.

Designed for intimate screenings of his films for influential guests, the theater had a maximum capacity of 50, but all 50 seats were custom-designed multi-position recliners that operated at the touch of a button. Each seat featured a lighted cup holder and retractable table. During a film, a gentle tap on a glowing button would bring one of Carrington's "furniture" girls running to take orders for any kind of food or beverage. Though located far underground, the theater's soaring twenty-five foot ceiling gave it a spacious feel. Embedded in the ceiling was a fiber-optic lighting system that lent the appearance of a starry night sky, complete with the Milky Way and an occasional shooting star.

Easing through the access hatch, Jamie found herself at the front of the theater, as expected.

Her goal was to reach a similar steel hatch located in the back wall of the projection booth. That hatch opened to a tunnel that would provide another path back to the main corridor. The theater was dimly lit, but she could see the door to the projection room, not more than thirty feet away.

As Jamie made her way through the rows of plush leather recliners toward the back of the theater, attempting to move as stealthily as possible, the stillness of the theater was suddenly shattered by a blaring alarm. The theater lights flared to full brightness, momentarily blinding her. The computer had spotted her.

Moments later, the alarm shut off as an armed two-man security team burst through the door at the far side of the theater. "Ms. Thatcher," the first guard barked. We request that you come with us. Mr. Carrington has ordered us to bring you to his office."

Jamie froze.

One guard remained stationed at the entrance, but the other began striding purposefully in her direction. The door to the projection booth was still ten feet away. She knew she couldn't make it, but had to try.

Jamie sprinted for the projection booth door and reached it just before the guard, but as she grasped its knob in her right hand, she felt the guard's fingers clamp down hard on her left arm. Jamie struggled against him, trying to pull away, but the guard's grip only tightened. She was captured.

"Wait," came a shout from behind her. It was Grat Dalton, knife in hand.

"The bitch is mine!"

The guards hesitated, confused, but Grat's position as Special Projects Director meant he clearly outranked them. Grat was steadily advancing. The guard released his hold on Jamie's arm and backed away.

The projection booth door was just behind her. She extended her hand again and clenched the knob. If she could make it through that door, she could be back in the access tunnels within seconds

But Grat was almost upon her. There was no time.

She eyed the gleaming blade in Grat's hand, still streaked with blood. He'd just murdered Nicole. She wondered how many others that knife had killed.

Grat was moving slowly, savoring the terror in her eyes. *I was right*, the thought popped into Jamie's mind. *Grat Dalton really is a psychopath. And I'm his next victim.*

Grat extended his left hand, ready to grab her, the knife gleaming in his right.

But then something happened that terrified Jamie even more than Grat Dalton's knife.

A monstrous shape suddenly appeared, seeming to drop through the ceiling of the theater. It looked to Jamie like a giant bat with dark leathery wings, fifteen feet across. The thing was descending, heading directly toward her. Jamie pressed her body tightly against the projection room door, trying to put as much distance as possible between herself and the apparition.

The beast uttered an unearthly screech that shook the room. Then it screamed one clearly discernable word, "STOP!"

Knife in hand, ready to plunge it into Jamie's defenseless body, Grat hesitated, turning toward the horror that had now landed beside him. "Do not kill her!" the thing shrieked.

The voice sounded familiar, and then Jamie saw the face. It was undoubtedly Kareina, but she had changed. Kareina's face had lengthened and distorted, gaining stubby, goat-like horns and jagged fangs. Her torso was no longer that of a human female. It looked more like a gaunt skeleton over which had been stretched a bone-tight hide of dark scaly leather. Enormous bat-like wings grated and rasped as she moved.

The guards were obviously as terrified as Jamie was. The one who only moments earlier had grabbed Jamie's arm began quietly inching away, then broke into a run for the theater door.

Grat was startled, but clearly not frightened. He took a step toward Kareina.

"Carrington ordered me to kill her!"

"When he told you that he didn't know Jamie had destroyed the SD card!" Kareina countered. "We can't kill her yet. The only remaining copy of the detonation codes is in her head. We have to take her alive!"

With Grat's attention momentarily diverted, Jamie saw her chance. With one smooth motion she swung the projection booth door wide and made a break for the access hatch. The hatch opened easily. Within moments of entering the projection booth she had scrambled through the hatch and down the access tunnel.

Seeing Jamie in motion, Grat moved to follow her.

"Let her GO, you fool!" Kareina shrieked again. "She can't get away!"

Jamie raced on hands and now-bloodied knees back to the main corridor, then ran to the elevator. She was breathing in ragged gasps, her body quaking violently as she waited for the elevator door to open.

The descent seemed to take hours.

What had she just seen? *Was that really Kareina?* Jamie had always known there was something strange about Kareina, but the thing she saw in the theater was clearly not human. *What is she?*

The elevator door finally slid open, and Jamie bolted for the emergency exit.

She undid the latches and turned the big wheel to undog the door. She pushed, but it did not move. She checked to make sure all the latches where clear then pushed again, harder. Slowly, the heavy steel door began to move. She leaned into it with all her strength and it finally opened wide enough for her body to slip through.

She was out!

Her heart was pounding, her whole body quivering, but she was out and she was alive.

She looked around for Roger.

There! A car was flashing its lights. He'd seen her.

She ran to him.

High overhead, a dark bat-like shape circled over Raven's Nest as Roger's BMW drove away. Satisfied that she'd seen everything she needed to see, Kareina angled the tip of a dark, leathery wing and banked to the left. Gaining altitude rapidly, she opened her mouth in an exultant roar.

FLYING OUT OF
BOULDER

Chapter Sixteen: The Flight

ERIN FLETCHER'S PRIVATE JET, EN ROUTE TO DALLAS

"What happened to you?" Roger asked, sensing Jamie's agitation as she slid into the BMW's passenger seat.

"I destroyed the SD card with the detonation codes," she said, still struggling to catch her breath, "but Carrington found out. One of his men just tried to kill me. I barely escaped."

Roger put the car into motion.

"Where are we going now?" Jamie asked. Her world had just disintegrated, but somehow she knew she could trust Roger implicitly.

"Our first step is to get you out of Boulder. This is Carrington's home base. His army could easily overwhelm us, and they *will* try to recapture you.

"We have a private jet waiting at Boulder Municipal. It will take us somewhere safe. My friends have a place in Texas they assure me is secure."

"Who are these friends of yours?"

"Just call them the resistance. They found out what Carrington is trying to do, and are attempting to prevent a worldwide disaster. I'll explain more when we're on the plane. For now, why don't you lean your seat back and try to rest. We'll be there before long."

Jamie gratefully complied. She could not sleep, but it felt good to rest. And for the first time in days she felt secure.

Boulder Municipal Airport is a small general aviation airport located three miles northeast of downtown Boulder. Coming into Boulder from the south, Roger took Foothills Parkway to Valmont Road, then headed east toward Airport Road.

Just before they turned onto Valmont, two black SUVs passed them going south on Foothills. They both bore the Carrington logo on the door.

Roger glanced over to Jamie and noted that she was still awake.

"We just passed two of Carrington's SUVs. They were headed south on Foothills."

"Do you think they saw us?"

"I hope not..." he said, then added hopefully, "We've almost made it to the airport. Just a few more minutes.

"Wait..." Roger said with apprehension, eyes locked on the rearview mirror, "We're not out of the woods yet. The SUVs must have hung a U-turn. They're following us."

He mashed the accelerator, then placed a call to Lys using the BMW's Bluetooth link to the iPhone in his pocket.

Lys answered on the first ring.

"This is Roger. Is everyone on the plane?"

"Yes, it's fueled and the flight plan is filed. We're ready to leave as soon as you get here."

"Ask Erin to have the pilot begin the preflight checklist. We're on Valmont headed your way, and should be there in a few minutes, but we're being followed by two black SUVs with the Carrington logo. They're staying well back, so I think they've been told to find out where we're going, but not apprehend."

Kareina must be planning to deal with Jamie personally, Lys thought. *We have to get her out of here quickly.*

Erin's blue and white corporate jet was parked on the tarmac, engines running. The pilot had just finished the pre-flight checklist when Roger and Jamie climbed aboard. By the time they'd fastened their seatbelts, the cabin door had been latched and the plane was in motion, taxiing to the runway.

Receiving clearance for takeoff, the pilot pushed the throttle forward until the twin Honeywell engines were each generating 7000 pounds of thrust. The engines' roar shook the cabin. As the pilot released the brake, the wheels began to roll, slowly at first, but the acceleration built quickly. When the airspeed indicator hit 80 knots, the pilot pulled back on the yoke and commanded the gear up.

The sleek craft floated off the field like a feather

in a breeze, runway lights dropping away and landing lights shining up into the night. The jet banked gently to the right, then shot skyward, climbing to 40,000 feet in about twenty minutes.

As they were climbing, Jamie glanced around the cabin. She recognized the craft as a Gulfstream G280. She'd flown in one with a slightly different configuration a few years earlier and knew it had a cabin rated best-in-class for a midsize corporate jet. Erin's jet was configured for nine passengers, six in leather reclining seats, and three on a leather side-facing divan near the rear of the plane.

When they reached cruising altitude, the five unbuckled their seatbelts and moved to the back of the jet to facilitate conversation. Jamie sat with Lys and Erin on the side-facing divan, while Michael and Roger took the recliners across the aisle.

Roger introduced Jamie to the other passengers, beginning with Lys.

Jamie had met Lys several times while she and Roger were dating, but Lys had just been a teenager at the time. It felt reassuring to see another familiar face in the plane.

Michael Fletcher, Roger explained, was a well-known author, having written several books dealing with the supernatural.

His wife Erin had been married to Rex Vanderberg, one of the wealthiest men in Texas. Her husband had been killed in a hunting accident two years earlier, making Erin an instant billionaire. She and Michael had been married one year, and now made their home in Scotland.

Erin took the drink orders, retreating to the galley at the front of the plane and returning with everyone's selection.

"I've never been served drinks by a billionaire waitress!" Roger quipped.

"Just here to serve," Erin smiled graciously.

Jamie had ordered a gin and tonic, and accepted it eagerly. She was still trembling.

She quickly filled the others in on her experiences since meeting with Roger that morning.

"Right at the end, something strange happened. I know I didn't imagine it, but it can't be real either." She described Kareina's entrance to the theater.

Lys smiled, "I've had a few encounters with Kareina myself. What you saw tonight was the real Kareina.

"Usually she uses her mind control powers to mask her true identity, but with Grat about to kill you she didn't have that luxury. When the alarm sounded, she would have headed directly to the theater. Kareina has the ability to slip partially out of our dimension and pass through walls and ceilings. Thank God she made it in time."

"What is she?"

"Kareina is an Archon," Erin explained. "The Archons are a race of beings from Hades, a dimension parallel to our own."

Seeing the look of confusion on Jamie's face, Erin described the Earth-realm's ongoing battle with the Archons. "There are many parallel dimensions in the universe, Jamie, and many of them are inhabited. Unfortunately, for the past 20,000 years, our Earth-realm has been a battleground in a war between several of these dimensions.

"The realm of Hades was once a beautiful place, rich in minerals and filled with awesome vistas. The Archons were highly intelligent and built tall, cloud-piercing cities. They considered themselves the most advanced of all the inhabited realms. But the ruler of Hades was overcome with ambition. He set out to conquer the other inhabited worlds, and establish himself as supreme lord over all.

"The first step was invading our world. The invasion force was massive. It included many legions of Archons, as well as a few renegade members of a race called the Irin. Joining this force was a horde of Nephilim—monstrous half-breed warriors, the mutant offspring of Irin fathers and human mothers.

"The devastation was unimaginable... Whole continents disappeared beneath the seas. Our race was decimated. It was from that era that our legends of Atlantis and the great flood were born.

"The human race was nearly obliterated, but in the midst of the destruction, our leaders appealed for help. In those days, there were still humans who had the ability to travel between dimensions. Fearing their battle was lost, the remaining human princes sent a delegation to Hi-Ouranos, realm of the Ancient Ones who rule the inhabited worlds. The Ancient Ones responded to their appeal and raised up a force to stop the invasion.

"A portal was constructed on what is now England's Salisbury Plain, and tens of thousands of volunteers poured through. They came from every inhabited world: winged Irin from Basilea, Gnomen from the crystal caverns of Alani, Mermen from Taverea, and Elvin warriors from the forests of Ayden.

"In a bitterly contested battle lasting centuries, the Archon advance was weakened, but the Archons refused to retreat. Finally, the Ancient Ones authorized a direct assault on Hades.

"From what the Irin tell me," Erin continued, "it was a time of incredible horror. In the end, the Archon forces were devastated, and the once-beautiful realm of Hades became a burned-out wasteland.

"As city after city on their world was devastated, the inhabitants of Abadon, the last great Archon city, moved underground, burrowing into an extinct volcano. There they established a new Archon culture centered on their hatred of the human race.

"In their twisted reasoning, the Archons blame the human race for the destruction of their world. That's why they're intent on invading our world and taking it for their own.

"They've captured millions of humans over the

years and made them slaves. All manual labor in Hades is now done by humans. But they also use their human slaves for their entertainment, torturing them for sadistic pleasure."

"The Archons have moved among us for thousands of years," Lys added, "tormenting human victims and plotting to destroy us. They form the basis of many of our oldest legends.

"Kareina is an Archon commander, sent to prepare the way for their invasion of our world. Before I found out what Kareina really is, I actually went with her to a party at Carrington's about two years ago. I almost didn't survive the evening. She's tried to kill me several times since."

"There are forces of evil in the world that are capable of terrible things," Erin continued, "but there are also forces of great good. When we get to Texas we'll introduce you to Eliel. She's is a member of an alien race called the Irin. She and her people have battled to defend our world from the Archons for thousands of years. Many have perished.

"But the warfare is now reaching a climax. We're now in a time when every one of us will need to choose which side we're on.

"Carrington aligned himself with evil because of the power he thinks it will bring him. Evil always promises power. It may seem enticing at first, even exhilarating, but evil is never satisfied. Evil begets evil, and leads to greater and greater darkness. Those that choose that route always end up enslaved and destroyed."

After finishing their drinks, they let Jamie stretch out on the divan for a brief nap, while the rest took to the recliners and did the same. Two hours after takeoff, the Fletcher jet gently touched down on the runway at the Addison Airport, nine miles north of downtown Dallas.

Chapter Seventeen:
Return to the Lake House

THE PINEY WOODS OF EAST TEXAS

Erin had reserved a Mercedes-Benz GL450 seven-passenger SUV from one of the rental agencies at the airport, and—by pulling a few strings—had arranged to have it waiting for them on the tarmac when they deplaned at 1:15 AM. The five transferred their bags from the plane, and were quickly underway.

Traffic at that hour was almost non-existent. Just outside the airport, the big SUV took the entrance ramp for the Dallas North Tollway headed north. Four miles later they exited onto George Bush Turnpike which skirted the northern edge of the city and connected them to Interstate 30 east of Dallas. Continuing eastward on the interstate, they made it to the Cedar Hills Lake turnoff just one hour after the plane landed.

Their destination was what Erin considered her "home away from home," a lake house owned by Derek and Piper Holmes.

When Holmes and Piper had been psychologists, the lake house had been their weekend getaway. Far enough from the city to feel truly isolated, it was a place they could leave their pressures and responsibilities behind and actually relax.

The main feature of the house was a large "great room" with an eighteen-foot knotty-pine cathedral ceiling and a wall of windows offering a full 180-degree view of the lake. On pleasant evenings, they'd enjoyed reclining side-by-side on the broad wrap-around deck, watching the sun set across the peaceful waters of the lake. On cool evenings they'd snuggle up on the couch in front of a crackling fire.

It was at the lake house that both Holmes and Piper first encountered the Irin. The lake house had also provided a secure refuge for Erin when her life had been threatened by her former husband.

In the past year, Holmes had added several extra guest rooms so the house could provide a safe haven for members of the synaxis in times of emergency.

The Mercedes pulled into the driveway of the lake house at 3:00 AM. Its five passengers were exhausted, but thankful to be there.

Holmes and Piper met them at the door.

Jamie had slept most of the way there, and was asleep again shortly after they arrived.

Jamie slept till ten the next morning, and was surprised to find a note from Piper welcoming her to the lake house, along with several changes of clothing in her size, laid out on the couch in her room.

Holmes and Piper had already finished their

morning workouts and had breakfast prepared when Jamie limped stiffly down the hallway. Roger had already been up for about twenty minutes, and instinctively went to her and held her gently. To his surprise, she returned the embrace without hesitation, melting into his arms with an eagerness he'd not expected. It almost seemed like their relationship was picking up where they'd left off many years earlier.

"Thatcher..." he sighed, tightening the embrace, "I know this last week was a nightmare in almost every way, but I'm so glad to be with you again. I didn't even realize how much I'd missed you until I saw you in the park last week."

Piper served breakfast to Roger and Jamie on the deck of the lake house: scrambled eggs, crisp bacon, whole wheat toast, along with coffee and orange juice. It was a beautiful spring day with clear skies and temperatures in the seventies.

Roger and Jamie ate in silence for a few minutes. Jamie was clearly troubled.

She finally looked up at Roger, "I feel totally lost, Roger." She appeared to be fighting back tears. "What am I supposed to do now? For the last twelve years, my life has been centered on Carrington and Raven's Nest. Now all of that is over."

"Are you really sorry? You know now what kind of person Carrington is. Would you rather still be with him?"

"It's not Carrington I miss. I've known for a long time he isn't a good person. But I loved my work.

"Carrington hired me right out of grad school with the challenge to design and build a computer network to control a huge underground complex he was building. He'd heard of my reputation in computer science and took me to dinner at Gary Danko's—at that time the top-rated and most expensive restaurant in San Francisco. I was overwhelmed.

"As we sat across the table from each other, savoring the cuisine and sipping some of the finest wines in the world, Carrington cast his vision for Raven's Nest. Nothing like what he was envisioning had ever been done. He promised me great freedom and unlimited resources. After several hours of conversation, I accepted his offer.

"I think Raven's Nest was the first thing in my life that ever challenged me and I rose to the occasion. I accomplished everything Carrington wanted and more.

"When the network was up and running, Carrington promoted me to his administrative assistant, tasked with maintaining the network and expanding it to his other enterprises.

"Raven's Nest was my life. But when I walked out the escape hatch last night, I knew I'd never see it again."

She reached over and took his hand. "I'm thankful to be with you, Roger. You don't know how many times I'd thought of you over the years. I wanted to contact you, but I knew you didn't have a place with Carrington, and I wasn't ready to leave Raven's Nest. I guess it's our same old story.

"But now everything has changed. Two weeks ago, I was confident, self-assured, and totally in control. But in the last week I've lost my sister, my job, my home, and what I thought was my future. I wasn't able to save anything. I'd packed a small bag last night with some mementos I wanted to keep, but I lost it in the access tunnels. I don't even know where. I have nothing."

She paused a moment, looking up into Roger's eyes, then added, "But it does feel good to be with you again."

As they finished eating, Jamie looked up and saw a flock of birds coming toward them across the lake— great white-winged birds soaring effortlessly in their direction. Approaching the house, three of the birds broke away from the rest of the flock while the others began to circle slowly overhead. The three spread their wings and floated gracefully down to a soft landing on the deck. They were not birds. They were Irin warriors.

Jamie sat frozen, her mouth open in amazement, eyes locked on the new arrivals. "They're *real!*" she gasped. "Everything you told me is true!"

As Jamie sat in stunned silence, Lys came out and welcomed the Irin. As their wings silently folded back into an unseen dimension, she began introducing them to Roger and Jamie.

The first was Eliel, whom Roger has already met.

Though she was small and almost delicate in appearance, Jamie sensed in Eliel great strength and intelligence.

The next was Rand. Jamie looked at her with awe. She was a stunning beauty—tall and slender, yet with an intensity about her that was a little intimidating. Dressed in a black belted tunic and leggings, Rand's piercing brown eyes, coupled with the long dagger strapped to her right thigh, gave her the appearance of an Amazon warrior. Her lithe body was crowned by a long flowing mane of dark, auburn hair.

The male Irin was equally striking. Araton was tall and muscular, with rich, dark-brown skin and closely shaved head. He wore a multicolored, two-piece garment reminiscent of a West African dashiki, with a metallic mesh belt cinched tightly around his waist. Attached to the belt, the hilt of a scimitar protruded from a three-foot-long steel scabbard.

Erin ran to the deck to greet the new arrivals, going first to Araton and giving him a warm embrace. Araton had saved Erin's life more than once, and would always hold a special place in her heart.

Piper invited everyone inside and served coffee.

As they took their seats in the great room, Araton explained the Archon plot to Jamie—how they planned to use the nineteen remaining bombs to bring an end to human civilization, allowing the Archons to invade the world.

"You did well to destroy the memory chip, Jamie,

but you must understand that it puts you in grave danger. You now hold the key to all their plans. Kareina will try to capture you and force you to give up the codes, and don't under estimate her. She has great powers.

"For the present, we believe you're safe here. The Irin guards overhead will prevent attacks by human collaborators like Carrington, and we hope we'll be able to shield you from Kareina's mental powers."

Roger was the first to ask the question all of them had been pondering. "But where does all of this end? Does Jamie have to stay here forever, confined to this house with Irin guards circling overhead?"

Araton shrugged, "We don't yet have an end-game. But we are committed to do whatever we can to keep Jamie safe. We'll do it for as long as it takes... and as long as it works. The Archons won't give up. They'll keep trying. But if Jamie falls into their hands, your world is finished."

Rand standing guard at the lake house

Chapter Eighteen: Surrounded

THE PINEY WOODS OF EAST TEXAS

Jamie went to bed early that night and slept peacefully. The next few days were a welcome respite. The second day at the lake house, she and Roger spent long hours talking and visiting with the others. The morning of the third day she was looking through the bookshelf in her bedroom and came across several books by Michael Fletcher. She spent the better part of that day reading.

At dinner that night, Jamie peppered Michael with questions about the book.

"Now you have to remember, Jamie," Michael cautioned. "When I wrote that book I had yet to meet my first angel. It was all just theory. Still, I'd say my conjectures were about 90% accurate."

Later that evening, Jamie and Roger sat on the lake house's broad wrap-around deck watching the sun set over the peaceful waters of Cedar Hills Lake as a trio of Irin warriors wheeled protectively far overhead. In the woods nearby they could see Rand, hovering effortlessly about twenty feet in the air, senses trained, alert to any

Archon presence. Knowing that Rand and other Irin warriors were stationed in the forest around the house gave them both a much needed sense of security.

The peaceful atmosphere of the lake house seemed healing.

As they relaxed side-by-side, Roger leaned back in his chair and studied Jamie for a long time.

"We have so many years to catch up on," he said, finally. "I've thought about you many times over the years, but I always pictured you working at some high-tech firm in Silicon Valley. I never dreamed you were right here in Colorado."

He paused a minute, then added, "Tell me about Raven's Nest. Living in Boulder, I've heard a lot of stories and wild rumors about the place. What was it like to live there?"

Jamie took a deep breath, not quite sure how to begin. "Let me begin with the good part," she said.

"When I started work on Raven's Nest, Carrington gave me almost total freedom. I threw myself into the project, sometimes putting in twenty-hour days, but I enjoyed every minute. With an unlimited budget and top contractors brought in from around the world, the complex was finished in less than three years.

"Amazingly there were none of the usual start-up bugs. Everything worked from day one. And the place was a dream.

"I'll always remember my first morning at the Nest. As I woke up, the computer slowly brought up the lights and greeted me with a pleasant, 'Good morning, Jamie.' I stumbled into the bathroom to take a shower, and the shower came on automatically—already set to the perfect temperature. The shower welcomed me with several minutes of warm, drenching rain, then a set of sixteen pulsating spray jets activated, perfectly adjusted to my body.

"Throughout the day, the computer would automatically sense my mood and change the color of the lighting. My favorite music was always playing. I felt I'd created my own personal paradise.

"For the first few months, life at Raven's Nest was intoxicating. My commute was a ten second-ride on a private elevator from my apartment to the Carrington Corporation office suite. We had a beauty shop on site, a masseuse on call, a fully-equipped gym and recreation center, and world-class chefs to prepare anything I desired. Everyone in the complex knew who I was and treated me like royalty.

"But after the first three months, reality began to set in. My fourth month there, Carrington seduced me into sleeping with him. During a stormy five-week affair, I caught my first glimpse of what Alexander Carrington was really like.

"About that time, Carrington began to host his now infamous parties, attended by the rich and powerful from all over the world. I only ever went to one of his parties, but still shudder when I think of it.

"The hardest thing for me to deal with was the

way Carrington treated the furniture."

"The furniture?" Roger asked.

"*Human* furniture," Jamie answered. "To be specific—young women paid by Carrington to lounge around the Nest in scanty attire. They're a regular fixture at the mansion, part of the décor. Carrington just calls them 'the furniture.' He hires the girls for one year, and when their year is over he discards them like last season's wardrobe, shipping them off to the harem of a Middle Eastern terrorist he calls the *sheik*."

Seeing the look of revulsion on Roger's face, Jamie recounted more of the Nest's troubling aspects: the way Kareina worked behind the scenes to manipulate and control Carrington, the disturbing presence of Grat Dalton, and Carrington's overweening lust for power.

Finally, she revisited the horror of her last night there. She described Nicole's brutal murder, the terror of being pursued through narrow tunnels in total darkness by a psychopath determined to kill her, and the final confrontation between Dalton and Kareina in the theater.

As she talked, Jamie felt like blinders were coming off her eyes—as if she was seeing for the first time the evil of the place. She'd been so caught up in the challenge of her job and the Nest's hi-tech luxuries she'd never stopped to consider what Raven's Nest had become.

Now that she was away from it, it no longer seemed like a luxurious mansion. It seemed like hell.

When Jamie finished her story, Roger shared his.

He told her about his years in medical school at Yale, his residency in Boston, and finally fulfilling his dream of moving back to Colorado. He talked about his wife and daughter and their tragic death.

"After Laura and Elise were killed, I was devastated; I felt I had nothing left to live for. There were a few times I even considered suicide.

"I finally decided to start over. I sold the house with all its reminders of Laura. I bought a beautiful new house, had it professionally decorated with very few mementos of the past, and I threw myself into my work. But I was numb on the inside. I guess that's where I've been the last three years.

"It wasn't until I saw you in the park that I felt I was coming alive again. It feels like I'm waking from a long nightmare."

On her fourth morning at the lake house, Jamie awoke with a splitting headache. Sitting at breakfast with Roger, she was in obvious distress.

"What's the matter?" Roger asked.

"I woke up this morning with the worst headache I've ever had. It feels like there's a steel band around my head. It's slowly tightening, squeezing," she winced. "It hurts!"

Roger gave her a painkiller, but it didn't seem to help. The pain came and went throughout the day.

That night Jamie didn't sleep well. She was

tormented in her dreams, one nightmare after another. Running through a labyrinth. Falling from a great height. Being pursued by grotesque monsters. Each time she awoke trembling, drenched in perspiration.

After breakfast, Jamie sat with Lys and Roger in the great room looking out over the lake.

She shared about the headaches and nightmares and then added; "Something else strange is happening to me. Since yesterday afternoon, it feels like there's something crawling through my mind. Not my brain, but my mind.

"I know it sounds crazy, but it feels like there is something moving through my thoughts. Sifting through them. Examining them. Is this the Archons, or am I imagining this?"

Lys and Roger had no explanation, so when Eliel arrived later that morning Roger told her what was happening.

Eliel immediately called a meeting.

Within ten minutes, Araton and Rand arrived. Lys, Roger, Jamie, Erin, Michael, Holmes and Piper all took seats. Eliel asked Jamie to share what she'd been experiencing.

Jamie briefly recounted the events of the last few days. "I've had enough mental discipline to put up barriers against them, but it's decidedly unpleasant. Could these sensations just be a psychological response to the trauma I experienced this past week?"

"I don't think it's psychological," Holmes replied.

"It sounds real."

"Our sentinels have reported increasing Archon activity in the area," Eliel responded. "It sounds like they're using their mind control powers to try to gain access your memory. I'll increase the guards to see if we can shut them out."

Days five through seven at the lake house were better.

But the eighth day was much worse.

Jamie's headache lasted all day, and no amount of painkiller availed.

Toward midday, the Irin guards overhead reported Archons moving in the woods near the house.

More Irin arrived, throwing a defensive cordon around the house. Their presence seemed to help. For a few days Jamie's condition improved.

By the end of that week, however, black SUVs bearing the Carrington logo were seen cruising the road in front of the house several times a day.

Another meeting was called, and Rand outlined the situation. "The Archons have dramatically increased their numbers, and their collaborators now have the house surrounded. We've had enough strength that they haven't attempted to physically take Jamie, but we've not been able to fully shield her from their mental attacks.

"But conditions are continuing to deteriorate. In the last twenty-four hours, the Archon supporters have begun closing ranks. We believe they're preparing to kidnap Jamie."

"What can we do?" asked Roger.

"We had thought the lake house would be safe, but Jamie is a high priority target for the Archons. I don't think we can fully protect her here. We estimate a full-on Archon assault on the lake house within twenty-four hours."

"Where can we go?" asked Jamie.

"There's only one place on earth where we have enough strength to fully protect you. Since the opening of the Iona portal, the island of Iona has become an Irin stronghold. There is enough Irin presence on the island that no Archon would dare approach."

Roger asked, "So we just fly halfway around the world to Iona?"

Lys added, "Is that even safe? Couldn't they just knock the jet out of the sky?"

"We deem the trip to Iona far safer than remaining here. Remember, the Archons need Jamie alive. They last thing they would do would be to try to kill her."

"I talked to Erin earlier today." Rand continued. "Her jet is being prepared as we speak. You'll leave here at midnight. The jet should be ready for takeoff by the time you get to Dallas. You can sleep on the plane and make it to Iona early tomorrow afternoon."

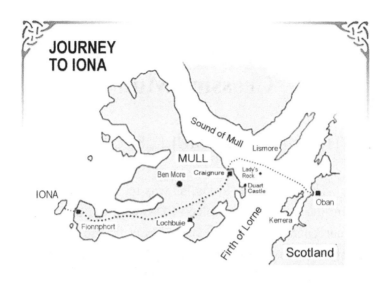

Chapter Nineteen:
Crossing Mull

THE ISLAND OF MULL, SCOTLAND

The drive back to Dallas was tense. Shortly after leaving the lake house, a black SUV with the Carrington logo careened out of a side road right in front of them and attempted to block their path, but as they watched, the big vehicle mysteriously skidded across the road into a ditch, leaving the way open. Then two more black SUVs began tailing them. They stayed on their tail all the way to Dallas. Several times the lead SUV charged forward as though attempting to ram them, but always pulled back at the last moment. They all knew that it was only because of the Irin guards accompanying them, cloaked in the invisibility of the shadow realm, that they made it to Dallas without incident.

As Erin had promised, the Gulfstream was fueled and ready to fly when they arrived at the Addison airport at 1:30 AM.

Eliel appeared next to the plane just as they were exiting the rented SUV. "That was an interesting trip," she smiled, "but I think you're okay from here. The Archons wouldn't dare to endanger Jamie's life by attacking the plane, and we don't think Carrington has had time to deploy his forces in Scotland. The other guards and I are going back to the lake house to make sure everything is secure there. We'll see you tomorrow evening on Iona."

Everyone in the group thanked her profusely for her help.

Erin, Michael, Lys, Roger, and Jamie boarded the plane and took their seats with a sigh of relief. They fastened their seatbelts and were sipping drinks as the plane taxied out. By the time the craft was at cruising altitude, they were all soundly asleep.

The G280's maximum range of 3,600 nautical miles put Scotland slightly out of range for a flight originating in Dallas, so the pilot made a brief refueling stop at Teterboro, a busy general aviation airport in northern New Jersey. Most of the passengers slept through the stop.

In the air again, the craft began its red-eye flight across the pond.

Roger had slept briefly on the flight from Dallas, but leaving Teterboro, he sat, wide awake, watching the others dozing peacefully. He hated flying and could hardly ever sleep on a plane. The rumble of the engines, coupled with the roar of the air slipping past the fuselage, grated on his nerves.

He fished a pair of Bose noise-canceling headphones out of the seat pocket in front of him and plugged them into his iPhone, then flipped through his music collection and finally chose Rachmaninoff's *Rhapsody on a Theme of Paganini.* As the familiar melody began to play, he leaned his seat back, closed his eyes, and tried again to sleep.

But his mind was in turmoil. The last few weeks had been like a surreal dream. There'd been his first encounter with the Irin, the reawakening of his relationship with Jamie, the long days at the lake house, and their present flight half-way around the world to save Jamie from an Archon attack. He had no idea where it was all leading, but he was glad to be with Jamie, and had no choice but to see it through to the end.

After thirty more minutes of insomnia, he made his way up to the galley and fixed himself a gin and tonic. Twenty minutes later he was finally asleep.

They awoke about an hour before landing and enjoyed a pre-packaged breakfast that had been loaded on board at Teterboro, along with several cups of strong coffee.

The sun had already risen when the Gulfstream G280 gently touched down at Oban and the Isles Airport, just six miles northeast of the city of Oban.

They quickly passed through Oban's makeshift version of customs and passport control. Their big white Hummer was waiting for them, right where they'd left it.

Erin dangled the keys in front of Lys, who still looked a little sleepy. "Will you do the honors?"

"With pleasure," Lys smiled, eyes brightening as

she eagerly snatched the keys from Erin's hand.

Erin called up the ferry schedule on her smartphone. "The next ferry to Mull leaves in an hour. I think we can just make it."

Oban, known as "The Gateway to the Western Isles," is a lovely town—reminiscent of a bygone era. At the end of the 19th century, Oban had flourished as a popular seaside resort and many of the buildings still had a Victorian feel. Gingerbread villas clung to the hillside while majestic old hotels lined the Esplanade. Along George Street, busy shops and restaurants provided a quaint backdrop for the fishing boats crowded against the quay.

Their ferry, The Isle of Mull, was just boarding when they arrived. The Isle of Mull was one of the largest ships in the Calmac fleet. Her gleaming white superstructure was accentuated by a distinctive red and black funnel towering above her decks, but her most notable feature was the company name proudly emblazoned across her black hull in huge white letters: Caledonian MacBrayne.

Lys drove the big Hummer down the entrance ramp, and they soon had climbed the metal stairway to the main passenger deck. By the time they'd taken their seats on the rear observation deck, the Isle of Mull had eased from her moorings and was churning its way across the peaceful waters of Oban harbor.

Watching the western shore of Scotland retreat behind them, Michael said, "Being on a ferry in Scotland always makes me thirsty. Anyone else care for a pint?"

Michael took orders, recommending the thick foamy *Velvet*, his favorite Scottish ale, then headed straight for the ship's bar. Ordering a pint of Velvet for each of them, he returned to the observation deck.

Driven by its eight-cylinder, 3100 horsepower Mirlees Blackstone diesel, the Isle of Mull was already making fifteen knots across the smooth water of the sound.

Taking a sip of the ice-cold Velvet, Michael savored its rich smoothness as the town of Oban faded into the distance.

The Isle of Mull soon passed out of the Bay of Oban into the broad estuary known as the Firth of Lorne. To the right they were passing the island of Lismore, marked by the picturesque Lismore Lighthouse.

Visible ahead off the port bow was their destination, the ship's namesake, the island of Mull. The hulking form of Duart Castle, ancestral home of the Clan Maclean, was perched on the cliffs above the shore.

A stiff, offshore breeze had begun to blow. The Isle of Mull's deck shuddered continuously as its massive engine thrust the big ship through the rising seas.

Lys stood at the rail on the port side of the ship, watching for a jagged rock just breaking the surface of the water. Seeing it, she called Roger and Jamie to the rail, and recounted the night she'd spent on the tiny rock.

Exiting the ferry at Craignure, on Mull's eastern shore, they pulled in to the Torosay Inn for an early lunch. The synaxis had eaten there on their first trip to Iona and had since made a point of stopping whenever they crossed Mull.

The pub had once been an old drover's inn and still retained its historic character, with rough cut stone walls, wooden floor and a huge open fireplace with a replica of an ancient claymore battle sword mounted above it.

The innkeeper came to the table to distribute menus and returned fifteen minutes later to take their orders.

Waiting for the food, Lys glanced at Jamie, "How's your head feeling?"

"So far, so good," she replied, hopefully. "I slept better last night than I have in weeks, and the headache is gone for the moment."

"We're almost to Iona," Lys smiled. "We should be there in less than two hours. You'll love Iona. It's a beautiful place, but best of all, the Archons can't touch you there."

The food finally arrived, and was superb, as usual.

As they prepared to leave, the innkeeper gave them a word of caution.

"If you're driving to the west you'd best take care. A sea fog is forecast to roll in sometime this afternoon.

"When a sea fog rolls in," he said, shaking his head, "'tis bad trouble on the roads. The roads on Mull aren't that well marked to begin with, but in a fog, you sometimes can't see the road at all. Run off the road some places and those peat bogs will swallow you like quicksand!

"And the fog can play mind games on you as well. When the light's just right in a deep fog, people often imagine seeing fairies... or worse."

The road to Iona was a winding, one-lane affair running the length of Mull. Being a one lane road meant that they had to pull over frequently to allow cars traveling the opposite direction to pass.

In spite of the innkeeper's words, the start of the drive seemed pleasant. The road wound its way through the mixed forest on the eastern side of the Mull, rising into the green but stark volcanic uplands that make up most of the island. The landscape was dramatic, and constantly changing, with desolate moorland and steep heather-clad hills. Ancient brooding castles, deep lochs, impassible bogs, and deserted glens all glided past as Lys guided the Hummer along the now familiar route.

To the right, they could see Ben More, which, since its recent eruption, was now a picturesque cone more than four thousand feet high in the center of the island. The eruption of Ben More had brought great devastation to some sections of Mull, but reconstruction was well underway and progressing rapidly.

Roger sat with his mouth open, awestruck. He had never imagined a place so desolate, yet so beautiful.

Then, without warning, with the sun still shining brightly overhead, the fog began to roll in.

It came in from the sea, enveloping Mull like a monster from the deep, creeping forward in a conquest that would end only when a favorable wind came to dispel it.

The sky above turned a sickly tallow color as low clouds started pouring over the mountains. They watched helplessly as a dense fog bank came rolling down the ridge toward them. Within moments, they were engulfed in a swirling, thick, impenetrable mist. The air took on a significant chill and there was little visibility ahead or behind.

Lys realized with horror that she could scarcely see past the end of the Hummer's hood

"This is as thick as a traditional London 'pea-souper,'" Michael quipped.

"I've never seen fog like this," Roger said.

"Here in Scotland it's not uncommon," Michael replied. "On the east coast of Scotland this is what they call a *haar*. It's a dense fog that forms over the sea, then is blown onto the land. I drove through one several years back near Edinburgh. It went from a bright sunny day to not being able to see five meters in front of you within a couple of seconds.

"Sea fog is not as common here in the Western Isles, but it does happen."

"How long does it last?" Lys asked.

"The length of time a *haar* will last is unpredictable. Sometimes it will lift within a couple of hours, but it can also last for days. It sometimes spends an entire day moving like a tide, backwards and forwards, up and down the length of a glen.

"Experiencing a *haar* can be a depressing thing. It feels as if no warmth remains amidst the fog. A *haar* is not only dark, dank and damp, but often so cold that it seems to penetrate your very bones.

"And like the innkeeper said, there's something decidedly eerie about a *haar*. It conjures up tales of the supernatural and causes people to hurry home to escape from its clutches. It makes you want to lock the door, switch on the heat, and close the curtains."

The *haar* dramatically slowed their progress across the island. Ordinarily the trip from Craignure to Fionphort took about ninety minutes, but only being able to see the edge of the road a few feet ahead, their progress across the island ground to a slow crawl, barely maintaining five miles an hour at times.

Lys squinted into the fog, gripping the wheel more tightly, "At this rate it could take us five hours to get to Iona."

Jamie groaned at the thought. She was in agony. Just before the fog rolled in, her headache had returned with a vengeance. *There must be Archons close by. If only we can make it to Iona!*

An hour passed. For Lys, the boredom was numbing. There was nothing to see but enveloping fog. At one point they came to a barricade in the road, barely seeing it in time to stop. A hand-painted sign was posted on the barricade with an arrow pointing left and the word DIVERSION."

"Diversion? Like in 'entertainment?'" Lys quipped. "I could use some of that. This fog is driving me crazy."

Michael laughed. "In Scotland, a diversion is not some kind of pleasant pastime. Diversion is the British word for 'detour.' They're probably still doing some construction work on the road. This section was one of the hardest hit by the pyroclastic flow when Ben More blew."

Mile after mile, the scene was unchanged, with the dark mist confronting them at every hand. The edge of the road came into view just beyond the Hummer's hood, and with the track constantly twisting and turning, Lys had to keep her eyes glued to it.

Jamie was barely conscious. Her head seemed ready to explode.

After about three hours the fog began to lift. The sky overhead was still dark and overcast, but beneath the overhanging clouds, they began to catch glimpses of the surrounding landscape. The scenery was not what they'd expected.

"This doesn't look like the road to Iona," Lys said, pulling over to the side of the road and killing the engine. "Where are we?"

Up ahead she could see the waters of a beautiful

loch. Perched on its shore were the crumbling ruins of an old castle.

To the right, through the trees, they could see an ancient circle of standing stones. Nine granite monoliths, set in a ring 40 feet in diameter.

"I know where we are!" Michael exclaimed. "This is Lochbuie, I've been here several times. On a clear day, this is one of the most beautiful places on Mull. Majestic mountains, lush woodland, a truly spectacular coastline. That castle is Moy Castle, built here in the early 1400s.

"We're in southern Mull," he continued, "near the coast. We must have made a wrong turn in the fog a few miles back."

"How do we get back to the main road?"

"There's only one road in and out of Lochbuie, I'm afraid." Michael replied. "We'll have to go back the way we came."

"Great," Lys sighed, "Back into the fog."

As Lys prepared to restart the Hummer, her eye caught sight of movement near the stone circle.

Noting that Lys's attention was fixed on the stones, Michael commented, "That circle of standing stones is thousands of years old, dating back to Neolithic times. It's the only stone circle on the island, and no one knows who built it. It's sort of the island of Mull's version of Stonehenge."

Just then, there was a loud thud on the roof of the

Hummer, shaking the whole vehicle. They all jumped, startled by the unexpected sound.

"What was that?" Roger said, peering out the window.

"I have no idea," Lys replied, "but I don't like it."

It happened again. There was still nothing visible.

Then Lys pointed toward the stone circle. "There's something large moving in the trees over there near the stones." She paused a moment. "Correction. Make that lots of things moving in the trees... and they're coming our way!"

The loud thud repeated, and the whole vehicle began to shake and sway.

"Something's landed on the roof!" Lys shouted, restarting the Hummer in an attempt to make a getaway. But a horde of Archon warriors suddenly surrounded them, leather wings thundering as they flew in a rapidly tightening circle around the Hummer.

Living gargoyles! Roger thought with horror as they came closer. Like the hideous stone carvings that adorned many medieval cathedrals, the beasts bore broad, deeply ridged foreheads, stubby, goat-like horns, and bulging reptilian eyes. Their thickly muscled jaws were spread wide revealing a double row of razor-sharp fangs.

Within moments, the monsters landed and mobbed the Hummer, pounding the windows with clenched fists and shrieking with rage.

Suddenly, Jamie's door was flung open and a dozen Archon hands clawed at her. One of the Archons slashed her seatbelt with a razor-sharp talon, and in a moment she was dragged, kicking and screaming, from the Hummer and dumped into the tall grass by the side of the road.

Before she could react, two eight-foot tall Archon warriors seized her wrists, and with wings beating violently, swept her into the air. Jamie was shrieking in absolute terror, pleading for help.

Roger was already out of the Hummer, running at top speed after her, screaming her name. The rest of the synaxis was not far behind. Roger tripped on the uneven ground but picked himself up and was running again, heedless of the danger.

Surrounded by a swarm of smaller demons, the two Archon giants flew Jamie high above the trees, carrying her toward the circle of standing stones.

Touching down in the center of the circle, they dropped her roughly on the ground and left.

For a moment, Jamie lay unmoving, stunned by the horror of her situation. The area between the standing stones reeked with the stench of burning sulfur, and the air was literally vibrating with the roar of Archon wings and the unearthly screech of their calls.

Finally, Jamie looked up to see Kariena standing over her, sword in hand. Kariena's thin, pale lips drew taut in a satisfied smile.

In a movement almost too quick to see, Kariena's left hand darted down and seized Jamie's arm in a powerful grip. With inhuman strength she jerked Jamie to her feet, nearly wrenching her arm from its socket. As Jamie screamed in anguish, Kariena glared at her with unmitigated hatred. For just a moment, the illusion of humanity was broken, and Kareina's face reflected the hideous monster she truly was. Her mouth opened wide, revealing a double row of jagged fangs. Her eyes narrowed to fiercely burning embers.

"Pathetic human bitch!" she hissed. "You thought you could thwart my plans!" Taking a firmer hold on Jamie's arm, she purred, "Now we'll go to *my* world, and you'll tell me *everything* I want to know."

As Jamie struggled futilely to get free, Kareina screamed, "Open the portal!"

More Archons appeared, filling the air. They flew in a narrowing spiral around the standing stones, a monstrous whirlwind of reptilian bodies and rapidly beating wings. The air reverberated with an unearthly shriek, and a dark swirling cloud appeared in the middle of the stone circle.

As Roger watched helplessly, Jamie Thatcher, along with the surrounding Archon horde, disappeared into the darkness.

As the mist dissipated, Roger finally made it into the stone circle and glanced around frantically, seeking some way to follow Jamie. Seeing none, he fell to his knees on the hard-packed ground.

Lys went to him and knelt beside him, placing her hand gently on his shoulder.

Roger was distraught. Through his anguished

sobs, he hoarsely croaked one word, over and over: *"Jamie!"*

"It's no use, Roger," Lys said numbly. "Jamie's gone."

KAREINA AT
LOCHBUIE

SECTION FOUR: DESCENT INTO HELL

Chapter Twenty: Weighing Options

THE ISLAND OF IONA

A sense of despair hung over every member of the group that met the next day at the St. Columba hotel. Present in the dayroom were Michael, Erin, Lys, Patrick, and the other members of the Iona synaxis, along with Roger Johnston. Also present were a number of Irin. Lys recognized Eliel, Araton, Rand, and Mendrion.

They all shared a sense of shock and hopelessness at Jamie's loss.

"I believe the fog was orchestrated by the Archons, as was the 'diversion' sign," Michael was saying. "When we retraced our route back to the main road, the diversion sign was gone and there was no trace of construction."

"They plotted this whole thing to take Jamie captive." Eliel agreed. "I can't believe we didn't see this coming. Jamie was so close to Iona. She was almost safe."

There was a stony silence in the room for several more minutes.

"Where would they have taken her?" Roger finally asked.

"To their own world," Eliel said. "A parallel dimension called Hades. A terrible place. It served as the inspiration for your legends of Hell."

Roger was silent for a moment, as though pondering something, then looked up at Eliel, "So if Jamie was taken to Hades, that means it's possible for humans to travel to these other dimensions?"

"Yes, if a portal is open."

"Ancient mythology records a number of instances when humans were kidnapped and taken to Hades," Michael interjected. "It was never a pleasant experience. The most well-known account is the story of Persephone. According to Greek mythology, the lovely young maiden Persephone was gathering flowers for her mother in the meadows near Enna when she was abducted by the king of the underworld. He carried her to the underworld through a cleft in the earth and raped her. Some myths say that Hermes found his way to Hades and rescued her, reuniting Persephone with her mother. It's only a myth, of course, but I've found most myths have some basis in reality."

"And for a more recent example of inter-dimensional travel," he added, glancing at Erin, "Araton took Erin and me to the Irin homeworld in the parallel dimension of Basilea last year. It's an incredible place!

I'm sure a much more enjoyable trip than the one Jamie is enduring."

A pall of awkward silence hung over the group for several minutes more. Roger tried to imagine what torments Jamie might be experiencing at that very moment.

Rand finally broke the silence. "In view of what's happened, I'm afraid we're forced to admit defeat. All of our efforts to save your world have been for naught. With Jamie a captive in Hades, the Archons will eventually extract the codes and complete their plans. I see no way to avoid it.

"I'll speak to the ancient ones. We may be able to persuade them to let the present synaxis members relocate to another realm, perhaps Basilea. You don't want to be in the Earth-realm when the Archons invade."

"I can't believe you people!" Roger slammed his glass down on the table beside him. "Are you just giving up?"

"You've told me that Lys has a gift that can open a portal to another world. You've also told me that humans can travel to these places. If Lys can open a portal to Hades, why can't we go in and rescue Jamie?"

"Absolutely not!" said Rand sharply. "You don't have any idea what you're proposing. You would be throwing away your life with no hope of success."

"I agree," added Eliel. "Any attempt to enter Hades would be doomed to failure."

"There may be a way to do it," Araton countered,

ROBERT DAVID MACNEIL

"but it would be perilous."

"Hades has a large human population," he continued, "numbering in the millions. They're slaves, captured by the Archons just as Jamie was. The Archons use them for manual labor. Many are also tortured for the Archons' amusement.

"But with such a large population of humans, there's a slight possibility that a few of you might be able to slip in undetected."

"If there's any chance at all, we need to try," Roger insisted.

"I agree," Lys said.

"If you're considering doing this, I need to tell you several things up front," Rand interjected, clearly upset, and looking deadly serious.

"First of all, none of the Irin can go with you. Our presence in Hades would be recognized immediately. Any Irin who enters Hades would be instantly attacked and destroyed.

"That means there can be no rescue mission for you if you are caught. Once you go through the portal, you are totally on your own.

"Second, once you get to Hades there's no guarantee you'll find Jamie. Hades is a big place—an entire world. It's your own world shifted into a parallel dimension. Your chances of finding Jamie are almost nonexistent.

"And finally, I can't over stress the danger you'll be in. Not only will you be beyond our help, but the odds are massively against your survival. We don't know a lot about present conditions in Hades, but we do know the Archons. They are highly intelligent with an incredible telepathic ability, and they are vicious sadists, capable of cruelty beyond anything you could imagine. In Hades, there are fates far worse than death.

"So before you choose to do this, you need to decide that you're willing to throw your lives away in what will doubtless be a futile attempt to save Jamie."

"It's not just Jamie," Lys countered. "It's the whole human race. If we don't save Jamie, our world will end. We have no choice but to try."

"I agree with you," said Araton. "But reluctantly."

Looking intently at Roger, Araton continued, "I do believe it's your destiny to make this attempt. But it's important that you count the cost before you go. As Rand has said, your chances are not good. To try to save Jamie—to try to save your world—you may all forfeit your lives."

Chapter Twenty-One: Planning

THE ISLAND OF IONA

The group sat in silence for several moments, pondering Rand's warning and Araton's exhortation.

Finally Lys asked, "If we do go to Hades, how *could* we know where to look for Jamie?"

Araton looked at Rand for a long moment, then replied, "I believe she's in the city of Abadon. It's the last true city in their world, and the only place Jamie could survive more than a day or two. The stone circle on Mull is probably linked to one in Abadon, which means if you go through the portal at Lochbuie, you should end up close to where Jamie is being held."

"So we go through the portal on Mull and end up in Abadon... but how will we find her once we're there?"

"That's more of a problem," Araton answered. "We don't really know much about Abadon. It's a large city, almost totally underground—burrowed into the soft rock of an extinct volcano. It's home to millions of Archons and millions of human slaves as well, but in all of our history, only one Irin has successfully entered the city, and he barely escaped with his life."

"I think I might be able to offer some help there," Michael interrupted. "I've been doing some research."

"Eliel once told us that some members of our race have a gift to see beyond our own dimension. When we weren't trying to burn them at the stake, we called them mystics and seers.

"These seers have had many visions of other worlds. Many of them saw with great clarity, but none had a framework to understand what they were seeing. They viewed scenes of astonishing beauty—worlds untouched by the Archon revolt—and gave them names like Heaven, Paradise, Valhalla, or Elysium.

"Over time, our concept of heaven developed—an idea that now pervades almost every religion. While some of the accounts were greatly embellished, what they saw was real. They were viewing realities beyond our world. Eliel told me that many of their descriptions of Heaven can be identified with real locations in Basilea, Hi-Ouranos, Ayden, Alani, or Taverea.

As centuries passed, these descriptions tended to meld together, becoming the various levels of the paradise our legends call Heaven. As I said, I've visited one of those worlds, and it was very real.

"That started me thinking. I wondered if the same thing could be true with our concept of Hell.

"So I started studying the ancient descriptions of Hell, and it's truly been enlightening. Almost every religion had some concept of a place of torment. Let me read you a few examples." Michael quickly pulled out his iPad, tapped the screen a few times, then read from his notes.

"The Greek and Roman Hell was called Tartarus, a deep black pit full of torture and suffering. In Roman mythology, Tartarus was reached by crossing a river guarded by a nine-headed monster.

"The Zoroastrian Hell was reached by crossing the Chinavat Bridge, the dividing line between the living and the dead. As the newly dead crossed over the bridge, their souls were judged and a bat-winged demon emerged from the pit to drag the wicked souls down into torment. Hell was described as a place of disgusting filth, where people are continuously tortured by demons.

"In some branches of Hinduism and Buddhism, Hell is called Naraka, a place of punishment based on a soul's karma. Naraka is divided into several levels depending on the sins committed during life. Naraka contains at least four levels, and in some traditions, many more. Punishments include having your flesh eaten by a serpent demon, and being boiled in hot oil.

"Diyu was the Chinese version of Hell. It consists of 18 levels of pain and torture. Names of the levels include the chamber of tongue ripping, the chamber of pounding, the chamber of dismemberment, the mountain of flames, and the chamber of the saw.

"Probably the most detailed description of Hell was penned in the 14th century by the Italian poet, Dante Alighieri. The first section of his epic poem, *The Divine Comedy,* is called *Inferno*. In it, Dante takes his readers on a guided tour of a place of dreadful torment. He pictured Hell as an immense circular pit surrounded by a river. His Hell contained 9 levels, with the torture on each descending level more hideous than the one above. Tortures included being locked in flaming tombs, being whipped by demons, submerged in feces, placed in a boiling lake, bitten by snakes, and dismembered. In the center of Dante's Hell, at the very lowest level, Satan himself was enthroned.

"I could go on and on, but I think you see my point," he said, looking up. "All of these descriptions are from different religions and diverse parts of the world, yet they have a surprising number of elements in common. I believe these seers were viewing a reality beyond our dimension, though they did not understand what they were seeing. In studying these accounts, and many more, I believe I've pieced together a fairly accurate picture of what we may find in Hades.

"On the far side of the city of Abadon, we should find a bridge over a boiling volcanic river. From the descriptions I've read, I believe the bridge may be decorated with stone gargoyles—replicas of grotesque monsters and demons. Beyond that bridge lies the place of torment, an immense circular pit, descending level after level, with the ruler of Hades enthroned at the bottom. On each level of the pit, Archons are continually subjecting human victims to unimaginable tortures. Each level is worse than the one above.

"If the Archons are trying to torture Jamie into

revealing the detonation codes, I think we'll find her in that pit."

"If there's even a remote possibility of rescuing Jamie, we have to try," Roger said. "Who's with me?"

Every hand went up. Every member of the group was eager to save Jamie, but Rand shook her head. "The more of you that go in, the more likely it is that you'll be noticed and captured. Only those who are absolutely essential should go."

"You can't go without me." Lys spoke up, "I'm the only one who can open the portal to get us out!"

"That's right," said Rand, "And the other person you need is Michael."

Erin caught her breath and reached out to grasp Michael's hand.

"From what Michael has said, he probably knows more about Hades and what you'll find there than any other human. Perhaps even more than the Irin. You definitely need him on the team.

"But the rest must stay here."

As Rand paused, glancing from Michael back to Roger and Lys, Mendrion stood and walked to the center of the room.

Mendrion was an imposing figure. His tall, well-formed body was lean and well-muscled, with a swarthy complexion and shaggy, dark-brown hair reaching almost to his shoulders.

Mendrion was a high-level Irin with some unusual gifts. He was the one brought in by Eliel to activate the gifts of the original synaxis members just before their journey to Iona. While the synaxis members did not know him as well as some of the others, they held him in high esteem.

Mendrion stood, looking at Roger, Michael, and Lys for a moment, then finally spoke. "When I was summoned here this evening, I sensed that this was the direction you would take. And while I have grave misgivings, I do feel it's the choice you had to make.

"There's not much we can do to help you, but we'll do what we can. For Lys, I believe it's crucial that we activate your next level of gifting. You are a singer, Lys, but you also have other gifts. We usually prefer to let those gifts activate on their own, as your life-force is restored, but I believe your next level of gifting will be important in this rescue attempt.

"Your next level of gifting is the gift of 'second sight.' The ability to sense things before they happen."

He stood and walked over to Lys.

She looked up in anticipation. Lys had known the Irin long enough to know she had nothing to fear.

Mendrion placed both hands gently on her head and held them there for a moment, then released them and returned to the center of the room.

"Was that it?" Lys asked. "I didn't feel a thing!"

"Activating a gift doesn't necessarily take long, and you don't always feel something," he smiled, "But you now have the gift of second-sight. At crucial moments you'll have a sense of what the future holds.

It's not a prediction of what *will* happen, but it's an understanding of what *could* happen if you make the right choices."

"I also want to offer something to Roger.

"Roger, your primary gift is to be what we call a 'sent-one.' There's no word for it in your language. It means something like envoy or ambassador, but much more.

"To be a sent-one means you have the ability to act as an Irin in certain situations. You can activate the gifts of others. You can organize a synaxis and blend the gifts of its members. It's a high calling, and a great responsibility. A sent-one may be called upon to lay down his life for others."

"You're not yet ready for that gift to be fully activated, but your gift does mean you have the capacity to carry a portion of the Irin life-force within your body.

"With your permission, I would like to deposit a measure of that life-force within you now."

"What's a Life-force?" Roger asked.

"Life-force is a kind of energy," he said, "but much more. It's the part of you that goes beyond physical existence, and it's what energizes all your abilities. In the wars of your distant past, the Archons inflicted genetic damage on your race. Your life-force was weakened, almost extinguished. When that happened, an important part of you died. You lost the use of many of your abilities, and your normal lifespan was drastically shortened.

"That's why the ancient ones sent the Irin to you. Through a synaxis with the Irin, a small portion our life-force can be transferred to you and over time, the damage inflicted on your race is partially reversed.

"What I'm offering you is a way to speed up that process. I can place a deposit of our life-force energy within your physical body. It could save your life, and the lives of the others."

"What does it do?" Roger replied, still dubious.

"When this life-force activates, you will experience a strength and alertness beyond anything you've ever imagined. It will clothe you in light, and give you power you can project into any blade you grasp. That power will transform a normal sword into a glowing weapon with the power to inflict instant death, even to an Archon. For a brief span of time, you will function as one of the Irin."

Mendrion paused a moment, letting Roger process what he had said, then asked, "May I give you this gift?"

Roger looked confused, but finally agreed.

Without saying a word, Mendrion, walked over and stood before Roger, then reached out his hand and placed it firmly on his forehead.

Then Mendrion faded from view, slipping into the concealment of the shadow realm.

As though responding to unspoken instructions, Roger closed his eyes, leaned back in his chair, and allowed his body to relax. His breathing deepened. He seemed to enter some kind of trance.

Minutes passed. Almost unnoticeably, a tremor appeared in Roger's eyelids, as though the tiny muscles in his eyelids were rapidly twitching. The tremor grew in intensity and spread. His fingers began to quiver. Then a violent tremor passed through his body. His whole body was now shaking. He was breathing in ragged gasps.

After several more minutes, the shaking gradually subsided. Roger sat motionless, breathing slowly. Finally, he took a deep breath and his body again relaxed. Thirty seconds later, his eyes popped open as Mendrion reappeared beside him.

"I'm not sure what just happened, but it felt really good," Roger said.

"You now have a portion of my life-force within you. At the right moment, you will know how to activate it. But I must warn you, there is a danger. When you choose to activate the Irin life-force, you will be, for perhaps several minutes, as one of the Irin. It will give you great power, but every Archon in the vicinity will view you as one of us, and will immediately attack. So use this gift wisely, and only when absolutely needed."

Chapter Twenty-Two:
Return to Lochbuie

THE ISLAND OF IONA

Later that evening, Lys, Michael, and Roger met with Rand and Eliel in the guest lounge of Mrs. Maclean's Bed and Breakfast. They'd asked the two Irin to meet with them to help them plan for their rescue attempt.

Eliel sat next to Rand, facing the three humans across the coffee table.

Though Eliel and Rand were two of their closest friends among the Irin, an obvious tension filled the room. It was clear that the Irin still did not agree with their decision.

Roger spoke first, "I know you don't think this is a good idea, and frankly, I'm not sure myself. I just know we need to do it. I'm hoping you will have some insights that will increase our chances."

Rand looked impatient. "To be honest, Roger, I'd put your chances of success at zero, and I really don't know what I could tell you that could improve them. As Araton said earlier, in all of our history, only one Irin has entered the city of Abadon and survived, and that just barely."

Eliel nodded agreement. "You don't understand what you're up against. You don't really know the Archons.

"Most of the Archons you've encountered have used mind control to disguise their appearance. Like Kareina, they look fully human, and it's easy to think of them as human. But they're not. They're evil beyond anything you've imagined."

Eliel paused for a moment, and Rand cut in, "Over the centuries, we've captured a number of Archons and had a chance to interrogate them. Let me tell you a little of what we know about them.

"First of all, Archons are totally alien. They don't fit any of your earthly categories. They're warm-blooded with a high body temperature, but in all other respects are reptilian. Their young are not born; they're hatched from leathery eggs.

"Only a small percentage of Archon females are fertile. Those that are not fertile become warriors, like Kareina. Those that are fertile become hive mothers. Like queen bees in a beehive, they're hidden away, pampered and protected. They lay all the eggs for the new generation. Since the Archon life span may run into thousands of years, they have no need for a high reproductive-rate. There are probably no more than five thousand hive mothers in Abadon, each producing three to five eggs every year.

"The Archon life-cycle affects everything about

them. Being reptilian, hive mothers don't have mammary glands, so Archon hatchlings aren't nurtured or nursed. Archons are never shown compassion. They are never taught empathy.

"To awaken their hunting instincts, every Archon hatchling is forced to hunt and kill its own first meal, and for thousands of years, every hatchling's ritual first meal has been a living human being. The Archons select a human slave—usually one that's too old or frail to work— and place it in a chamber with an egg that's about to hatch.

"When the hatchling emerges, it is ravenously hungry and drawn to the warmth of the human body. The terrified human tries desperately to get away, and for a while it seems to succeed. But newborn Archons are able to fly within hours of hatching, so the human really has no chance. Eventually, the human is caught and eaten. So every Archon's first act is pursuing and devouring a living human being."

Rand paused, eyes glancing at Michael, then to Lys. "So when an Archon sees one of your race, what comes to mind is the excitement of their first hunt. That first meal imprints indelibly on their psyche the idea that humans are prey to be tormented and destroyed."

"That's all you are to them." Eliel added. "You are not fellow-creatures to be treated with respect. You exist only to be tortured and killed. The Archon language has no words for empathy or compassion. To the Archons, the torture of human beings is a form of recreation. Given the chance, they will hunt you and kill you."

The three humans sat stunned.

Eliel looked from Michael to Lys again, and then to Roger, and paused a long time before speaking. "Over the last two years I've come to view the members of this synaxis as my friends. I've lost many friends in the battle with the Archons, both human and Irin. I have no desire to lose more, especially when there is virtually no hope of success.

"I know you feel driven to try to rescue Jamie, but you don't have to do it. You've already done far more than anyone had a right to ask. Come to Basilea and live out your lives in paradise, perhaps even start a human colony there. Why throw away your lives for nothing?"

Michael was quiet for a moment, then responded. "Eliel, how could we live our lives in Heaven knowing our world has been plunged into Hell?

"I've read many descriptions of Hell, and if Hades is anything like what our ancient seers portrayed, the thought of going there definitely scares the hell out of me! And you're right; we don't know what we're heading into.

"Maybe we're insane to even consider this. But our whole world is at stake, and we have no choice but to try."

"I understand," Rand said finally, her voice softening. "In your place, I would probably do the same, but we had to let you know what you're facing."

"I know how you view this," Roger replied. "But with your knowledge of the Archons, there may be some practical things you could help us with. For example, what kinds of things should we take with us?"

"Take as little as possible," Rand answered. "You want to blend in with the human slaves, and they probably won't be wearing backpacks. And no weapons you could take from this world would be of any help against the Archons, so you need no weapons, other than the life-force you received from Mendrion.

"You also don't need to take any provisions. A human being is fully capable of surviving several weeks without food, and at least three days without water. Frankly, I don't see you surviving longer than three days in Hades."

"What about clothing?" Lys asked

Rand shrugged, "I have no idea what the slaves of Abadon wear."

Michael smiled, "All the medieval artists who portrayed the torments of Hell showed the victims totally naked, but I doubt that would be the case within the city. While some garments may be provided to the slaves, I imagine many of them would be wearing the clothing they were captured in. My advice would be that we dress simply, and dress light, since we can count on it being hot."

"I agree," Eliel said, "and be as inconspicuous as possible."

LOCHBUIE, ISLAND OF MULL

The next morning they loaded into the Hummer and made their way to Lochbuie, with the rest of the synaxis following in other vehicles.

Michael had been right. Without the obfuscating blanket of the *haar*, Luchbuie was beautiful.

Once known as the "Garden of Mull," the tiny village of Lochbuie is situated at the head of a rugged bay, surrounded by majestic mountain peaks on three sides. The area is famous for its lush woodlands, broad shimmering beaches and abundant wildlife. They'd spotted stags, rabbits, and pheasants, with golden eagles soaring overhead as they drove into the village.

Standing beside the Hummer on the broad, sandy beach, Roger contemplated the beauty of the scene. *Only its remote location has rescued this place from being a tourist mecca with high-rise condos lining the shore.*

In place of condos, the shoreline at Lochbuie featured the hulking ruin of an ancient castle built on a low rock platform at the head of the Loch. Moy Castle had been constructed in 1450 by Hector Reaganach Maclean, 1st Laird of Lochbuie. In 1752, when the threat of inter-clan warfare had ended, the family moved to the much more comfortable manor house nearby, and allowed the castle to fall into ruin.

The focus of every member of the synaxis was on the small stone circle located on the grounds of the manor house, under the watchful gaze of Ben Buie, the tallest mountain in the area.

Estimated to date back to the late Neolithic Age, the circle is made up of nine granite slabs, set in a ring about 40 feet in diameter, positioned with their flatter faces towards the inside of the circle.

There were also three solitary stones set in the field at different distances from the circle. The nearest of these outlying stones was 17 feet away to the southeast, and just three feet tall. The second outlier was a spectacular monolith nine feet high and set about 130 feet away to the southwest. Also southwest of the circle, 350 away, was the third outlier, itself over six feet in height. Eliel had explained that the outlier stones were positioned to "tune" the portal, aligning it to a specific location in Hades. In this case, they believed it to be aligned with a portal entrance just outside the city of Abadon.

They parked by a seaside picnic area and ate their last meal together. They'd decided to eat just before entering the portal, since they didn't know when they'd eat again.

The beautiful surroundings stood in stark contrast to the task before them. They ate in silence, pondering the horrors they might be about to confront. "I feel like we're eating the 'Last Supper,'" Michael said, uncomfortably.

Finishing the meal, they walked in silence to the stone circle.

Just before entering the circle, they stopped and embraced. Erin held Michael tighter than he'd imagined possible, making it difficult for him to breathe. Patrick held Lys close, with almost as much fervency. When at last they parted, Michael, Roger, and Lys entered the circle and walked to its center.

The three looked at each other, and back to their friends standing beyond the monoliths.

"Are you ready?" Lys asked.

"As ready as we'll ever be," Roger answered.

"I feel like I'm at the top of a roller coaster, about to make the first plunge," Michael said. "From this point, there's no turning back."

Taking a deep breath, Lys opened her mouth and began to sing. At first, her voice sounded weak, scratchy, and a little hoarse. But as she sang, it strengthened. Unlearned words flowed out, creating a wormhole between the dimensions.

A black cloud appeared and swirled around them, increasing in speed and intensity.

The darkness hovered around them, then closed in. And suddenly, they were gone.

Chapter Twenty-Three:
Into the Abyss

HADES, REALM OF THE ARCHONS

They felt they were falling … a long, slow fall into darkness. Then, suddenly there was solid ground beneath their feet.

The three glanced around, trying to orient themselves. As the darkness cleared, they found themselves in the center of a large circle of standing stones, much larger than the one they'd left on Mull.

A barren wasteland stretched to the horizon under a dark, overcast sky that slowly pulsed with dull, red light. The place was oppressively hot. Clouds of yellow, sulfurous dust scudded across the desolate plain.

Far to the right stood the crumbling ruins of many ancient structures. From the great heaps of rubble on the ground, it must have once been a magnificent city with shining towers piercing the clouds. Now only jagged skeletons of dark, twisted steel stood vigil above the lonely ruin.

Gazing across the plain, they could see no life on the ground, but leather-winged, pterodactyl-like creatures wheeled slowly high above.

Immediately behind them, a jagged mountain rose abruptly from the plain, the front range of more dark peaks beyond. Several volcanos were erupting in the distance, spewing clouds of ash mixed with glowing cinders into the already darkened sky.

"Welcome to Hades," Lys muttered.

On a cliff face, just 300 feet away, yawned the gaping maw of an immense cavern.

"That would make a convincing gate of Hell," Michael said.

"It's obviously the entrance to wherever they took Jamie," Roger responded, pointing to a well-worn track leading directly from the stone circle to the cave entrance. "Let's get moving, but stay alert."

"Wait!" Lys cautioned. "Something really big is moving in our direction, just inside the cavern entrance."

The three crouched behind the upright slabs of stone and watched in horror as a genuine monster emerged from the cave.

They knew what it was as soon as they saw the immense horned head, gaping jaws and yellow cat-like eyes, alert and intelligent. It was a visage they'd all seen pictured in books since they'd been little children. Its legends had been portrayed in movies. Its fearsome angular head had adorned the prow of warships in many ancient nations. The thing emerging from the cavern was the human race's worst nightmare, recounted in the mythology of every people-group on earth.

As it emerged from the cave, the creature raised

its head on a long, sinuous neck and swung it slowly from side to side, its alert eyes surveying the horizon. Then with a roar that shook the ground, it belched a thick plume of flame and smoke high into the air. There was no doubt. The creature standing before them, less than 300 feet away, was a genuine fire-breathing dragon.

The beast raised two great leathery wings toward the sky and thrust them downward in a powerful stroke that lofted its body into the air. Another stroke lifted it higher and drove it forward with startling speed. The dragon traced a great circle overhead, then wheeled and flew off in the direction of the distant volcanos.

As it faded into the distance, the three humans gasped simultaneously. They looked at each other and laughed, realizing they'd all been holding their breath since the dragon emerged.

"I knew it!" Michael exclaimed, grinning like a little boy. "Dragons are real! They had to be! Every culture on earth had legends of dragons. Creatures just like that once terrorized our planet. I suspect they're the highest rank of Archons. Sort of what archangels are among the Irin."

Sobering somewhat, he added, "We must be careful. Where there is one dragon, there are probably more. And this could be just the first of the ancient horrors we encounter."

With Roger leading the way, they slowly approached the cavern entrance.

To the left of the entrance were several low

structures. A gang of 30 slaves were involved in some kind of building project, chipping rough-cut volcanic rock into blocks, and then mortaring them into place. The slaves looked emaciated, barely able to lift the tools they were using. Watching over them were five human overseers, who looked like they could be bouncers at some seedy strip-club. They carried no whips or obvious weapons, but it was clear that the slaves were terrified of them.

The overseers had been watching the three friends approach and were talking among themselves in hushed tones. One of them abruptly turned and sprinted into the cavern.

"I think we've been noticed," Michael observed.

The other bouncers continued to watch them intently as the three passed the construction site and headed into the cave.

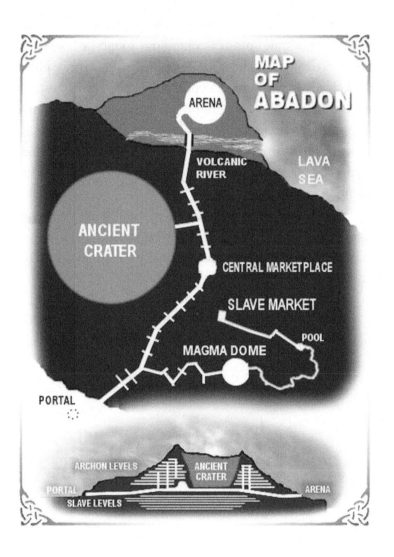

Chapter Twenty-Four: Captured!

ABADON, CITY OF THE ARCHONS

The cavern was immense. Its entrance, arching several hundred feet above them, was shaped like an open mouth, frozen in an anguished scream.

Looking up at the top of the gateway, Michael muttered, "This reminds me of a line from Dante's *Inferno*. In Dante's poem, there was an inscription over the gate of Hell: 'Through me you pass into the city of woe. Through me you pass into eternal pain... Abandon hope, all ye who enter here.'"

"That's cheerful!" Lys chided nervously.

They passed through the entrance into the darkness beyond, the well-worn path wandering downward into the depths of the cavern through a wasteland of black, twisted, volcanic rock.

As they moved further along the path, the light began to dim. Roger saw no sign of any artificial light sources, and the light from the entrance, large as it was, could not penetrate much further. *Would they have to complete their mission in darkness?*

As his eyes grew accustomed to the gloom,

however, he found that there was light in the cavern. An eerie, red glow seemed to emanate from the rocks themselves, bathing everything in a dull crimson light. *Some form of bioluminescence?*

The light was dim, but once his eyes adjusted, he could see well enough to make his way through the cavern.

As they moved forward, what appeared to be a natural cavern transitioned into a tunnel burrowed into the heart of the mountain. While not as large as the cavern entrance, the tunnel was still immense, 40 feet wide and at least 60 feet high. Many smaller side tunnels branched from the main one.

Roger glanced at Michael. "Where do you suggest we go from here?"

"The present-day city of Abadon is almost entirely underground," Michael said. "Its maze of corridors, vertical shafts, and tunnels are burrowed into this mountain. From what the Irin speculate, more than ten million Archons live here like bees in a hive. The Archon section of the city is located on the scores of levels above this one. Below this level is the realm of slaves, and there are probably millions of them also.

"I believe this tunnel is the central corridor, sort of the "main street" of Hell. It should run straight through the mountain and out the other side. I think we'll find the place of torment just beyond the end of this tunnel.

They continued down the passage for several

hundred feet, then paused to look around. The heat was oppressive. All three were drenched in perspiration.

"Any idea how much further it is?" Lys asked.

"I think we're just getting started." Michael replied. "We haven't passed any Archons yet, and only a few slaves, so we probably have not entered the main area of the city yet."

"I hate to be the bearer of bad news, but I think we're being followed." Roger said.

All three looked behind them to see, shrouded in the cavern's gloom, two of the bouncers they'd seen back at the construction site were headed their way.

"Maybe they're just going home for lunch," Lys said hopefully. "After all, this is the main street of the city."

"There's one way to find out," Michael replied. "Let's take a detour and see if they follow us."

Just ahead, a rather large side tunnel branched to the right. Michael led them down it for several hundred feet, then turned and looked back. The bouncers had taken the turn also.

Still not convinced, Michael took the next tunnel to the right.

"Don't get us lost in here."

"Getting lost is the least of my fears. If they are really following us, we're in trouble."

Looking back, the bouncers had again followed their lead, and were steadily narrowing the distance. The three walked faster, but the bouncers increased their pace also.

They passed a side tunnel branching sharply to the left. "In here," Roger said, "Then run like hell."

The three took the turn, then sprinted through the tunnel in near-darkness. They were in a more populated section of the city now. Slaves slowly plodded the Stygian corridor, eyes downcast, seeming to pay no attention to the three as they ran past. They made several more turns, but the bouncers were still on their trail.

The labyrinthine maze of corridors took them through an industrial area, with the clatter and clank of unknown machinery assaulting their ears. Passing the entrance to several large chambers, they saw slaves chained to heavy equipment in unendurable heat.

In one cavern, molten metal was being poured into molds, with glowing sparks filling the air. Loud metallic clangs rang out, the sound of an anvil being repeatedly struck with a hardened steel hammer.

Leaving the industrial area, they took another turn, and found themselves in a natural cavern. It appeared to be an ancient lava tube, running straight ahead for several hundred feet.

At the end of the tube, they saw light.

Moving toward the light, they emerged into an immense chamber, more than 600 feet in height. Fixtures attached to the roof bathed the floor in brilliant light. It was the only place in Hades where they'd seen artificial illumination.

The three stopped for a moment, stunned by the

sight before them. "We're in an ancient magma dome." Michael said, "I've seen pictures of some back on earth, but none on this scale. There's a magma dome in an extinct Icelandic volcano that's been opened as a tourist attraction. It's huge, big enough to hold the statue of liberty. But this is far beyond that. The floor of this chamber must cover several acres."

They looked around in awe. They were in the bowels of a volcano.

The area within the dome was a miniature ecosystem, with waterfalls spilling down the rough walls into artificial lakes, shimmering gold and crystal mineral deposits and soaring columns hundreds of feet high, created when stalactites hanging from the cave roof had met stalagmite formations building from the cave floor thousands of years earlier.

Unlike the dull red of Abadon's tunnel system, here the artificial light revealed incredibly rich palettes of mineral oxides: wine-red lava scars, terracotta ridges of frozen stone and stunning curtains of yellow and orange—the chromatic spectrum of fire, perfectly preserved in the heart of the planet.

Michael muttered, "I think we're catching a glimpse of what Hades was like before the destruction of the great wars."

"It's beautiful," Lys agreed.

The floor of the chamber was alive with activity. There was the continual hum of irrigation pumps. Slaves were scurrying between hundreds of cultivation racks, each towering ten levels high.

"It's an indoor hydroponic farm." Michael observed. "I was wondering where their food came from."

The floor of the chamber covered five acres, all under intense hydroponic cultivation. To the left they passed large vats of foul-smelling greenish slime.

Cultivation racks brimmed over with many kinds of grain and leafy plants. Michael recognized corn and tomatoes, racks of alfalfa and soybeans, rice, barley, and onions.

"This is huge," Michael said, "but this could never provide enough food for the population of this place. There must be dozens of farms like this one."

At the far end of the immense chamber, a steaming waterfall made a 600-foot fall into an artificial lake. Cooled by its descent, the lake water was merely tepid, cool enough to support a large population of freshwater eels and blind cave fish.

Around the outer wall of the chamber were animals: pens and cages filled with grunting pigs, lizards, rats, snakes, and scrawny chickens pecking in the dirt. There were smaller cages full of chirping crickets and grasshoppers.

Darting between the cultivation racks, they looked back to see one of the bouncers drawing close.

Looking ahead, there were two exits to the magma dome. On the left, a large artificial tunnel led back toward the city. But the other bouncer had run ahead and was now standing in the center of that corridor, watching them intently while speaking into some sort of communication device.

The other exit from the hydroponic farm appeared to be another natural lava tube. They headed in that direction.

Leaving the hydroponic farm, they passed into an undeveloped region of the cavern. With the artificial light now behind them, they were forced to slow their pace until their eyes adjusted again to the dull red glow of Hades.

As they moved beyond the end of the cleared path, progress became more difficult. For close to an hour they scrambled over stalagmites and boulder fields, though vaulting galleries, going ever deeper into the heart of the planet. At times they were forced to crawl on hands and knees as the cavern roof dipped almost to the floor. They felt the weight of the mountain above them—what might be thousands of feet of solid rock—and wondered if they would ever find their way back again. Looking behind them, however, the two pursuers still maintained the chase.

"Have you wondered why they're not overtaking us?" Lys asked.

"Yes, it feels almost like we're being herded, driven in the direction they want us to go," Michael replied.

Their pursuers were just behind them now. They

had no choice but to keep moving.

Squeezing through a narrow passage that ran for several hundred feet, they arrived at the shore of a small, dark pool under a dome of sulfurous flowstone. And there, waiting for them, were five more bouncers.

"We're trapped," Roger blurted, glancing frantically around but seeing no place to run.

"What have we here... escaped slaves?" the largest of the bouncers taunted gruffly, as they moved to surround them.

"Check their shoulders, see who's they are."

One by one, Lys, Michael, and Roger were roughly grabbed. Powerful hands pulled their sleeves back, examining their left shoulders, looking for some kind of identification mark.

Finding none, there was a flurry of conversation.

"There's no registration. They're not slaves!"

"How could they be here if they're not slaves?"

"Maybe they escaped their captors before they could be taken to the slave market."

The two bouncers who had been trailing them arrived. One of them, obviously the leader, spoke up, "You're right, Armando. They are not slaves. I saw them come through the portal. They were not brought here by the Archons. They came here on their own."

"That's the stupidest thing I've ever heard. Who chooses to come to Hell?"

"The point is, what are we going to do with them?"

The leader spoke again. "I say we take them to the slave market. We'll get a healthy percentage of the sale price for bringing in fresh meat." Grabbing Lys by the wrist, he added, "I already have a buyer in mind for this one. A buyer who will pay well."

Chapter Twenty-Five: Jamie and Kareina

IN THE PIT OF HELL

Kareina stood in a volcanic cavern before a glowing pit. At the edge of the pit stood two of her subordinates, holding Jamie Thatcher's arms in a vice-like grip. Ten feet below, at the bottom of the pit, seethed a pool of white-hot lava. The stench of sulfur filled the air and the heat was suffocating.

While Kareina continued to cloak her true identity with the mentally projected illusion of a human female, her assistants made no such pretension. Each of the monsters stood more than seven feet tall, ferocious and bestial in form. Their jaws hung open in a vicious grin, revealing a double row of fangs, and their green reptilian eyes shone with cold malevolence. Jamie winced as their powerful talons dug deeply into the soft flesh of her upper arms.

"Jamie, I'm growing weary of your resistance," Kareina said. "I'm only going to ask this one more time. Give me the detonation codes NOW."

Jamie refused to make eye contact or even acknowledge the demand. She knew what was coming.

Glancing at her subordinates, Kareina growled, "Let the human bitch taste the fires of Hades."

Responding to their commander, the two monstrosities jerked Jamie from her feet and held her, suspended by her wrists in the superheated air rising from the pit. The blast of heat brought excruciating pain. Jamie felt like she was being roasted alive. As wave after wave of the searing heat engulfed her naked body, she looked pleadingly at Kareina, and whispered one word, *"Please!"*

With no trace of compassion, Kareina drew her lips taut in a satisfied smile, enjoying the sight of Jamie writhing in anguish. Finally, when she sensed Jamie was about to lose consciousness, Kareina barked, "Release her!"

The subordinates released their hold and dropped Jamie, feet-first, into the pit.

As Jamie's feet came in contact with the lava, they did not sink beneath its surface, rather the flesh of her feet and lower legs disintegrated in a cloud of bloody steam. Her bones instantly carbonized and shattered in an explosion of unbelievable pain.

Jamie somehow remained upright on the disintegrating stumps of her legs for several seconds. Then, as her body began to fall forward, she instinctively raised her hands to break her fall, but her hands and forearms also dissolved on contact with the lava.

With nothing left to slow her fall, Jamie's body continued its inexorable descent toward the surface of the fiery pool.

Time seemed to slow. Jamie felt she was suspended in space, her movement almost imperceptible. For what felt like hours, she watched as her body inched closer to the seething surface.

Her hair sizzled, crackled, and burst into flame. Finally, her face disintegrated in howling agony as it came in contact with the churning lava.

A few seconds later Jamie found herself back in her cage, her body trembling, but unharmed.

Since arriving in Hades, she'd been gang-raped, eviscerated, drawn and quartered, burned at the stake, and impaled. She always awoke unharmed in her cramped three by five foot steel cage. None of it had actually happened, but thanks to Kariena's mental powers, every torture felt totally real. She had lived every moment of it, fully conscious, and Kariena repeated the process several times a day. Every day brought new agonies.

Only her mental disciplines had allowed her to survive. But she knew she was growing weak. They were wearing her down. She knew the time would come when she would tell them anything they wanted, just to make the pain stop.

Chapter Twenty-Six:
Slave Market

ABADON, CITY OF THE ARCHONS

The trek back into the city took more than an hour and the bouncers kept a firm grip on each of them. There was no chance of escape.

Entering the slave market, the bouncers split the three up. Four of them led Michael and Roger down a long dark corridor. Lys was taken to what appeared to be some sort of admitting room. The bouncers released their grip on her arms and thrust her in. Then, pointing to a bucket of water and a filthy sponge laying on a crude wooden bench, they told her to undress and bathe. They remained at the door, watching her.

Lys hesitated, glancing around the room. There was no way of escape, and it was clear the men had more than enough strength to force submission if she resisted.

Choose your battles wisely, Lys. You can't win this one.

Lys turned her back to the men and undressed, then made a perfunctory effort at bathing, quickly running the foul-smelling sponge over major areas of her body. When she finished, she found they'd taken her clothing. In place of her clothing, they gave her a sleeveless smock-like garment that hung loosely around her body, tied with a slipknot above each shoulder. The garment was made of a coarse, brown fabric, similar to burlap. It was filthy and reeked of urine, and was distinctly uncomfortable. She had no choice but to put it on.

Leaving the admitting room, they led her through the slave market, keeping a tight grip on her wrists.

The market was made up of five parallel hallways, each holding 40-50 slaves of every race and age, all sitting chained with their backs against the wall. Most wore smocks similar to hers, but a few were naked. *Could Jamie be here?*

Passing the entrance to each hall, Lys looked frantically for Jamie, but didn't see her. What she did see literally made her sick. Men, women, and children were all mixed together, waiting in this place of shame and filth for their turn at auction.

The majority were young—mid-to-late teens, or early twenties. Some were cursing and thrashing their chains. Others were moaning or weeping. Some just sat, eyes downcast, hopeless.

The stench was overwhelming. A brief glance confirmed what her nose had already suspected. There were no bathroom facilities in the slave market. Slaves were forced to sit, chained in their own excrement, until the slavemaster's servants made their way down the row, dousing them with buckets of water to wash the accumulated waste down the drains. *The whole place is one big toilet!*

Lys's captors led her past the five hallways to a side chamber about twenty-five feet square. One of the bouncers held her arms in a vice-like grip while the other clamped manacles to her wrists. They then chained her in a standing position between two stone columns on a broad, raised dais in the center of the room.

The bouncers left.

She scanned the room, searching for a possible avenue of escape. There wasn't much to see. Dark, roughhewn walls carved from native volcanic rock. No furnishings. No decorations of any kind. *I guess I'm the decoration here... strung up for all to see.*

The rock floor, worn smooth over the course of many centuries, had a small drain in one corner. A coating of filth surrounding it provided ample evidence that the floor of this chamber also served as a toilet for those unfortunate enough to be chained here. The place stank.

Her arms were already beginning to ache. Lys pulled against the chains, but they were firmly attached. *This has got to be a bad dream. I look like Fay Wray waiting for King Kong!*

Sometime later a man came in. He was large and solidly built, and appeared to be in his late fifties, with a graying crew-cut and a face creased like worn leather.

Stepping onto the dais, he introduced himself as

the slavemaster, head of the largest slave market in Abadon. "You need know only one thing while you are here," he spat, studying her without pity. "Until you are sold, your life is in my hands. Obey me without question.

"I can inflict pain like you've never imagined. I can make you wish you'd never been born. So if you want your time here to be as painless as possible, choose to obey me, and obey me quickly.

"Let's begin with you telling me your name."

Lys hesitated, not wanting to cooperate, but the slavemaster slid a copper rod with a blue glowing tip from a holster on his belt and casually tapped it against one of her bare legs.

Lys's world exploded in agony. The pain from the rod was like nothing she had ever experienced. She screamed in anguish. Tears came to her eyes. She felt her leg was on fire, yet looking down, there was no scar or mark.

"I ask again," the slavemaster said firmly, as the pain gradually subsided, "What is your name."

The pain inflicted by the rod had shaken her. This was another situation where she could not win. Resistance brought unendurable pain, and there was no way of escape.

"My name is Lys Johnston, that's L-Y-S... J-O-H-N-S-T-O-N," Lys said through the tears, spelling it out when she saw that he was scrawling it in thick letters on a wooden plaque he carried.

He asked her a few more questions, jotted more

words on the wooden plaque, then hung it around her neck with a leather thong.

"Please," Lys begged, as he turned to leave, "I'm trying to find my friend. A woman named Jamie Thatcher was brought to this place through the portal. Has she been here?"

"I've not heard that name," the man said coldly, "But your friend's plight is no longer your concern. You have troubles enough of your own."

His tone softened slightly. "I've put you in this private gallery for a special showing. A great man has shown interest in you, Praetor Hewett, the head slave in all of Abadon. To be considered for purchase by Praetor Hewett is a great honor, especially for a female slave. He rarely tortures his slaves, and he has great favor with the Archons, so they won't try to have their way with you while you're under his protection. There are far worse fates in Hades than to be Praetor Hewett's slave."

The slavemaster began to leave, then turned back, eyeing her almost with compassion. "I'll give you some advice Ms. Johnston, and you would do well to follow it. First, forget the life you had before you came here. It's over. Gone. In this world you have no identity, no history, and no rights. You are nothing more than a piece of living tissue up for sale on the auction block. The sooner you accept that fact, the easier your life will be.

"When you leave this market, it will be in chains. The man who buys you will be your master. You would be wise to try to please him, for you will exist at

His discretion. If he chooses to torture you for his amusement, no one in this universe will come to your aid. If he kills you, he will suffer no penalty. In this world you are no longer a person, Ms. Johnston; you are *chattel*, your owner's legal property, and he is free to do with you as he will.

"But serve your master well and show him respect," he shrugged, "and he may occasionally show you some kindness.

"But most important," the slavemaster continued, lowering his voice, "never allow yourself to even *think* of escaping. There's no place to go, no place to run. They *will* catch you, and you don't want to see what Archons do to runaway slaves."

At that, the slavemaster pivoted abruptly and left the chamber.

As Lys stood helpless, spread-eagled between the stone columns, the slavemaster's words began to sink in. She'd read about the horrors of slavery in ancient Rome, and in the American South before the Civil War, but had never stopped to consider what it would feel like to actually be sold as a slave. Now she knew. It felt like death.

What if the slavemaster was right? What if there is no way out?

She thought of her parents back in Dallas. With both Lys and Roger both enslaved in Abadon, they would never know what happened to their children.

She thought of her cozy room in the guesthouse

on Iona, of Patrick, Catherine, and the other friends she would never see again.

For the first time in her life, Lys felt truly lost. Rand had warned her that if they were captured, there could be no hope of rescue. She remembered Michael's comment as they entered the city, "Abandon hope, all ye who enter here."

The prospect of life as a slave overwhelmed her. Slavery meant she could no longer direct her own life. She would never have the freedom to take a leisurely shopping trip or plan a vacation. She would never wake up on a sleepy Saturday morning, stretch out in bed and ask, *What do I want to do today?*

Her life would now be controlled by her master. She would exist to satisfy his whims, and the price of disobedience would be dreadful pain.

Worst of all, enslavement meant she'd failed in her mission. There would be no rescue for Jamie.

The Archons would inevitably wear Jamie down. She would reveal the detonation codes, and the Earth-realm, along with everything Lys knew, would be destroyed.

With that thought, something in Lys snapped.

Deep in the core of her being, one word reverberated with resolute determination: *NO!*

That CANNOT happen, Lys told herself. *There IS a way out of this. There must be!*

Lys surveyed the room around her again, as if hoping to see an answer. She had always believed she could find a way out of any situation if she kept trying. Many times in her life she'd persevered and been rewarded with success, long after others would have given up. But how could she do that here?

Realistically, she knew there was little hope of escape from within the slave market. The Archon system of slavery had endured for thousands of years. The guards were highly skilled at controlling the Archons' captives, and the slavemaster wielded the threat of excruciating pain.

But Praetor Hewett might be a possibility. From what the slavemaster said, it sounded like Hewett might be a decent man.

She didn't know if it was her "second-sight" gift activating, or just her imagination, but Lys suddenly had a strong impression that Praetor Hewett was the key to her freedom.

She mentally went through the steps before her. She would need to find a way to escape, locate Michael and Roger, then rescue Jamie and get back to the portal without being recaptured. It seemed ludicrous, but Lys did have an advantage none of the other slaves here had. She could open the portal. She did have a way to escape. But only if she lived long enough.

Chapter Twenty-Seven: Auction Block

ABADON, CITY OF THE ARCHONS

Twenty minutes later, a set of floodlights blinked on, bathing the dais in brilliant light.

Showtime, Lys thought to herself wearily, squinting her eyes against the light. *And I'm the star of the show.* She drew in a deep breath and let it out slowly.

I'm not sure what's going to happen, but I hope it happens soon.

Her arms were aching, her legs burning with pain, and she was starting to need to pee. But there was no relief in sight. She'd been standing spread-eagled between the pillars for more than an hour. *I just want this to be over!*

After a few more minutes, the slavemaster came into the chamber, accompanied by a man more disgusting than any Lys had ever imagined. Praetor Hewett looked more like a derelict off the street than the greatest man in Hades. Several of his teeth were missing, and others were rotting away. Wisps of stringy, unwashed hair fell in greasy tangles from his balding head, and it was obvious from his foul stench that bathing, mouthwash and deodorant use were not a part of his daily routine.

Hewett was a large man, well over six feet. His misshapen face was cradled by thick wattles of fat slung beneath his multiple chins. His corpulent body reminded her of nothing so much as a large toad.

Yet the slavemaster showed him great respect.

After conversing with the slavemaster in muffled tones, the toad stood back and appraised her carefully.

Finally, hoisting his ponderous bulk onto the dais, he began his examination, first reading the plaque that hung around her neck. "Lys Johnston. Age: 28. Provenance: unknown. Price: 50 shekels of silver, firm."

"50 shekels!" He feigned a gasp, glancing at the slavemaster. "You must think you have a treasure here. That's nearly twice the normal slave price."

When the slave master made no response, he turned back to Lys. "I've never paid 50 shekels for a slave girl in my life! I shall see if she's worth it."

The Praetor reached his pudgy hands up and felt around her head, running his grimy fingers through her hair. "Blonde hair, that's always a plus," he muttered. "Not platinum, more a light ash-blonde. And the eyes. Not blue, exactly. More of a steel gray. I'd prefer blue, but this isn't bad."

He looked in her ears, examined her eyes, then instructed her to open her mouth. His stubby fingers spread her lips as he examined her teeth. "They seem in good condition. Okay, let's see the rest of her."

As the toad stepped down from the dais, the slavemaster complied, and with a quick movement of his hands undid the knots at each shoulder that secured her slave garment. To her horror, the smock rapidly fluttered to the floor, leaving her fully exposed before the leering toad.

Lys realized she should have known this was coming, but somehow it took her by surprise. Displayed like a slab of meat before this grotesque ruin of a man, she'd never felt more vulnerable, or more degraded.

She struggled to turn away, but the chains binding her arms to the columns were tightly stretched. *What the slavemaster said is true,* she thought, tears of anguish flowing down her face. *In this place, I'm not a person. I'm just a mass of living tissue with no identity and no rights... not even the right to keep a shred of clothing on my body.*

Seeing the shock and hopelessness in her eyes, the toad said coldly, "Welcome to Hell, Ms. Johnston. Don't expect things to get better."

Hewett stood back and casually surveyed his potential purchase, tilting his head slightly to the side and muttering to himself. "Pleasing overall appearance... Athletic, but still feminine... Appears to be in good health..."

As though running through a mental checklist, he began pacing the room, stopping occasionally to view her from different angles. He circled the dais several times. "No obvious scars or deformities... Generally well proportioned, though a bit too narrow at the hips for my liking... Skin quality is okay..."

As the toad continued his dispassionate critique of her naked body, Lys trembled with revulsion. She longed to spit in his face, scream obscenities at him, and let him know what a hideous monstrosity he was. But once again she had the strong impression that Praetor Hewett would be the key to her freedom. *But will he choose to buy me?*

Finishing his examination, the toad paused, as though deep in thought, then glanced at the slavemaster, "40 shekels."

The slavemaster made no response.

"45?" Hewett asked.

"Sorry, Praetor," the slavemaster said. "My price is firm. There's an Archon master coming in later today who'd probably give me 60 shekels, but I'd hate to think what he'd do to her."

The toad paused again, weighing his decision.

Finally he spoke. "Very well, I'll take her. Have your servants prepare her while I arrange the payment."

The bouncers returned and painfully tattooed an eight-digit number across the back of her left shoulder. "This is for your protection," one of them confided as she winced in pain. "It identifies you as the property of Praetor Hewett."

They re-clothed her in the filthy slave smock and replaced her manacles with handcuffs, binding her hands in front of her. They also fastened shackles to both ankles and connected them with a 12-inch length of steel chain.

Suitably prepared, they led her back to the admitting room, where Praetor Hewett was waiting, holding a package of some kind under his left arm.

He looked at her coldly for a moment, then said, "Walk beside me where I can see you at all times." They headed out into the main cavern.

Lys discovered that with the ankle cuffs and chain she could walk with a fair degree of freedom, though noisily, but the 12-inch length of the chain prevented any attempt to run. The toad led her through a maze of tunnels to a ramp leading down to another level.

This can't be happening to me. Lys told herself. *It can't be real.*

They passed several other slaves being led through the corridors, bound hand and foot in similar chains. Others wore only ankle chains and were carrying heavy burdens or otherwise serving their masters. But many had apparently achieved a sufficient level of trust that they were allowed to walk the corridors of Hell unchained.

They passed through more tunnels, all lit by the dim red glow that seemed to come from the rocks themselves, then down a side passage. Twenty feet ahead, the passage ended at a massive wooden door. The toad unlocked it, swung it open, and motioned for Lys to enter.

The room was spartan, to say the least. There was a sleeping mat along one wall and a crudely built wooden armoire along another. An open door on a third wall revealed rudimentary toilet facilities. The room was carved from the soft volcanic rock, the walls grimy and rough, but the floor had been worn smooth by decades of use. Being underground, of course, there were no windows.

"Is this where you live?" Lys asked.

"Oh my! No!" the toad laughed heartily, his wattles of fat jiggling. "I only use this little room for matters that require utmost privacy. You'll see why we're here in a few moments.

"I have chambers like this all over the city," he said with pride. "I call them my 'bolt-holes.' I got the idea from a Sherlock Holmes story I read as a kid. They come in quite handy at times."

Locking the door behind him, Hewett reached into a pocket and withdrew a key ring with two keys. He threw them onto the sleeping mat. "Sit down there and take your chains off."

Lys complied. This was one command she was only too happy to obey.

She fumbled with the keys, fingers trembling. Identifying the key to the handcuffs, she slid it into the lock and gave a firm twist. The lock popped open. One hand was free. She repeated the process with the other hand, then the ankle cuffs. As one-by-one the chains fell off, she felt a sense of freedom returning. *Maybe Hewett really isn't a bad guy.*

Freed from her chains, Lys breathed a sigh of relief, rubbing her ankles and wrists to try to restore circulation.

The toad stood over her, watching in silence for several minutes.

"Now," he said, looking at her intently, "take that slave garment off."

Chapter Twenty-Eight:
The Iron Maiden

IN THE PIT OF HELL

Jamie awoke again in her cramped cage, drenched in perspiration, her body quaking uncontrollably.

The tortures were unrelenting. Today Kareina seemed to focus on the medieval torture devices of the Spanish Inquisition. She'd experienced the rack, the wheel, the thumb screw, and the infamous iron maiden.

That had been the worst. After binding her tightly, Kareina's subordinates had lowered her into a narrow iron casket. Sharpened spikes had been attached to the lid, positioned to penetrate her body as it closed. One spike had been positioned over each eye, four over her chest, and four more over her abdomen.

Kareina gave the word for the lid to be closed, and it began to slowly descend. Jamie shut her eyes and prayed to whatever gods there might be for strength. When the first of the spikes had just touched her body, the lid stopped its descent. Jamie squirmed, trying to turn away, but she was bound firmly in place.

Kareina spoke again, softly this time, "It doesn't have to be this way, Jamie. You don't have to suffer.

Just give us the detonation codes and all of this will end.

We'll set you free."

Jamie remained silent. *This isn't real,* she told herself. *It's an illusion. I can resist this. I MUST resist this!*

"I'll make a deal with you," Kareina continued. "You don't even have to give me the whole list. Just give me the next five numbers. I'll lift this lid and take you back to your own world."

Kareina paused, waiting for a response, but there was none. Jamie contemplated how many tens of thousands of people would die a horrendous death for each number she revealed. She bit her lip until it bled, but remained silent.

Finally Kareina barked, "Close the lid… and close it slowly!"

One by one Jamie felt the spikes penetrate her body. She screamed in agony 'till she had no breath to scream. Death did not come quickly. Jamie was pinned, held immobile in a place of excruciating pain for what seemed like an eternity. Finally life seeped from her body and she awoke in her cage.

Kareina usually held four torture sessions each day, then left Jamie isolated in her cage for the night. She was given no food, only an occasional cup of tepid, foul-smelling water.

Jamie was determined to keep resisting, but it was getting harder. Her mind now seemed fogged, barely conscious even when she was awake.

But every day she resisted was one more day of survival for her world. This truly was one life for billions. But how much longer could she hold on?

Chapter Twenty-Nine:
The Toad

ABADON, CITY OF THE ARCHONS

Hearing the Toad's command, Lys hesitated, eyes wide; staring up at him in horror.

Taking a step toward her, a tremor ran through Hewett's ponderous bulk as he repeated his demand. "Take that smock off... *now!*"

Lys glanced desperately around the room, but realized she had no choice but to obey. There was nowhere to run, nowhere to hide. She was totally at his mercy. With trembling hands, she slipped the slave garment over her head, then looked up to meet his gaze.

For a long moment the toad leered at her, crouched before him, naked and terrified. Finally with a sigh of resignation, tossed the package he'd been carrying onto the mat beside her.

"Put these on," he said.

Lys tore the package open. The package contained her own clothing: undergarments, jeans, sandals, and a T-shirt.

She looked up at the toad in confusion. "I don't understand..." she began, then chose to take advantage of the offer before he changed his mind. She quickly pulled on her clothing.

"Don't think I'm not tempted to use my advantage over you in more pleasurable ways, Ms. Johnston, but I have no time for that at the moment. And I apologize for the little games we had to play back at the market. When someone in my position buys a slave as attractive as you, certain things are expected to be done. If I had not, suspicions would have been raised, and that can be fatal. Fortunately I didn't have to play that kind of game to purchase your friends."

Lys had finished dressing, but was still confused. "You purchased my friends also?"

"Yes, now follow me and I'll lead you to them."

Walking to the large wooden armoire along the wall, he explained, "This little room is not only in an out-of-the-way location, it has certain connections that have often proved valuable." He pushed the armoire aside, revealing a hole, three-feet high and four-feet wide, carved into the soft volcanic rock. "Go in there, and follow the tunnel till it ends. I'll move the armoire back into place and follow you."

Lys complied again, hoping against hope that what the toad said was true. The tunnel twisted and turned, and descended again to a lower level. Lys crawled on hands and knees. The dim illumination was barely enough to show the way. After a sharp jog to the left, she entered a room about fifteen-feet square. She stood up, awaiting the Praetor, who arrived a few moments later.

Opening a concealed trap door in the center of the floor, the Praetor lowered himself through, and instructed her to follow. He moved with surprising agility for a man of his girth.

Climbing down the ladder, Lys found herself in another fifteen-foot square chamber. Two figures lay sleeping on the bare floor. As she stepped off the ladder, one of them stirred and looked up at her in the dim light. "Sis?" a familiar voice asked, then exclaimed, "Sis! It's *you!*"

As Roger scrambled to embrace his sister, Michael woke also, and soon they both held her tightly, bombarding her with questions while the toad looked on impatiently.

"Now," Hewett said finally, "It's time we talked."

Sitting with their backs against the rough rock wall of the subterranean chamber, the three friends listened as Hewett spoke.

"As you have seen, there are many slaves in Abadon. No one knows the precise number, but I'd estimate at least ten million. The Archons use them for manual labor, but also as playthings, to torment and kill for their amusement.

"I was captured 40 years ago and brought to Abadon as a slave. I was only 14 at the time. Most of those who are brought here as slaves are dead within a few years; but somehow I survived. I learned to work the system; and I rose to the top. I've been given favor by the Archons and am respected by every slave in Hades. But there's only one thing in the universe I really want." He paused, looking at each of them, "I want to go home."

"The Archons are constantly bringing human captives here to replenish their slave supply, but you three are different. You were not brought here by the Archons. One of my operatives saw you arrive. You came here on your own. That means you know how to open the portal, and that also means you know how to escape.

"I don't know what you've come here for, but I'm willing to help in any way I can. I do make one demand, however: Take me back to your world when you leave."

Lys, Roger, and Michael looked at each other and nodded in agreement. "We'll take you with us if you help us find the person we're looking for."

The three quickly told Hewett about Jamie's kidnapping, and explaining the urgency to rescue her before she was forced to reveal the detonation codes.

"We know they'll use all their powers to force her to reveal them.

"We suspect she's held in a place of torment, a circular pit with many levels where humans are tortured and killed."

"You're describing the arena," Hewitt said. "It's just outside the city. It's a long walk from here, but I can take you there if you'd like. But rest here for tonight. I'll bring some food and refreshment. We'll see the arena in the morning."

The next morning the toad led them through a tangled maze of passages that led back to the main corridor. From there, they began a long trek that would lead them to the arena, and hopefully, to Jamie Thatcher.

Chapter Thirty: Crossing Abadon

ABADON, CITY OF THE ARCHONS

As they approached the center of the city, the passageway widened and the ceiling now arched more than 100 feet above their heads. The corridor also become more congested. The air above them swished with Archons darting past at high speed, while on the ground, slaves—many hobbled with rattling chains—slowly trod the passage, headed toward assigned destinations.

"We're almost to the central marketplace," Hewett said.

Just then, a fury of dark flapping wings and high pitched shrieks exploded around them as four Archons dropped into the corridor from a vertical shaft over their heads. The monsters quickly darted away toward the marketplace.

Looking up in alarm, the three saw that just above them an enormous vertical shaft at least forty feet wide seemed to stretch upward into infinity. The upper levels were alive with darting movements: swerving, twisting blurs. Hideous screeches echoed down from the cavernous chambers above.

"That shaft leads up into the Archon sections of the city," Hewett continued his commentary. "There are dozens of shafts like that."

From time to time, several of the Archons from the higher levels would fold back their wings and dive into the shaft. In a dizzying display they dropped, plunging downward at high speed then, spreading their wings, they swept into the corridor and quickly darted away, somehow dodging other Archons who were flying equally fast in the opposite direction.

The corridor before them enlarged into a huge gallery that obviously had once been another magma dome. Though not as big as the hydroponic farm it was still immense, with a roof soaring three hundred feet above a broad plaza.

"This is the central marketplace of Abadon," Hewett explained.

Along the sides of the cavern were various markets and shops. Storefronts were also carved into the gallery wall six or seven stories high, many accessible only to flying Archons, and to slaves terrified enough of their masters to brave the precarious narrow stairways carved into the cliff face. The friends watched in horror as a few slaves were struggling to climb the stairs while carrying heavy loads to Archon shops high above.

The open plaza between the shops bustled with

activity. Hundreds of slaves were plodding across the plaza, heads down, carrying out menial tasks. The air overhead was filled with swarms of Archons, flitting from store to store. A few high-level Archon lords were making a stately promenade across the plaza, each accompanied by a band of eager minions.

"These shops are reserved for the Archons," Hewett pointed out. "Slaves have their own marketplace on a lower level. The slaves you see here are carrying out tasks for their masters, most of them delivering goods to the Archon shops."

"What kinds of things do they sell here?" Michael asked.

"Many of the items are similar to what you'd find for sale in your world," Hewett responded. "Food, household items, cookware…"

Pointing to the shop they were just passing, he said, "This is a clothing store. While the Archons tend to view clothing as an unnecessary encumbrance in everyday life, they do like to dress up for special occasions." The front of the store was hung with a variety of floor-length robes, most of which were of a coarse black fabric. Many of the garments were trimmed with rich leather and decorated with complex patterns of shining metal studs.

"That next shop is an arms supplier. Being a warrior culture, weapons are always in demand." The display at the front of the shop featured a variety of swords and knives. Lys noted that several of the knives featured razor-sharp obsidian blades. She cringed, remembering Kariena's attempt to kill her using a similar blade. *Did Kareina purchase that knife here?*

Moving on to the next shop, Hewett said, "This store specializes in instruments of torture. Very popular. Notice the display of copper rods with blue glowing tips. That's a recent Archon innovation. Pain by nerve induction. Highly effective. While the arena is the primary place of torment, most masters find pleasure in torturing their slaves at home also."

"I thought the slaves all lived on the lower levels." Michael remarked.

"Slaves who work in the industrial area and in food production live on the lower levels. They've pretty much developed their own culture and suffer much less abuse. But most of the Archons also keep household slaves who live with them in their chambers on the upper levels. Living in close proximity to their masters, household slaves are tortured much more frequently," Hewett sighed, shaking his head. "They tend to wear out quickly, but it keeps the slave markets busy."

The next shop in line was obviously a jewelry store. The display at the front of the store featured diamonds, colored gemstones, and a variety of other items. "The Archons love to decorate their bodies with all sorts of jewelry. For a society based on their hatred of the human race, it's surprising how many of the items are human artifacts.

"A few years back, the big thing was shrunken

heads. They'd take a human head, remove the skull, then dry the flesh to shrink it to a fraction of its former size. It's still not uncommon to see a high-level Archon lord parading through the marketplace with four or five human heads dangling from a chain around his neck.

"More recently, the big thing is necklaces made from human teeth. The ones that come with gold and silver inlays are especially in high demand. When polished properly, they can be quite stunning."

"Where do they get the human body parts?"

Hewett was silent for a moment, then replied. "You'll see."

As they made their way through the marketplace, Roger stopped, suddenly alert. Amidst the clamor of the teeming market, his ears detected a new sound; a thin wailing—wild and indescribable— so indistinct and faint that it repeated more than once before Roger could be sure it was more than his imagination. But the sound came again... and then again, becoming more distinct each time it repeated.

It began as a doleful wail, as though a strong wind was twisting its way through distant caves. Then it increased in volume, becoming a wild shriek clearly audible over the other sounds in the marketplace. It died down, then began once more.

This time it was unmistakable, and like nothing any of the friends had ever heard: a keening wail, raw and primitive, resonating through the cavern.

Chills rippled down Roger's spine as the sound trailed off.

Hearing the sound, the toad instantly dropped to the ground and sat frozen, his face blanching.

"Banshees!" he hissed. *"Get down!"*

Michael knelt beside him. "So that's the wail of a banshee," he muttered. "I've read about wailing banshees, but I never thought I'd actually hear one. The ancient Celtic legends say that when you hear that sound, someone is about to die."

"That's more true than you know," said Hewett.

"What's a banshee?" Lys asked, crouched low beside them.

"They're a caste of female warriors, notorious even among the Archons for their great strength and cruelty. You don't want to mess with a banshee. They respect nothing. Not even I am safe when there are banshees about.

"That wailing sound is the cry of a banshee hunting party drawing near, and they're coming to make a kill. Michael is right. When you hear that sound, someone is about to die."

Most of the slaves in the plaza had frozen in place and crouched down. Many were visibly trembling. Even the Archons stopped their activity and flitted to the storefronts or found perches along the face of the cliff, clearing the air for what was approaching.

Suddenly, a group of three banshees tore into the

marketplace from a side tunnel, flying at high speed, darting and weaving. They were the largest Archons any of the group had yet seen. Though it was difficult to judge size as the banshees wheeled through the marketplace at breakneck speed, Michael estimated they must each have a wingspan of more than twenty feet.

The banshees were true monsters. Over nine feet tall had they been standing upright, their lean, muscular bodies were covered in gleaming black reptilian scales. Sinuous barbed tails lashed from side to side as they flew.

The lead banshee's piercing green eyes burned with a chilling mixture of intelligence and cruelty. Her jaws spread wide as she howled, revealing a double set of long jagged teeth.

Hewett whispered. "They're about to choose a slave to kill. Keep your heads down and stay close to me. Whatever you do, don't look at them until after they've made their selection."

The three banshees circled the market several times, loudly screeching, flying low over the throng of slaves filling the plaza. Some of the slaves covered their heads, a few unshackled slaves broke for the nearest side tunnel, desperate to escape death. The banshees were searching for a victim, and it would be the first slave who did something to catch their attention. Finally they found what they were looking for.

An emaciated boy, not more than thirteen years old, was struggling to pull a cart loaded with goods toward one of the larger Archon shops when he made the mistake of glancing up at the banshees. That was enough to seal his fate. The three flew silently in a great circle around him, then swooped down on him from the rear.

The lead banshee abruptly seized the boy by the waist, grabbing his body with powerful talons that pierced his flesh, then swept him into the air. The startled boy screamed in agony and began flailing his limbs, struggling to get away. As the other two banshees hooted and cheered, the lead monster flew the boy at high speed around the edge of the marketplace several times, mere feet above the slaves crouched on the floor. She held the boy at arm's length for all to see her prize, then began rising in altitude, wings beating a smooth, even tempo.

As she rose higher and higher above the floor, the boy's desperate shrieks grew louder until they reverberated from the walls. Finally the banshee reached the peak of the ancient magma dome, higher than a thirty-story building. She circled the immense chamber several more times then turned the boy to face her. Her green eyes flashed with fire as she let loose a keening howl that shook the cavern.

The terrified boy was whimpering piteously, tears streaming down his cheeks, pleading for his life. "Please... please *let me go!*"

Fixing her eyes on him, the banshee's thin gray lips broke into a sadistic smile as she purred, "Certainly!"

Abruptly seizing him by his right arm, she swung the boy around in a great circle, building up momentum, and let him go.

The doomed boy cartwheeled halfway across the market, shrieking in mindless terror. Slaves on the plaza below rushed into the side corridors to avoid being struck by his falling body. The three banshees flew alongside the boy most of the way to the ground as he plummeted to his death.

Archons perched on the walls all around the marketplace hooted their approval.

A group of slaves were already heading in the boy's direction to remove the body as the banshees darted into a side corridor and disappeared.

Roger and his friends were stunned by the display of brutality. "Why didn't anybody stop them?"

"Stop them?" Hewett replied. "From killing a slave? Remember, this is Hades. It's not encouraged to interrupt slaves while they are carrying out their duties, but it's definitely not forbidden.

"When the owner of the boy is identified, the banshees will be required to reimburse the owner for the loss, but there will be no other penalty. A boy like that can be purchased for five or six shekels so the loss is negligible, and as you could see, all the Archons in the market enjoyed the spectacle."

Seeing the horror on their faces, the toad shook his head, wattles quivering. "What you just saw was nothing! Wait 'till you see the arena."

Leaving the market center, they continued on the main corridor as it led toward the city's exit.

As they passed a wide corridor that branched to the left, Hewett paused a moment. Glancing at Roger he said, "Let me show you one more thing before we get to the arena."

A two-hundred yard trek down the side corridor brought them out onto a balcony, three hundred feet above a circular, gravel-covered field that stretched before them for more than half a mile. The field was situated at the bottom of what must been the central crater of the ancient volcano. The walls of the crater formed immense cliffs that surrounded the field on every side, rising upward for thousands of feet. The pit was open to the elements, and was illuminated by the dull light of Hades' perpetually overcast sky.

"This crater was once a pit reaching deep into the earth," Hewett explained, "but for thousands of years it's been the dumping ground for tailings from excavations in the city. That debris gradually filled in the depths of the crater, creating the broad field you see now.

"Two hundred years ago the floor of the crater was leveled to create a training ground for Archon warriors. Young fighters are now apprenticed here and taught the skills of battle."

Gazing out across the ancient crater, the friends saw throngs of Archons engaged in swordplay and mock battles.

On the far end of the field, a seething mass of

Archon warriors had just risen into the air and was swiftly gaining altitude.

High above them, other Archons were soaring in vast formations. Thousands were swirling just above the rim of the crater, moving in perfect concert with each other as they flew in ever-expanding circles.

The rising swarm of Archons began to twirl in a clockwise direction. They were joined by thousands more streaming from caves around the perimeter of the crater. The air above the training field was suddenly filled with a living maelstrom—tens of thousands of darting bodies circling higher and higher.

Gaining momentum, they continued to increase their altitude until they joined the formation circling just above the rim of the crater. Then more Archons streamed into view from beyond the crater rim, further enlarging the gathering Archon storm. A spinning vortex made up of hundreds of thousands of warriors now darkened the sky.

Then, responding to some unknown silent signal, the apex of the swirling mass of warriors began to stream off towards the east in a snaking column so long and so thick it appeared like a trail of smoke.

It was one of the most awesome displays Roger had ever seen. "That's amazing," he said. "What are they doing?"

The toad looked at him in silence for a full minute, then replied. "These are Archon armies preparing to invade your world."

Chapter Thirty-One:
The Arena

ABADON, THE PLACE OF TORMENT

For more than an hour the group continued their trek across Abadon. The Archon presence was lighter here, and the only slaves present were those being led in chains toward the arena.

As they drew near the city's exit, its crimson gloom was replaced by the comparative brightness of the planet's surface. The path leaving the city wound upward between enormous, convoluted blocks of hardened lava. Finally exiting Abadon, the three friends gasped. Before them, silhouetted dark against the overcast sky, was an immense dragon, its angular head raised high on a serpentine neck, eyes fixed in their direction.

The dragon was not alone. Standing twenty feet to the left of the dragon stood a hideous nine-headed monster. Aligned behind the dragon and the monster were two rows of other repugnant beasts: gryphons, harpies, manticores, gorgons, chimeras and hydras. They all stood in strange silence, unmoving.

In a moment of relief, the friends realized what they were seeing. The path ahead of them passed between two rows of enormous gargoyles, adorning an ancient stone bridge that arched above a deep canyon. The stone dragon and nine-headed monster, each at least twelve feet tall, stood as sentinels over the entrance to the bridge. The smaller beasts, still more than nine feet tall, were arrayed on either side of the broad walkway that ran down the center of the bridge. Two more twelve foot tall gargoyles, a basilisk and a Minotaur, served as sentinels on the far end.

Hewett led the way as they crossed the bridge, dwarfed by the monstrous menagerie on either side. Passing the scowling visage of a gorgon, with its coiffure of writhing serpents, Lys wondered if the beasts towering over them were only mythological creatures, or if the gargoyles represented actual horrors inhabiting this dimension.

The bottom of the canyon was lost in rising clouds of steam, but the sound of surging, rushing water from its depths told them this was the boiling volcanic river Michael had predicted.

The path from the bridge led down a gradual slope, winding through a wasteland of black, twisted, rock—the remains of an ancient lava flow. The stench of burning sulfur was heavier here and breathing was becoming difficult. Exiting the lava flow, they found themselves on a broad, paved esplanade overlooking the arena.

The panorama before them was both breathtaking and horrifying. Jagged volcanic peaks surrounded them on three sides, with more volcanos in the distance. From the erupting volcanos, columns of smoke mixed with glowing ash billowed skyward. White-hot lava gushed from several peaks, pouring down the mountainsides in rivers of liquid fire, then cascading in blazing torrents to a sea of molten lava in the valley below.

Just below them, quarried into the surface of a broad plateau situated high above the fiery sea, was the arena, a vast bowl-like depression, close to a quarter-mile across, illuminated by the surrounding volcanic fires. Its interior was terraced, forming nine concentric rings, each level alive with the activity of hundreds of bat-winged Archons.

At the center of the pit, on the lowest level, was a raised dais where a winged figure sat enthroned. Behind him, two dragons stood guard, and before him, at the foot of the dais, stood two monstrous giants. Four more dragons wheeled slowly overhead.

The most horrifying element of the entire vista was the sound. Above the roar of the volcanos, the atmosphere reverberated with an unceasing cacophony of human shrieks, howls, agonized screams, and pleas for mercy rising from the pit below.

Michael had seen this vista portrayed many times. It had been painted by a number of medieval artists. It was a portrait of Hell.

As Hewett and the three friends stared out across the expanse of the pit, an Archon guard noticed them and came to investigate. "Out for a stroll, Praetor Hewett?"

The toad answered casually, "I've just purchased three new slaves, and have brought them to view the arena. I want to impress them with the need for absolute obedience."

"A good strategy, Praetor!" The Archon laughed, "Keep them in fear and they'll serve you well."

The toad waited until the Archon guard walked away, then began to describe the arena. "The arena exists primarily for the entertainment of the Archons, but as the head slave of the city, I can tell you that it's the most effective tool for slave training ever devised.

"The top level is reserved for minor offenses and punishments are relatively harmless. Slaves can be beaten, lashed, confined in cramped cages for hours at a time, or forced to swim through pools of human excrement. Archon masters always find an excuse to bring new slaves to this level. It's unpleasant, but they survive. And a visit to the first level lets new slaves witness the punishments awaiting more serious offenses on the lower levels. From that point most slaves are highly motivated to obey.

"The arena has nine levels," he continued, "with each descending level bringing more extreme tortures. At the second and third levels, for example, slaves might be suspended over pools of boiling lava, branded with hot irons, staked to the ground while lines of slaves carrying heavy weights are forced to march back and forth over their naked bodies..."

As Hewett continued to describe the torments of the arena, the three friends looked at each other in horror. Roger was aghast that Hewett could speak so casually as he described scenes of unimaginable cruelty. Hewett not only accepted what was taking place in the arena, he seemed proud of its efficiency. It occurred to Roger that the arena had been an accepted part of Hewett's world for most of his life. The torture of slaves was an everyday event. He'd grown callous to it.

The toad was continuing his description, "At still lower levels, slaves are mutilated. Their bodies are pounded with hammers until bones break, stretched on the rack until joints dislocate, forced to wade through pools of boiling tar, or thrown into pits crawling with scorpions and serpents. Of course, slaves never fully recover from that kind of torture, but it's still useful since it serves as a warning to others.

"The lowest level is a place for extreme torture and execution—usually reserved for runaway slaves or those who attack their masters. Slaves are flayed alive, impaled, sawn in two, burned at the stake, and worse.

"Of course, to the Archons, the torture of human beings is great entertainment, so when an Archon master grows weary of a slave for any reason, they always find some excuse to bring them here for punishment."

The appalling scene before them, coupled with the toad's casual description of its horrors, was overwhelming. Lys feared she was going to vomit. She turned her head away to avoid witnessing the torments taking place in the pit, but she couldn't close her ears to the anguished cries from its depths.

"This really is Hell," she muttered. "And these are the *damned!*"

Chapter Thirty-Two: Waiting for Night

ABADON, THE ARENA

Michael had turned away from the arena in revulsion, but at last his curiosity forced him to look. On every level, unspeakable cruelties were being inflicted. In addition to the torturers and victims, each level was also thronged with leather-winged spectators, moving from scene to scene, gawking at the tormented captives and sometimes joining in the torture.

"Who is that seated on the throne in the middle of the arena?" Michael asked. "It looks like an Irin!"

"That's Lucifer, the shining one," the toad replied. "He used to be an Irin. In fact, he was one of the highest Irin in Basilea, but he broke one of their strictest rules. He led a group known as the Grigori. Many thousands of years ago they left Basilea, invaded the Earth-realm, and intermarried with human women. For his crime, he was banished from Basilea. Now he is the master of the arena, and his hatred of humankind knows no limits.

"The giants before him are two of his sons. They're nine feet tall, and built like oak trees—incredibly strong, and the quintessence of evil. In your realm, the ancient Hebrews called them Nephilim, which means 'fallen ones.' The Greeks called them demigods, the mutant offspring of an Irin father and a human mother. Terrible creatures. Developing Nephilim grow so rapidly in the womb they quickly become too large for the birth canal, so when they're fully developed, they have to claw their way out of the uterus. Their first act in life is killing and eating their mother.

"Since none of Lucifer's wives ever survives childbirth, he and the other Grigori are constantly prowling the slave markets, seeking new mates."

Glancing at Lys, he added, "So, Ms. Johnston, you can be doubly thankful that it was Preator Hewett who purchased you at the market, and not one of the Grigori."

"Dante's *Inferno*," muttered Michael as he surveyed the scene. "That old poet got some details wrong, but he *saw*. The man truly was a seer. What must he have thought the first time he had a vision of this place?"

Just then two Archons came down the path from the city, dragging a human female, a girl, not more than 16 years old. The girl was thin, almost anorexic, with a pretty face and a disheveled shock of flaming red hair. Dressed in a filthy slave garment, she was kicking and screaming, pleading with her masters in piteous tones not to take her to the arena, but the Archons ignored her pleas. As they pulled her down the ramp toward the second level, her sobs faded into the din rising from the pit.

The three friends had to fight their natural impulse to intervene. They knew any attempt to rescue the girl would have been doomed to failure. There were dozens of Archons around them on the esplanade, and interference with the punishment of a slave would have brought an instant and violent response. The girl would still have been tortured, and they would have been captured or killed, thwarting their mission to save Jamie.

"Isn't there anything we can do to help these people?" Lys asked.

"Your first priority must be to secure your own world." Hewett responded. "If the Archons take over the Earth-realm, your whole world will be like this. But succeed in driving the Archons from your world, and the supply of slaves here will be cut off. Then things will have to change.

"Now about your friend." Hewett turned to Roger, "There is a small chamber just off the lowest level reserved for special cases. The most horrendous tortures of all take place in that room, but the process is less entertaining for the Archons. In that room, prisoners are kept in cages, and not harmed physically.

"Instead, the Archons use their mind-control powers to make the prisoners vividly experience the tortures of all the other levels. For the victims, the tortures feel totally real. They feel every bit of the pain, but there's no actual physical damage, so the victims can experience torture after torture, day after day, week after week, enduring unending agony until, at last, they are driven mad. From what you've told me, I suspect that's where we'll find your friend.

"It would not be wise to go down there now. There's too much activity," Hewett said, with a glance around the arena, "but when Lucifer leaves this evening, things will quiet down. We'll come back tonight."

Re-entering the city, Hewett took them to another of his hidden chambers, where they spent the next few hours talking. Hewett went into great detail describing life for the slaves of Hades, but he also had many questions about the Earth-realm.

"Where do all those slaves come from?" Lys asked.

"A small percentage were born here to other slaves, but most slaves don't live long enough to bear children. The vast majority of the slaves you've seen here were taken captive in the Earth-realm."

"But how could so many people simply disappear without being missed."

"People disappear all the time," Michael interjected. "I was just reading an article about it last week."

"Did you know that in the United States alone, close to a million people are reported missing each year, with 800,000 of those teenagers and children. Most are never found. It's the same in every country, and the vast majority of the missing are young. Experts say that eight million children worldwide go missing every year.

"Half of the missing kids are written off as runaways. Twenty-five percent are abductions by family members involved in custody disputes. Then there are kidnappings by strangers and kids taken by human traffickers.

"But the numbers unaccounted for are still staggering. With eight to ten million people disappearing every year, it's not hard to see how the Archons could abduct hundreds of thousands and it never be noticed."

Lys was horrified by the revelation. "I had no idea anything like that was happening."

"Most people don't, but it *is* happening," Michael replied. "In the United States alone, hundreds of thousands are enslaved by human traffickers every year, but only a tiny fraction ever makes the news."

"It appears," Hewett observed, "that Hades has already established a strong presence in your world."

"I hate to say it, but you're right," Michael said. "There are Archon collaborators in our world who would love nothing more than to turn our Earth into a copy of Hades."

Listening to Michael's explanation, Roger was quiet for a while, then smiled wistfully, "I know this is off-subject, Michael, but I have to say it. When you talk, you remind me so much of Jamie. Sometimes when we were dating, her photographic memory would drive me up the wall. She never forgot anything! But I loved to hear her talk. I'd get her on a subject and it sounded like she was reading from a book." Roger was surprised how much he missed her.

"Speaking of Jamie," Michael looked at Hewett, "how will we get her out of that hell hole tonight? Won't she be guarded?"

"Once the activity of the day is over, there's very little security at the arena." The toad replied. "Any slaves remaining in the pit will be securely locked in cages. And besides," He laughed, his wattles jiggling, "who tries to break into Hell?"

Chapter Thirty-Three: Rescue

ABADON, THE ARENA

The Archons were gone from the arena, their entertainment for the day ended. Crews of slaves were hard at work cleaning up the carnage.

Scores of dead bodies were being carried up the ramps to the top of the arena, where they were tossed unceremoniously from the edge of the plateau into the fiery lava sea below.

Other slaves lugged heavy buckets of water down the ramps, where they sloshed the worst of the blood and gore into drains spaced around each level.

Walking among them were human overseers, armed with the same kind of copper rod the slavemaster had used on Lys. One slave had been tottering under the weight of a large water-filled bucket. Attempting to set the bucket down to catch his breath, the slave accidently tipped it, causing the bucket to upset and spill, the water sloshing over the edge of the ramp and onto the terrace below.

In a moment, an overseer was on the scene. With a sharp rebuke, the overseer pressed his copper rod firmly into the man's chest. The slave let out a bloodcurdling cry and fell to the ground, clutching his chest and writhing in agony. The overseer turned and walked away.

Having personally experienced the pain induced by the copper rod, Lys gasped at the overseer's cruelty. *The torture in this place never ends!*

Hewett led them down ramps from level to level, going ever deeper into the arena. They tried not to contemplate what had transpired on these terraces earlier in the day.

From the lowest level, a corridor led into the depths of the mountain. The toad pointed toward it, then led the way. The tunnel ran straight for about a hundred feet, ending in a small anteroom hung with a variety of tools, implements of torture, and slave smocks. Several buckets of brownish, tepid water sat in one corner. An archway led to another room, long and narrow, with steel cages arranged along the left-hand wall.

The first cage held a man in his thirties lying naked in a fetal position, an expression of hopeless agony frozen on his face. Roger didn't have to examine him. The man was obviously dead, and had been for several hours. Rigor mortis had set in.

The next three cages were unoccupied.

In the fifth cage, a naked young woman lay on her side, one arm draped across her face. She appeared to be dead also, but then her body trembled slightly and her arm shifted, revealing her face. It was Jamie.

Leaning close, Roger whispered, *"Thatcher!"*

There was no response. Roger crouched down; pressing his face against the bars of her cage. *"Thatcher!"* He said again, louder. "It's me. It's *Roger*. I'm here with Lys and Michael. We've come to rescue you."

Jamie groaned weakly as one eye flickered open. A faint smile of recognition appeared on her lips, and she began weeping silently.

Roger reached through the bars and gently took her hand. "We need to get her out of here."

Michael had been examining the cage door. It was secured with a large padlock. He tested it, trying to pull it open, but it held securely. "Does anyone see a set of keys?"

Lys brightened. "Just a minute," she said as she sprinted back through the archway. A moment later she returned, a ring of keys jangling in her hand. "I noticed these hanging on the wall in the anteroom when we came in." She passed the keys to Roger.

Roger accepted them gratefully, and immediately began trying them in the padlock. One after another he inserted the keys and attempted to open the lock, but it remained unmovable. Finally, he slid the last key on the ring into the lock. He hesitated a moment, holding his breath, then gave the key a firm twist. There was a distinct click, and the lock popped open.

"An unwritten law of the universe," Michael laughed. "It's always the last one you try."

Quickly removing the lock, Roger swung the cage door open.

Jamie had lapsed once more into unconsciousness.

He lifted her gingerly from the cage and took her vital signs. "She's alive, but not doing well at all. She needs food, and some serious medical attention. Most of all, she needs to get out of this place.

"Lys, bring me one of those slave smocks from the anteroom and help me get her decent."

Lys appeared a few moments later with the cleanest smock she could find. As Roger helped Jamie to a sitting position, Lys slipped the garment over her head.

"How do we get her out of the arena without someone spotting us?" Michael asked.

Roger glanced at Hewett, "Is there a back way out of here?"

"I'm afraid not," Hewett replied. "The only way out is the way we came in. But as you saw, there were no Archons around, and most of the slaves are occupied with their assigned tasks. We just need to be careful not to arouse the suspicion of any of the overseers."

Roger remembered the lines of slaves carrying dead bodies out of the arena. "I think she'll pass for dead if no one looks too closely," he muttered.

With Roger clutching her hands and Michael holding her feet, they joined the stream of slaves removing bodies from the arena, making the long climb to the top. Hewett and Lys dumped the water from two of the buckets onto the anteroom floor, then each took up an empty bucket and followed behind Roger and Michael as they slowly made their way up the ramps.

Reaching the esplanade, Jamie moaned again and her eyes flickered open.

Finding a sheltered area along the low wall surrounding the esplanade, they laid her gently on the paved surface. Roger crouched close, again checking her pulse. She remained stable.

Carefully picking up her frail body, he carried her in his arms as they followed the path upward through the lava field, and then made their way across the stone bridge, passing between its hideous gargoyles.

As they entered the city, Hewett led them down a series of ramps, descending at least ten levels, then through a maze of corridors to a chamber similar to the one where he had first taken Lys. "This is another of my little bolt-holes," he said with pride. It was plain and sparsely furnished, but it had sleeping mats along two walls.

"Let Jamie rest here," Hewett said. "I'll go and bring back some food and refreshment. You should all try to get some sleep. It will be a long journey to the portal if you're carrying her."

It was a long journey, and tense. They headed out the next morning, fully expecting Kareina and her horde of demons to surround them at any moment, determined to once again take Jamie captive. None of the friends had any doubt that the Archons were scouring the city. They had no choice but to trust Hewett to know the best routes to avoid them.

Because of the need to avoid detection, Hewett led them by a circuitous route, through side tunnels, down more ramps, and across the lowest levels of the city, choosing areas where Archons rarely come. Around mid-day, Hewett brought them to another of his bolt-holes and left to procure food. He returned an hour later with a basket containing a pot of vegetable stew, a loaf of stale brown bread, and a jug of nondescript red wine.

Jamie revived a little and was able to eat and drink small amounts, but still did not speak.

Chapter Thirty-Four: Hewett's Story

ABADON, CITY OF THE ARCHONS

As they huddled in the cramped chamber eating the spartan fare of Hades, Lys couldn't take her eyes off Hewett. He ate noisily, devouring his food with reckless abandon, crunching up a piece of half-cooked carrot with his mouth open wide, while a dollop of stew oozed down his multiple chins, seemingly unnoticed. It was hard for her to imagine Hewett ever being anything more than a grotesque monster. *How will he ever adjust to life in the Earth-realm?*

Finally she asked him, "Tell me about yourself, Hewett. What were things like for you when you were growing up?"

Before responding to the question, Hewett gulped down the huge gob of food in his mouth, wiped his chin on his sleeve, then let loose with a humongous belch.

He smiled, obviously satisfied with his meal, then leaned back against the wall and got a faraway look in his eyes, as though revisiting a treasured memory.

"I had a wonderful childhood," he said.

"I grew up in a little town just outside Niagara

Falls, New York, called the Town of Niagara.

"It was a great place. We lived in a small house just off the main highway. There was a big field behind our house, and in the summer it was full of wild strawberries. I'd gather them by the bucketful.

"My dad had a big vegetable garden and we also kept chickens. I helped him work the garden. We grew the best sweet corn in the county and had fresh eggs every morning."

Hewett seemed almost in a trance. In his mind he was a thirteen-year-old boy again.

"There was this great restaurant just down the road called the Whistle Pig," he continued. "They served enormous hot dogs wrapped in crisp bacon and smothered in cheddar cheese. I can still taste them.

"At the back of our field was the Great Forest—at least that's what I called it. It went on for miles. In the summers my best friend Joey and I would spend hours exploring it. We'd build forts and play army. We'd swing from vines and pretend to be Tarzan.

"Winters were even better. When the lake-effect snows blew in, we'd get drifts six feet high to play in and burrow through.

"In the winter we'd often sneak down to Joey's basement. It wasn't a finished basement, just a couple of old couches and a threadbare carpet spread out over a bare concrete floor, with piles of boxes and old tires at the far end. The only lighting came from two bare light bulbs affixed to the open joist ceiling. Joey's dad went down there to smoke cigars, since his mom didn't allow smoking in the house. It was damp and dark and musty, but for two thirteen-year-old boys, it was our own personal heaven.

"We'd sneak a couple of beers from the fridge at my house, then sit around smoking his dad's cigars. We thought we were real men.

"One day, we were rooting through some boxes in the back of the basement and found an old Ouija board. Joey knew how to use it.

"We put the planchette on the board and both of us rested our hands on it. It suddenly started sliding around, pointing to letters, spelling out words. At first I thought it was Joey moving it. I know now we had encountered an Archon, operating from within the shadow realm.

"At first it just seemed spooky. We'd play with the board for a while then put it away, but in a few days we'd get it out again. Something about it always drew us back.

"It knew things... sometimes very practical things!" Hewett beamed. "The Ouija board told me where my dad hid the keys to his liquor cabinet, so Joey and I progressed from cheap beer to the good stuff.

"It also revealed where Joey's dad kept his collection of old Playboys. After that, Joey and I spent hours stretched out on the threadbare carpet surrounded by stacks of Playboy magazines—two thirteen-year-old boys in a dank basement exploring the forbidden mysteries of female anatomy!" Hewett smiled contentedly at the memory, as though still viewing some of those debauched pictures in his mind.

"The Ouija board began to tell us things before they happened. One night it told us Joey's mom was going to be hurt in a bad car wreck. The next night she was almost killed when a drunk driver slammed her car. We began to take the board very seriously.

"One day we asked the Ouija board who it was. It spelled out its answer, 'I am Abacus, the spirit of the board.' It confided that some in our world would call him a demon, but he assured us we didn't need to be afraid of him. He said most humans don't understand about demons. He just wanted to be our friend. He told us he had lots of friends at our school.

"Just after my 14th birthday, the demon told us that some of his other friends were having a Halloween party and invited us to come. He said they were meeting at 11:00 p.m. at the old fire-pit in the woods and promised that at midnight, he would materialize so we could see what he really looked like. It sounded like a great way to spend Halloween.

"I snuck out of the house and met Joey in his backyard at 10:30 Halloween night. It was bitter cold, but we knew how to dress for winter.

"Everyone in school knew about the fire-pit. It was way out in the woods, a circle of big boulders with a pile of ashes in the center. Rumors were that a witchcraft coven met there and they all danced around the fire naked. Of course, none of us really knew who built it, but from time to time there were fresh ashes in the center.

"We got there and there were a bunch of guys from school already there, clustered around a roaring fire.

"They acted like they were expecting us, and invited us to warm ourselves around the fire. It felt good to be accepted by those guys. I was always a chubby kid and not very popular. I recognized a few of the guys from school, but the oldest was someone I'd never met. The others called him Ashton. We sat and talked and Ashton told us ghost stories as we sipped whiskey from a big flask Ashton passed around. I remember thinking this had to be the best Halloween ever.

"About 11:45 Ashton stood and announced that it was time to summon the demon.

"Ashton seemed to know what to do. He told us to circle the fire. On the far side of the fire a mangey old dog was staked to the ground, whimpering in the cold. Ashton pulled out a long butcher knife and knelt beside the dog.

"Joey cried out in alarm, 'Are you going to kill that dog?'

"'You want to see the demon don't you?' Ashton sneered. 'We have to make a sacrifice at the stroke of midnight! ...Or maybe you should have just gone trick-or-treating with the little kids!'

"It was almost midnight. Ashton placed his hand

on the dog's body. It seemed to calm it. 'Now, call for the demon to come!' he shouted.

"A few of the guys laughed and began to chant, 'Come demon! Come demon!' Then the others began to join in.

"You have to remember, we were just stupid kids, just fooling around, and it was midnight on Halloween. I don't think any of us really expected anything to happen.

"At the moment of midnight, Ashton plunged the knife into the dog's body. It let out a piteous squeal as it died, sounding more like a pig than a dog. As it died, everyone in the group was startled by a flash of lightning and a rumble that sounded like thunder. A dark mist began to swirl around us. Then out of the center of the fire, the demon arose—rising spectrally at first, then taking shape and solidifying.

"It spread hideous bat-like wings and flew in a big circle around the fire-pit. And suddenly it was joined by others. A horde of demons were flying around us. Most of the guys screamed in terror and ran off into the woods. I'm sure most of them were peeing their pants.

"But Joey and I and a few others stayed, transfixed by the unearthly spectacle taking place around us. *After all,* I thought to myself, *this demon is our friend.*

"Without warning, several of the demons swooped down, grabbed us with their talons and flew us directly into the blazing fire. We were screaming and thrashing our arms, trying to pry the monsters' claws from our bodies, terrified that we were going to be burned.

"But the demons flew us right through the fire into a long tunnel of silent darkness. We eventually found ourselves at the great portal of Abadon.

"The demons who captured us are called gatherers. Their job is to kidnap humans in the Earth-realm to replenish the slave supply here. Mostly they take kids. There were five of us captured that night. They drug us, kicking and screaming, through the city and chained us to a wall in the slave market. We were terrified.

"The next day we were sold as slaves."

"Did they torture you in the arena?"

"Many times." Hewett shivered at the memory.

"The first year was rough. The first few months I was tortured at least weekly on the first level of the arena, then later on the second. Six months in, they dragged me down to the third level, tied me to a post, and used a hammer to break off some of my teeth. I was in agony for months.

"Of course I made out better than Joey..."

Hewett looked down, shaking his head.

"The kid would not learn. He kept trying to escape. Finally he took a knife and tried to attack one of his Archon masters. The last I saw of Joey they were dragging him down to the lowest level of the pit for execution. I'm not sure what they did to him, but I could hear him shriek for hours."

Hewett leaned his head back against the wall for several minutes, then looked up, as though awakening from a dream. "I'll be glad to be away from this place," he said wearily. "I never thought I'd see home again."

As Hewett pondered the thought of going home, a troubled look came across his face, as if for the first time contemplating what he might find when he returned. "I'm sure home has changed a lot... My folks would be in their eighties now, if they're even still alive. My sister, Katie, in her sixties." He sat for a moment, deep in thought.

"What will you do when you go back?"

"Believe it or not, when I was little I dreamed of being a doctor, but I know it's too late for that. I never even made it out of junior high."

He paused a moment, looking thoughtful. "All I remember of home was the fun I had as a kid. I hadn't really thought about what I'd do when I get there."

Sensing his concern, Lys said, "Don't worry, Hewett. We'll help you find something. The important thing is to get away from this place."

It was evening when they arrived at the secret room to which Hewett had first brought Lys. Hewett had been uncharacteristically silent through the afternoon, but again he left them in the hidden chamber while he went to procure food. Hewett was gone much longer than usual, but finally returned with their provision.

Michael sat next to Lys as they ate, a look of

concern on his face. "Something's not right," he murmured. "We saw back at the lake house the effort Kariena took to capture Jamie. I'd have thought Kariena and her minions would be scouring every square inch of Abadon in a frantic attempt to find her, but we haven't seen a trace of them."

"I just assumed Hewett knew routes the Archons wouldn't search," Lys said thoughtfully, "but you're right. This does seem too easy."

Roger was carefully monitoring Jamie's condition, feeding her as much as he deemed safe. She wept from time to time, but still made no effort to communicate.

"Tomorrow morning," Hewett told them as they ate, "we should make it to the portal."

Chapter Thirty-Five: Followed!

ABADON, CITY OF THE ARCHONS

For a long time the next morning they made their way up ramps, climbing from level to level, finally emerging on the main corridor through the city. By the time they got there their legs were aching and they were breathing heavily, but none of them thought of resting. They were almost free.

Hewett was still acting strangely, much quieter than usual.

"Are you okay?" Lys asked him as they stopped to catch their breath.

"I'm fine," he said abruptly. "I just need to get you to the cavern entrance."

Looking around him, Hewett gestured down the corridor. "That way! We should be to the entrance in about forty-five minutes."

Almost immediately, their attention was drawn to the sound of shouts and screams coming from the path ahead. The source of the tumult was a mixed group of humans and Archons, moving rapidly in their direction.

Hewett and the four friends quickly ducked into a narrow side tunnel, then peered cautiously around the corner to see what was causing the commotion. As the group came into view, Lys recognized immediately what was taking place

Five gatherers were driving and dragging a group of ten newly-arrived slaves toward the slave market. The slaves each wore a steel collar clamped tightly around their neck. Each collar was connected by a five-foot length of chain to the collar of the slave in front and by another chain to the slave behind. Together they formed a fifty-foot line of misery—ten slaves strung together like ornaments on a necklace, being driven toward a destiny more horrendous than any of them could imagine.

Two of the seven-foot tall gatherers walked at the font of the line, guiding the human chain down the corridor. Three more of the grotesque monsters followed the group, using copper rods to drive them forward, inflicting intense pain on any who hesitated.

Lys was taken aback by the age of the slaves. The oldest was a boy about seventeen, who looked from his build like he could have been a high-school football star. The youngest was a pretty oriental girl who couldn't have been more than twelve. All were wide-eyed, confused and terrified, shrieking in pain as they ran to stay ahead of the Archons wielding the copper rods.

As she watched them pass, Lys wept silently. She knew exactly what lay ahead for these children and there was nothing she could do to help them. *Stay focused, Lys. Your whole world depends on getting Jamie safely out of here.*

As the line of slaves disappeared into the distance, Hewett led the friends back into the main corridor. It now looked deserted as far as they could see.

They were almost out.

They began walking faster, with Roger carrying Jamie's limp body. They were all anticipating the joyful reunion that awaited them on the other side of the portal.

Twenty minutes later, however, Michael stepped close to Hewett with a look of alarm, "I think someone's following us."

"Are you certain?"

"I've heard noises behind us several times. When I look back, I catch a glimpse of movement, but it quickly stops."

"This could be bad. We need to find out who it is."

Hewett led them into another side corridor to await the follower.

"There's the noise again," Michael whispered.

It was the sound of cautious footsteps grating on the loose gravel along the edge of the main corridor. Their mysterious follower was getting closer.

Leaving Jamie and the others in their hiding place, Roger turned back to the main corridor to face their pursuer.

A figure emerged, walking in a crouch, sliding stealthily along the edge of the corridor. It was the teenage girl they'd seen being dragged into the arena. The disheveled shock of flaming red hair was unmistakable.

As Roger stepped out of the side corridor to confront her, the girl cringed and began trembling violently.

"Why are you following us?" Roger demanded.

"I'm not followin' anybody, mister. I'm running." She glanced around in terror, eyes darting like a frightened animal. "I know they'll kill me but I don't care. I can't stand this place."

Then she added, "Are you going to turn me in?"

Lys had come out of the side corridor to stand beside her brother. "No, honey, I promise we won't turn you in."

"Who are you people?"

"We're running too," Roger said.

Lys went to her, placing one hand gently on her shoulder. The girl flinched. "We saw you being taken into the arena two days ago, but there was nothing we could do. We're so sorry."

"T'wasn't your fault," she said. "You couldn't have done anything."

"What's your name?" asked Lys.

"They call me Casey."

"This is your lucky day, Casey. Come with us. We have a way out of this place."

Moving forward again, with Casey following tentatively behind, they at last saw the proverbial light at the end of the tunnel. The cavern entrance was just ahead. After days in the dim crimson light of Abadon, the perpetually overcast sky of Hades was unbelievably brilliant.

They made their way slowly up the winding path, the cavern roof now arched hundreds of feet above them.

"I'm thankful old Dante was wrong on that one," Michael quipped, thinking again of the inscription over Hell's gate. "We entered the inferno, but we never abandoned hope. Now we're on our way home."

Finally they could see the vast desolate plain before them. More importantly, they could see the ancient circle of standing stones just 300 feet away. It was just a short walk to the portal.

As they exited the mouth of the cave, however, three seven foot-tall Archon guards stepped toward them from the left with drawn swords.

"They've been waiting for us," Rodger muttered. "We've been found out."

Chapter Thirty-Six: Betrayed!

ABADON, CITY OF THE ARCHONS

Seeing the Archon guards, the four froze, with Casey taking a step back into the cave.

The guards began silently moving in their direction, spreading out to surround them.

Hewett's response was immediate. He gallantly stepped to the fore, drew his sword with a flourish, and extended it in the direction of the guards. He then paused a moment, smiling, and swung the sword around toward the four friends.

"Just as we agreed, my Archon lords!" he shouted. "In exchange for my reward, I've thwarted the escape of the dark haired woman, and delivered to you two exceptional slaves. One is a doctor, the other a man of great intelligence. You can have them both. And as an extra bonus, the red-haired girl is a runaway slave. I'm sure she'll give you great pleasure at the lowest level of the arena!

"The blonde I'm keeping for my own pleasure. If you check her shoulder, you'll see that I own her!"

The friends stood motionless, open-mouthed, searching for words to express their shock and confusion. They'd been betrayed!

Finally, Lys said, "Hewett... why?"

Hewett looked at her with what seemed to be genuine regret, "I've watched you all carefully since we met, Ms. Johnston. When I saw that you offered a way of escape, I wanted that more than anything, but as I spent time with you, I realized that I don't fit in your world. I'm not like you. I never could be. As we talked yesterday, I realized that in your world, I'd be considered a freak. A grotesque monster with no useful skills.

"But here in Hell, I *rule!* I'm a man of position! Everyone in this city respects me. I have a harem of six lovely slave girls who obey my every command. I could never have anything like that in your world!

"So the decision was simple. I could go with you and become an object of loathing and ridicule, or I can use your presence here to enhance my position still further. I've chosen the latter.

"In exchange for betraying you, I'm getting spacious new living quarters. Big enough to enlarge my harem. There'll be a room there just for you, Ms. Johnston, and you'll never be lonely. I'm planning to spend a great deal of time with you. After all," he laughed, wattles jiggling, "I paid fifty shekels of silver for you!"

"You bastard!" Lys screamed in rage and drove the hardest punch she could into his immense gut. Then, seeing that his stomach was too well padded for her fist to produce an effect, she brought her knee up forcefully into his groin.

Startled and hurt, the toad staggered back a step and dropped his sword.

The three Archons were moving in quickly to take control of the situation, but Roger Johnston was faster. He knew this was his moment of destiny. As he snatched up the toad's fallen sword, the Irin life-force activated within him. His body began to glow with a brilliant white light. He felt a life and energy he'd never imagined possible flowing through every part of his being.

Roger hadn't handled a sword since a fencing course his second year in collage but the Irin life-force more than compensated for his inexperience. Shifting the blade in his hand, he willed the life-force energy to flow through his hand and out to the end of the sword. The blade began to glow with a brilliant white light.

The toad instinctively reached out to Roger to retrieve his sword, but with his unexpected new strength, Roger dispatched him with one flick of his wrist. The glowing sword slashed deeply into the toad's abdomen, which erupted in greasy flames. Praetor Hewett stood for a moment, mouth open, uncomprehending, then fell over backward, dead.

But Roger had already turned his attention to the perplexed Archons. The Archon guards had killed many humans, both in Hades and the Earth-realm, but they'd never seen a human with the life-energy of an Irin. They held back for a moment, hesitant to approach him.

High overhead, a dragon had also noticed the display of Irin energy, and was diving in their direction.

Seeing the dragon, Roger shouted, "Lys, get to the stone circle and open that portal NOW. You must get Michael and Jamie out of here!"

"Not without you!"

"There's no time to argue!" he shouted as the three Archons moved to surround him. "Get that damn portal open now or we'll all be dead. I know what I'm doing."

The Archon guards were far more experienced with a sword, but Roger had the advantage of the Irin life-force. One touch of his glowing blade would bring instant death.

Roger slashed at one of the Archons, who quickly backed away. Then, as another Archon moved close behind. him, he swung around and drove his glowing blade home. The Archon exploded in flames.

The two remaining Archons moved more carefully now, but continued to press the fight. The dragon was getting closer.

"Lys, *GO!*" Roger screamed again. "We're out of time!"

Lys hesitated another moment, but knew Roger was right. She and Michael half carried Jamie into the circle of standing stones, where Jamie collapsed unconscious. Casey followed a few steps behind, still terrified.

Lys took a deep breath and prepared to open the portal.

Standing in the center of the great slabs of rock, the now-familiar flow of unlearned words poured from deep within her, rising to a crescendo that reverberated between the dimensions. The overcast sky parted, and light beamed into the darkness, illuminating the four.

But Lys's eyes were still fixed on Roger. So far, he was holding his own, but the Irin life-force was beginning to fade.

With tears in her eyes, Lys cried, "Roger, come *now*, it's not too late! You can make it!"

Roger glanced at the circle of stones and noticed the portal had begun to open. It was just 200 feet away, two-thirds the length of a football field. If he ran, he might just make it, but it was taking all of his effort to keep the Archons at bay, and the dragon was almost upon him.

He thought of Lys, and of Jamie, who he now realized had always been the love of his life. He thought of Michael and of the friends waiting beyond the portal. He thought of Casey, her innocence stolen, barbarically tortured in the arena at an age when she should have been texting with friends and cheering at high school football games. Finally, he thought of the Archon threat to the entire Earth-realm, of the arena being duplicated thousands of times over on every continent. *Hell on earth!* Roger knew what was at stake, and his choice was clear.

The dragon had paid little notice when the portal opened. That was a regular event here. It had not even noticed Lys, Jamie, Michael, and Casey standing illuminated in the center of the stone circle. The dragon was fully focused on him. As long as the Irin life-force remained, it appeared to the dragon that one of the hated Irin was doing battle with Archon guards in the very heart of Hades. That held the dragon's attention. If Roger were to try to join the others, the dragon's attention would shift, imperiling them all.

"I can't go with you, sis," Roger shouted. "Tell Jamie I love her... I've always loved her!"

The Irin life-force was nearly depleted, but Roger remained the focus of the dragon's attack. As the four felt themselves drawn into the now-open portal, the shadow of the dragon fell across Roger. A bellowing roar split the air; then a torrent of dragonfire spewed from the beast's mouth, instantly vaporizing both Roger and the Archon guards.

Chapter Thirty-Seven: The Vigil

LOCHBUIE, THE ISLAND OF MULL

Though Rand had said there was little chance of their friends surviving more than three days in Hades, the Iona synaxis had come prepared to stand vigil at the Lochbuie portal for at least a week, hoping for their friends' return.

They'd rented both rooms at the small Lochbuie bed and breakfast, and slept in shifts while maintaining a constant presence at the portal.

Patrick, Erin, and Catherine, however, refused to leave the portal. They stayed in the Hummer, taking turns napping and watching the stone circle, retreating to the bed and breakfast only to shower and use the restroom facilities.

Araton, Rand, and Eliel joined with the synaxis members in their vigil, standing watch in shifts but alert to call on other Irin should the need develop.

The second day at Lochbuie, a storm moved in and a cold rain fell most of the day. Through the long afternoon, the group maintained their soggy watch, walking the cold muddy ground, umbrellas in hand, or huddled in their cars. One of the few shops in the tiny village of Lochbuie was the *Old Post Office and Lochbuie Larder,* which served delicious, home-cooked food. While most of the group welcomed a hot meal on such a cold damp day, Patrick found he had no appetite. His focus was only on Lys.

The third day was partly cloudy and cool, with a few showers in the morning. Patrick rose early, stretched, walked to the bed and breakfast to freshen up, then returned to the Hummer. He spent most of the morning sitting in the Hummer with the windows open, eyes fixed numbly on the mysterious stone circle, hoping against hope that something would happen.

Weary from sitting too long, he spent the afternoon pacing the white sand beach, barely noticing the beautiful surroundings. His gaze kept returning to the standing stones. *What is Lys doing now? Is she even still alive?*

The day passed with no activity at the portal. That evening, Patrick returned to the Hummer and reclined the seat in a futile attempt to sleep. Discouragement was clearly setting in. The thought struck Patrick that the portal might never open. He might never see Lys again. He might never even find out what happened to her.

The fourth day dawned bright and sunny. Though by Rand's estimate, there was now little hope Lys was still alive, Patrick was determined to maintain the vigil till the end.

Early that afternoon, Patrick, Angus, and Araton were standing together beside the portal when Araton suddenly stiffened, becoming totally alert.

"Something is happening," he said softly. "I'm sensing a faint vibration in the earth." He paused, listening intently, then concluded, "The portal is about to open."

Angus ran to alert the synaxis members who were taking their turn to rest in the bed and breakfast. They came streaming out the door of the little guesthouse in less than a minute.

The vibration had increased. They all felt it now.

"Do you think it's them?" Patrick asked hopefully.

"It could be," Araton said, resting his hand firmly on the hilt of his scimitar. "but it could also be another horde of Archon warriors. We won't know which it is until the portal opens."

As they watched, a tenuous mist formed between the standing stones. The mist quickly thickened and began to rotate and expand, until it formed an ominous whirlwind. As it swirled, it spread to fill the space between the upright stones. Then, with a sound like a crack of thunder, a shining brightness appeared in the center of the cloud, increasing in intensity until the synaxis members had to shield their eyes.

When the light finally faded, four bedraggled figures were left standing on the muddy ground between the monoliths.

The members of the Iona synaxis quickly rushed to meet them.

Patrick got there first, throwing his arms around Lys, squeezing her body tightly and lifting her into the air. Erin arrived next and embraced Michael, clinging to him like she'd never let him go, tears of joy streaming down her face.

The rest of the group quickly attended to Jamie and Casey. Jamie seemed barely alive.

Peter Flannigan, a medical doctor who had just moved to Iona from Northern Ireland to join the synaxis, quickly took her vital signs and pronounced her weak, but stable. Angus lifted her limp body and gently carried her to the Hummer.

Glancing around, Patrick asked, "Where's Roger?"

"He's gone, Patrick..." Lys searched for something else to say but could not find the words. Finally she repeated, "He's gone. He gave his life for us."

"We need to get going," Erin said abruptly, releasing her hold on Michael. "As long as we're on Mull, we're vulnerable. This portal could open again at any moment and we could be engulfed by hundreds of Archons. We must get to Iona as quickly as possible."

The journey to Iona was tense. Erin drove the Hummer as fast as she dared on the narrow, twisting roads of Mull. Michael had taken the front passenger seat, while Patrick and Lys sat in the back on either side of Jamie. Casey and Catherine occupied the third row. The rest of the synaxis followed behind in separate vehicles.

As she drove, Erin kept glancing out the side window, fully expecting that at any moment they'd be inundated by hordes of Archon warriors trying to recapture Jamie, but it never happened. They finally arrived at the ferry and drove down the ramp.

As the ferry pulled out into the Sound of Iona for their brief voyage home, Lys glanced at Michael. Their eyes met briefly, and she knew they were both thinking the same thing. *This was too easy. Why didn't Kareina come after us?*

The seas were calm, and the crossing to Iona was without incident. As they exited the ferry on Iona, they all breathed a huge sigh of relief.

Chapter Thirty-Eight: Casey's Story

THE ISLAND OF IONA

Being late spring, both of the hotels on Iona were filled to capacity, so Lys and Catherine took Casey to Machair Cottage. After a hearty meal and shower, they provided her with a nightgown that was several sizes too large, and fixed her a makeshift bed in the guest lounge.

There had been a last minute cancelation at Mrs. Maclean's Bed and Breakfast, so Michael and Erin installed Jamie in the vacant room, but stayed with her through the night.

The next morning, Kathrine Campbell overslept and came out of her room to find Casey already awake, standing at the guest lounge window, mouth open. She was a pathetic sight, with frazzled red hair straggling halfway down her back, borrowed nightgown dragging the floor, and pale, emaciated arms clutching the window frame for support.

"I've never been any place like this before," she said in a hoarse whisper.

"The beach is pretty, isn't it?"

"I didn't mean the beach, I meant this whole place. As soon as we got off the ferry I felt it. I feel safe here. I've never felt safe before... anywhere."

She turned to Catherine and asked, "Can I stay here?"

"Don't you have a family, parents that are worried about you?"

"I don't have anyone," she replied with downcast eyes. "My mom was real sick most of the time I was growing up and finally died when I was ten. After that, my dad got drunk all the time and beat me. I finally couldn't take it anymore. Just before I turned 15 I ran away and never went back."

"Where did you go?" Catherine said, with genuine compassion.

"I lived on the streets mostly. I'm from Chicago, and a lot of kids live on the streets there. It's pretty rough. I got raped a few times and beat up plenty. Sometimes in the winter I'd sell myself to strangers for food or a place to crash. I hated the things the men would do to me, but it gets cold in Chicago, and it felt good to be warm.

"Then one night I was walking through an alley and two men grabbed me. I thought they were cops, but it was worse, they were Archons. They took me... down there."

"How long were you in Hades?"

"I don't know. Must have been six months, at least.

"The gatherers took me through a portal and sold me to the slavemaster. I was chained to a wall for two days till it was my turn at auction." Casey shuddered at the memory.

"Two Archons bought me and used me as a house slave when they weren't doing other things to me. But after a while they seemed to get tired of me, and started taking me to the arena.

"I'd never know when they would take me there, or what I'd done wrong. But it happened more and more. I was in terror all the time. When I woke up in the morning, I never knew if I'd be tortured that day. They evidently didn't think the first level was bad enough, so they started taking me to the second. The screams coming from down below let me know where I was headed. So I decided to run. I didn't care if they killed me. I had to get away."

She was silent for a long time, then looked up at Catherine. "But I feel safe here."

"You are safe, my child," Catherine said warmly. "This is the one place on earth where the Archons can never touch you again."

"You've been a victim of the Archons all your life, Casey. They've tortured you since you were a wee bairn. The Archons wanted to destroy everything good in your life. That's what evil does. Going to Hades just brought it all to a new level, and let you see what they were really like.

"But there's a Presence on this island that's so

strong that no Archons would ever dare to come here. In this place, the sadness of all your years can begin to evaporate."

Seeing tears welling in Casey's eyes, Catherine went to her and held her gently, caressing her hair. Casey melted into her arms, welcoming the security of her embrace.

Catherine Campbell had only recently been told she had the gift of *singer*, but in a sense she'd always known it. For most of her life she'd known that when she sang certain things, the atmosphere in the room shifted. People changed. The Presence came.

She had never had words for it, but she knew her songs had great power. Some of the most powerful were the ancient Gaelic lullabies her mother had sung to her when she was a child.

Perhaps the most powerful of all was one that translated into English as "deep peace." It was a simple song that had been passed on from mother to daughter over many generations, some say even from the time of Columba. The ancient Celts had understood many things about the forces of nature and the power of song.

She remembered a time, years ago, when she had been hunting on Mull with Malcolm and Angus. Angus had fallen from a cliff, broken his leg, and was in agony. Knowing they were miles from the nearest road, Malcolm headed off to get help while Catherine stayed with Angus. Not knowing what else to do, Catherine felt prompted to sing *Deep Peace.* She sang it over him for close to an hour, cradling his head in her lap. By the time she finished singing, his leg was healed.

As she held Casey in her arms, Catherine somehow knew that was the song this lost child needed at this moment.

Cradling Casey gently, Catherine whispered, "Let me sing over you a lullaby my mum used to sing to me when I was a wee bairn. It's an old Scottish blessing that calls on all the forces of creation to bring peace and wholeness to your life."

"I'd like that," Casey said faintly, relaxing still more and resting her head against Catherine's shoulder.

Holding Casey in her arms, Catherine began to sing softly,

"Peace! Deep Peace!"

Catherine repeated the phrase, then repeated it again, her lips forming the words gently as a mother might sing to a newborn infant. And as she did, a tangible sense of peace filled the room.

Catherine began the first verse.

"Deep peace, of the gentle rain to you;
Deep peace from the flowing air to you.
Deep peace from the quiet earth to you.
Deep peace of the ancient hills to you!
Deep peace, my child, deep peace!"

Catherine could feel Casey continuing to relax in her arms as she sang. She held her more closely and began to rock her gently. She repeated the chorus and repeated it again.

"Peace! Deep Peace!"

Sensing the Presence filling the room, she began the second verse.

> *"Deep peace of the silent night to you.*
> *Deep peace from the smiling stars to you.*
> *Deep peace of angels guarding you.*
> *Deep peace of the King of Peace to you.*
> *Deep peace, my child, deep peace!"*

Over and over again Catherine sang it, first in English, then in Gaelic, then in English again, the words flowing out in a haunting Scottish melody. As the song continued, Casey felt her fears begin to ease. The air in the room seemed to thicken. Casey began to breathe very deeply. It felt like some kind of energy was flowing into her body. Healing was taking place.

When the sense of the Presence finally lifted, Casey looked up at Catherine with tears trickling down her cheeks. "I never felt anything like that before." Looking into Catherine's eyes, she asked again, pleading, "Can I stay here?"

"My wee one, we dinna have much room here, but if you don't mind sleepin' in the guest lounge, we'd love to have you stay. In another month our new home on the other side of the island will be finished and there'll be plenty of room for all of us."

Just then the door opened, and Lys walked in, arms loaded down with packages.

"Where have you been?"

"Shopping! What else does a girl do when she escapes from Hell?

"I went in to the village to buy Casey some new clothing. They don't have much selection on the island, but we can go online later and order more things from Oban."

Walking over to Casey, Lys studied her a moment in mock seriousness, shook her head and said, "That oversize nightgown doesn't do a thing for you, and you are NEVER putting on that slave smock again. It's much too drafty for this climate!" She handed Casey the pile of packages with a smile. "See if these will fit."

Casey was speechless, but quickly recovered enough to begin ripping open the packages. As she pulled out each item and held it up for Catherine to see, she was speechless no more. It was like watching a little child opening presents on Christmas morning. Between the "oohs" and "ahs" and exclamations of "Thank you," Lys could hardly get a word in edgewise!

Finally, Casey went to Lys and embraced her, weeping tears of joy, then turned to Catherine and embraced her again. "Nobody ever did anything like this for me," she said. "Thank you both so much!"

"You are very welcome, Casey," Catherine said. " You've been cheated out of so much in life, but Lys and I talked late into the night last night. We and the rest of our friends here are going to make sure things are different for you from now on."

Lys looked at Casey for a long moment, then finally spoke, "How's this for a plan, Casey? Let's eat breakfast, then we can take your slave smock down to the beach and *burn* it! Later today we'll go online and buy you more clothing."

Chapter Thirty-Nine: Healing

THE ISLAND OF IONA

Michael and Erin stayed with Jamie through the night, taking turns sleeping on the overstuffed chair and ottoman by the window.

Jamie slept fitfully, tormented by nightmares.

Around 4 AM Jamie awoke, but remained silent, laying on her back staring blankly at the ceiling.

"Can I get you anything?" Erin asked, noticing she was awake. Jamie did not respond.

"Michael!" Erin whispered, and then more loudly, *"Michael!"* …trying to rouse him from his sleep.

Michael grunted, then sat up, rubbing the sleep from his eyes. "How's she doing?"

"Not much change. Can you fix her some tea? …with a spoonful of sugar, and just a little brandy."

"Be right back," Michael said, suppressing a yawn.

From the guest kitchen there came the clatter of cups, the sound of running water, and the hum of a microwave. Michael returned a few minutes later, bearing two cups.

"I made one for you too!"

"Thanks," Erin said, taking a quick sip of hers before tending to Jamie.

Stroking Jamie's head, she said, "We made some tea for you. Why don't you sit up and give it a try?"

Jamie seemed agreeable, so Erin helped her to a sitting position and arranged the pillows behind her back. Jamie still had not spoken.

Erin held the cup till she was sure Jamie could handle it. Jamie's hands were trembling, but received the cup gratefully and began slowly sipping its sweet contents.

Finishing the tea, she extended the empty cup to Erin.

"Would you like more?"

Jamie nodded.

"I'll make her a fresh cup," Michael said, "and there's a package of shortbread cookies on the counter. I'll bring some of those too."

They stayed up with Jamie for close to an hour. Jamie finished both cups of tea and nibbled one of the shortbread cookies, then seemed ready to sleep again. Erin rearranged the pillows, and Jamie turned over, assuming a fetal position, and was quickly asleep.

"She seems so weak and so frail. What happened to her?" Erin asked.

"She has quite literally been through hell." Michael said. "You wouldn't believe the things we saw there. And Jamie definitely got the worst of it. She's in pretty bad shape."

"What do you think is wrong with her?"

"When I first saw her, she had a number of shades attached, but they seem to have left of their own accord when she set foot on Iona.

"It's a given that she's suffering some kind of post-traumatic stress disorder.

"But I'm sure there are also physical issues. I don't think she'd eaten for days before we found her, and she's been locked in a cramped cage. On top of everything else, the level of stress she's been under can tear up your body in any number of ways."

"What do we need to do?"

"I think we need to get the whole synaxis together."

The twelve members of the Iona synaxis agreed to meet in the guest lounge of Mrs. Mclean's Bed and Breakfast at 7:00 that evening. Holmes and Piper arrived in Iona late in the afternoon and planned to join them.

By 6:45, Jamie was seated in an armchair that had been pulled into the middle of the room. Michael and Erin stood protectively beside her.

Catherine and Lys came in, followed by a steady stream of others.

When Eliel and Rand arrived, they went directly to Lys and Michael and embraced them, tears welling in their eyes. "We're so glad you're okay," Eliel said. "I didn't think there was any possible way you could even survive, but you did it. You saved your world!"

"We almost didn't survive," Lys responded, welcoming the embrace and shedding tears of her own. "Only Roger's sacrifice made that possible." Lys shuddered as visions of Hades flashed in her mind. Glancing from Eliel to Rand, she added, "You were right in everything you told us. It was more horrific than any nightmare. Thank you for warning us."

Holmes and Piper arrived. More synaxis members were crowding into the room.

Being a purpose-built bed and breakfast with six guest rooms, the guest lounge at Mrs. Mclean's was spacious, with three plush sofas and two rockers gathered around a fireplace with a beautiful hand-crafted oak mantle. Nevertheless, the group gathered this night stretched its limits, with every seat taken and much of the floor space crammed with bodies as well.

With five of the guest rooms rented out to synaxis members, and Jamie in the sixth, they had the place to themselves.

Jamie sat numbly. Physically, her condition remained unchanged. She was still uncommunicative.

Erin welcomed everyone, and described Jamie's condition. "We've seen some remarkable instances of healing when a whole synaxis comes together, but I don't know that we've ever dealt with anything as serious as this. Jamie has multiple physical issues, but after the torture she's been through there are also some psychological ones." Glancing at Holmes, she asked, "Do you have any idea how we should proceed?"

"I think I'd yield to Eliel on that."

All eyes turned to Eliel as she walked to stand in front of Jamie. She studied her for a moment, then placed her hands gently on Jamie's head. A hushed silence filled the room as they waited for Eliel to speak.

"Her physical injuries are not life-threatening," Eliel said at last, "but she's in psychological shock. I sense great fear. While she consciously knows she's among friends, there's a part of her that anticipates more torture at any moment. She's isolated herself, trying to cut off contact for self-protection.

"Piper, you have the strongest healing gift here. Come and place your hands on her head."

Piper did as Eliel requested. Standing behind Jamie, she lightly rested both hands on Jamie's head. The response was immediate. Jamie's whole body stiffened. The muscles in her arms began to twist and contort, as though snakes were battling beneath her skin. A look of terror came across her face. She was breathing rapidly, her heart pounding. She began to perspire profusely.

Piper looked at Eliel in alarm.

"It's okay. This is part of the healing."

After a few minutes, Jamie began quaking violently, and at last let out a tortured shriek that shook the room. She screamed until she was out of breath, then screamed again, a bloodcurdling cry. The screaming went went on and on, and the shaking intensified to the point that Piper could barely keep her hands fixed on Jamie's head.

Eliel motioned for the members of the synaxis to gather around Jamie. As they did, Jamie seemed to feel a sense of protection. The violent tremors eased, and the screaming was replaced by wracking sobs.

"Now, Lys and Catherine, step closer, and begin singing."

Lys and Catherine stood on either side of Jamie and opened their mouths to sing. It was a simple melody, one neither of them had ever heard, yet they sang in unison, unlearned words flowing out of their mouths. As they sang, the song shifted and became more complex. Lys carried the melody, while Catherine shifted to harmony. It was the most beautiful song Lys had ever heard, yet she didn't know one word before it came out of her mouth. All she could do was yield to the flow that rose from deep within her being.

As they sang, the atmosphere of the room changed. The air thickened, and the Presence came.

Lys had felt the Presence on the island many times, but this was different. More powerful. More intense.

The Presence filled the room. Several members of the synaxis dropped to the floor, overwhelmed. Others sat down voluntarily, unable to stand.

Still Lys and Catherine continued to sing. As they sang, Jamie's sobbing stopped, and a look of peace came over her face. Finally Jamie looked up at Lys and then to Catherine and smiled. Then she opened her mouth and began to sing also. Unlearned words flowed from deep within her, as the song rose to a crescendo in perfect three-part harmony. On and on it went. And then it was over.

All present stood or sat in stunned silence, unable to move.

Moments later, the Presence seemed to lift.

Lys, Catherine, and Jamie looked at each other in awe. None of them understood what had just happened.

Jamie spoke first. "Thank you," looking at Catherine, and then to Lys, tears again trickling down her cheeks. "Thank you! I don't know what just happened, but thank you. Ever since I left Hades, I felt like I was still locked in the cage and the torture could resume at any moment. I didn't know if I'd ever get out. But as you sang, you unlocked that cage and set me free."

"How are you feeling?" Eliel asked.

"Whole," Jamie said, smiling faintly, "And at peace.

"I still remember everything that happened in that horrible place, but its power over me is broken now. I know I'm safe. And the Archons will never again have the ability to control me."

She rose from the chair and embraced Lys and Catherine, then turned and held Piper tightly. And then all the members of the synaxis joined in.

Jamie glanced around the room, and suddenly looked troubled. "Where's Roger?"

"He's gone," Lys said. "He gave his life so we could escape. His last words were to tell you that he loved you. That you've always been the love of his life."

Jamie was silent for a moment, then nodded. "And he was always mine. I can't believe I've lost him a second time."

"He's not lost," Eliel interjected. "You will both see him again."

What do you mean? Lys asked

"There's still much you don't understand about the universe. Your brother died an innocent death, giving himself to save those he loved. There's no greater love than that. Because of that, Hades cannot hold him."

Seeing the look of confusion on their faces, Eliel added, "Trust me. You will see him again." With that, she turned, and was gone.

Chapter Forty: Resolution

THE ISLAND OF IONA

The synaxis members stayed up most of the night, talking and sharing. Lys, Michael, and Jamie all took turns relating their experiences in Hades.

As their gathering broke up, Lys and Jamie walked out to the beach. There was a full moon, and the waters of the Sound of Iona were peaceful.

At first they didn't say much. They just stood together for a long time, looking out across the water to the distant mountains of Mull. Their shared experience in Hades had created a bond between them that few others could understand.

Both were thinking of Roger, and wondering what Eliel's cryptic words had meant. Finally, Jamie asked, "Did you understand what Eliel said about seeing Roger again?"

"I don't have a clue what she meant," Lys smiled wistfully, "But when she said it, something inside me sensed it was true."

"But didn't you say you saw him incinerated?"

"That is what I saw... or at least what I think I

saw," Lys replied, "but being around the Irin, I've learned that there are always possibilities beyond anything we can imagine. I don't know what Eliel meant, but I do know Eliel and I trust her implicitly. She wouldn't have said it if it weren't true. I don't know where or how or when, but I am certain we will see Roger again."

The first light of dawn was already painting the eastern sky when they returned to the house.

"Why don't you stay here for what's left of the night instead of making the trek across the island," Jamie said. "There's plenty of room to stretch out on a couch in the guest lounge."

"I think I might just take you up on that." Lys smiled. "I'm exhausted. Catherine went back hours ago to be with Casey."

Jamie slept until well past noon the next day, and woke up in turmoil. Her body was again convulsed with agonized sobs. She kept screaming one word over and over again, "No! ... *No!... NO!"*

Her tortured cries rose to a shriek, then faded to a lingering moan; then she screamed again, even louder.

Lys, Erin, and Michael came rushing in, to find Jamie sitting up in bed, a look of terror on her face. Erin sat down beside her and held her, comforting her.

"Were you dreaming of the tortures again?"

"No," Jamie sobbed, "It wasn't the torture. It's what I *did!"*

"What do you mean?"

"I've been sorting through the memories of my last hours in the cage. Toward the end I was so numb, barely conscious. Since the rescue, my mind has blanked those last hours out. I haven't been able to remember a thing.

"But it all just came back to me in a dream. I remember it now. In the last torture, they were driving nails into my flesh and the pain was so bad, I just couldn't take it anymore.

"Erin, I hope this was just a nightmare, but I think I gave them the codes."

There was a long moment of silence as the weight of Jamie's words sank in.

"If that's true, then it's all been for nothing!" Lys muttered hopelessly. "We've lost."

"It would certainly explain the ease of our escape," Michael commented. "Kareina's minions weren't on our tail because she'd already gotten what she wanted."

"I pray it's not true," Jamie said, "but I've got to know for sure, and there's only one way to find out. Erin, can I use your phone to call Colorado?"

Erin retrieved her phone, turned it on, and rested her index finger lightly on the "on" button to unlock it. She handed the phone to Jamie and stood back to allow her to make the call.

Jamie quickly tapped in Carrington's private number.

Alexander Carrington had been up since four that morning.

This would be an historic day. After a long and frustrating delay, the plan was finally coming together. Following a brief consultation with Grat, he made his way to his office.

He'd only been at his desk a few minutes when his phone rang.

He answered it on the first ring. "Yes."

A familiar voice spat his name, "Carrington?"

Instantly alert, his lips drew taut in a satisfied smile. "Well Jamie, it's so good to hear your voice. Kareina stopped by yesterday and told me all the fun you two had together last week. Did you enjoy your little sojourn in Hell?"

"You can go to Hell, you bastard!" Jamie shot back, then added, "I just need to know one thing. Did Kareina bring you the codes?"

"That is confirmed," Carrington said, gloating. "I have the full list on my desk right now. In fact, Grat just left from helipad two. He's gone to New Mexico to pick up the next nuke. Kareina has chosen Boston as the next city to be hit. It should paralyze all of New England.

"Our little mushroom should sprout just east of Boston Common mid-morning tomorrow. I've had cameras placed around the city so we'll have a front row seat. Pity you won't be here to enjoy the show."

He paused a moment, imagining Jamie's frustration, then continued. "You can't stop us now,

Jamie. With the 19 bombs in that bunker, Kareina and I will remake the world." He mashed the lock button to end the call.

About an hour later, Carrington got a call from Grat. He sounded frantic. "It's *gone,* sir! The New Mexico facility... it's gone! Wiped off the map! I was still 50 miles out when I saw the mushroom cloud."

As Jamie entered the final numbers of the seventeen digit detonation code, she imagined the look on Carrington's face when he got the news.

The day Jamie discovered the 19 nukes in the back room of the New Mexico facility; she immediately formulated a plan to stop him. Her plan of choice was to destroy the detonation codes, rendering the bombs useless. But as her dad used to say, "Always have a backup."

Jamie's contingency plan for a worst-case scenario where Carrington got the detonation codes had required some preparation, but it had not been hard. Before leaving the New Mexico facility, she wired the arming device of the sixteenth canister into the Carrington network. Once she deciphered the Russian labels on the wiring harness, it had taken only a few minutes. She'd run the connecting wires along the back of the canisters, and in the poorly lit vault they were virtually undetectable.

Completing that task, she knew there was still one more thing she had to do. Thinking of Becky, she'd walked purposefully to the end of the row and opened the last canister. Using a pocket screwdriver, she quickly unfastened the nuclear device from its stainless steel shell.

Carrington was still seething with rage when his phone rang again. As he answered, he was distracted by a sound. A loud hollow "clunk" resounded from somewhere overhead, followed by a prolonged rumble. The room was getting darker. The 4-inch thick steel blast shutters were sliding into place over the windows of Carrington's office. He jammed his finger down on the cancel key, but all controls had gone dead.

Jamie's voice was on the phone. "Carrington, I wanted you to know that I destroyed the New Mexico facility."

She paused to let it sink in, then continued, "But you were wrong about it holding 19 bombs. There were only 18. I brought one of the nukes back to Raven's Nest.

"It's hidden in the deepest access tunnel and wired into the network. I'm tapping the detonation code into the computer as I speak." She paused a moment, tapping in sixteen numbers, then continued, "I wanted you to know that before you die, you bastard."

She waited another moment, then added, "This is for Becky!"

Jamie tapped the last number into the keypad.

Everyone in Boulder Colorado felt the earthquake

and saw the huge cloud of dust rising over one of the mountains south of the city. With the suitcase nuke planted in the deepest access tunnel and shielded by tons of granite, the blast was 98% contained. Little radiation escaped.

But everything inside the steel blast doors of Raven's Nest was instantly incinerated, including Carrington.

Chapter Forty-One: Columba's Prophecy

THE ISLAND OF IONA, PRESENT DAY

Jamie, Lys, Erin, and Eliel met with Holmes and Piper over breakfast at the St. Columba Hotel the next morning.

"So you planned from the beginning to blow the New Mexico facility if Carrington got the codes?" Erin asked.

"I'd hoped I wouldn't have to do it. It was my desperate, last-ditch, eleventh-hour, back-up plan if all else failed." Jamie replied. "With the nukes tied into the computer network, I thought I had everything covered, but there was a catch. I hadn't foreseen the fact that I'd be in Hades when Kariena got the codes. Being in another universe, I had no computer access. I couldn't detonate the bomb from there. Of course, I also hadn't foreseen that I would be reduced to a human vegetable, virtually unable to function!"

"So if you hadn't made it out of Hades when you did, Carrington's plan would have worked?" Lys asked.

"That's right," Jamie replied. "The destruction of our world would have begun this morning."

"So by sacrificing his life, Roger really did save the world," Lys muttered.

"That is often the price for overcoming evil," Eliel said.

"Then is it really over?" Jamie asked. "The Archons are finally defeated?"

"This has been a major victory," Eliel said, "but the war is not yet over. The Archons spent close to seventy years laying the groundwork for this plot, and they're not going to be happy that it failed.

"But you aren't the only one with a backup plan. I'm sure the Archons already have another plan in motion. That's why we must continue to plant synaxis groups in every nation on earth."

Piper glanced at Jamie, "What are you going to do now?"

Jamie answered without hesitation. "I've been thinking about that a lot. I'm a fair chopper pilot, and I'm great with computers, but I have no family, no job, no home, nothing to go back to.

"If it's true that the Archons are not yet defeated, there's really only one thing I want to do. I want to join you… if you'll have me."

She looked across the table, at Holmes, Piper and Eliel, then continued with a rising intensity in her voice. "I want to join the synaxis. I'll do anything you want and go anywhere you ask. I want to see the Archons driven out of our world forever."

Lys rested her hand reassuringly on Jamie's

shoulder.

"That's how we all feel," Holmes answered, "and we're happy to have you join us."

"I think for the next few months, at least, you should stay here on Iona." Eliel added. "There'll be plenty of room in Iona House, and I believe there is still more healing to be done."

"I'd like that," Jamie smiled.

As they finished their meal, Patrick came running in. "Erin, come quickly! We've found something at the excavation site."

"What is it?" Erin asked as they all rose from the table.

"We've been excavating for the foundation of the new addition when we found what seems to be a small stone casket or vault. It was buried about three feet down, so it's been there a long time. It has an inscription on the lid. I think it may be some form of ancient Gaelic."

"I'll get Michael and meet you there," Erin responded. "If anyone on the island can read it, it will be Michael."

Fifteen minutes later they all arrived at the excavation site.

The casket appeared to be carved from native stone, and was still in its place at the bottom of the trench, half-buried in the damp, hard-packed soil. The lid was a stone slab, two feet by three, and about two inches thick. It was sealed in place with black pitch. Patrick's workmen had carefully brushed the top of the lid free of dirt and debris, revealing an inscription that was clearly visible.

Michael eased himself into the trench, then crouched down, and traced the letters of the inscription with his index finger as he read. Then looked up.

"Are you sure this was not put here recently, maybe within the last year?"

"There's no way it could be recent. As I told the others, it was buried three feet down, and the soil showed no sign of being disturbed. Why do you ask?"

"Well, the writing is in ancient Gaelic, but the inscription is very odd."

"How's that?"

"It simply says, 'The Word of Columba for the Iona Synaxis.'"

"Do we need to report this to the National Trust for Scotland?" Lys asked. "I mean, this could be a major archeological find."

"Normally, I would say yes," Michael replied, "but in this case I would not. This appears to be a personal message addressed to us."

They all looked to Eliel who was watching the events with uncharacteristic silence.

"Do you know anything about this?"

"Let's just say that you were right in your assumption. This is a personal message for you, left by Columba himself. No one else need read it."

After more discussion, they decided to leave the casket where it lay, but to pry the lid open to expose the contents.

Michael took pictures of the casket from many angles, then they brought in tools and carefully broke the seal. With the seal broken, the lid lifted easily.

Inside the casket, half submerged in dark brackish water, was what appeared to be a block of black stone.

Carefully lifting the object from the casket, the workman carried it to the nearly completed Iona House and rested it gently on the floor of what would soon be the main living area.

The group crowded around as Michael performed his examination. Michael began by turning the object over, carefully examining its smooth surface for any trace of a further inscription or message, but found none. What he did find surprised him.

"This isn't a block of stone at all. It's a heavy object coated with a layer of black pitch. Pitch was often used in the ancient world as a water seal, to protect objects from the elements."

After taking more photographs of the object, he began chipping away the thin layer of pitch. The pitch was brittle with age and easier to remove than expected.

Inside, wrapped in thick layers of linen cloth, were a stack of thin gold plates, inscribed with a message from Columba in ancient Gaelic.

Michael arranged the tablets in order on the floor before him, and glanced up at Eliel, who nodded for him to proceed.

Adjusting his glasses, Michael examined the inscription carefully for several minutes without saying a word, gently tracing each line of symbols with his index finger.

Finally a hush fell over the room as Michael began to read.

"This day is the last day of my present life, and on it I rest after the fatigues of my labor. This night at midnight, I shall go the way of my fathers. For the High King himself has invited me, and in the middle of this night shall I depart, for so it has been revealed to me.

"Soon I will be in Hi-Ouranos, the highest heaven. I will see with my own eyes the twenty-four elders, myriads of angels, the High King himself, and all of those who have gone before me.

"But before I depart, I must leave this message for those who will come after.

"Iona of my heart, Iona of my love, I know that in days to come, this monastery will be destroyed and the portal allowed to close. The sound of the singers will be replaced by the lowing of cattle and the bleating of sheep. But ere the world come to an end, Iona shall again be as it was.

"A synaxis will form again and the portal will be re-opened, but it will be in a perilous time. I have been shown it in a vision.

"Men and women will fly in the air without wings.

"Every race of mankind will become more wicked and all classes will be addicted to robbery.

"Falsehood and deceit will prevail.

"Great carnage shall be made, justice shall be outraged, multitudinous evils and great violence shall prevail.

"Severe weather and famine shall come. People oppressed for want of food, shall pine to death. Dreadful storms shall afflict them. Numberless diseases shall then prevail and remedies will fail.

"Many will regret the days they have lived to see.

"Then a great event shall happen. Stars will fall from the sky and a deluge shall drown the nations. A more sorrowful event could not possibly happen. The sea at one tide, shall rise up and cover Ireland and the green-headed Islay. But Columba's Isle shall rise above the flood.

"To you who find this, I give this word. When you see these events draw near, know that you have entered the time for the restoration of all things. For your world to survive, the great

portal in the south must again be opened.

"But first must come the restoration. These events may bring total destruction, but they also can bring the restoration of all that was lost. To survive this time the chosen one must find a way to appear before the High King.

"When the time of crisis comes, do not hesitate. You must go the High King himself. Only in Hi-Ouranos will the answer be found."

EPILOGUE

The Return

THE ISLAND OF IONA,
TWO MONTHS LATER

Though there was no one present to see it, the massive stone slabs atop *Cnoc nan Carnan* began to vibrate, almost imperceptibly at first, but gradually increasing in intensity until the whole hill seemed to tremble.

Then the hill started to glow. The green heather and the dark earth below turned transparent. The ground became as clear as glass.

Accompanied by a sound like the rumble of distant thunder, a shaft of light shot skyward—a pillar of white light that pierced the clouds overhead. And a wormhole formed—a glowing tunnel that penetrated into the depths of the sky, beyond Basilea, beyond even Taverea, it extended all the way to Hi-Ouranos, the highest of all realms.

Answering the light from the earth came a light from the heavens. Through the wormhole, a shaft of brilliant light flooded the island of Iona. The light was more than white. It was a shimmering rainbow of blinding radiance, brighter than the brightest day.

When the light finally faded, a lone figure was left standing between the stone slabs of *Cnoc nan Carnan.*

They'd been living in Iona House for three weeks.

The week after they moved in, Patrick and Lys announced their engagement, which was a surprise to no one. They'd decided to hold their wedding on Iona. Erin was flying both sets of parents to Scotland in August for the ceremony, and they'd be flying in style in the Fletcher jet.

Casey had blossomed during her weeks on Iona. No longer the cringing and malnourished waif, she looked healthy and was positively effervescent.

Casey and Catherine had bonded from the start. Catherine was teaching her to hunt, as well as instructing her in the culinary arts. Catherine was also looking into some homeschool curriculums to bring Casey up to speed academically.

Casey's legal status was still a little dicey. She'd lived on the streets of Chicago since she was 14 and had no identification of any kind. She now found herself living in a foreign country without a passport. Erin's lawyers had tracked down Casey's birth records and pulled some strings to get her a temporary ID but were still sorting out the details.

The day they moved into Iona House, Casey

celebrated her seventeenth birthday, which she was delighted to learn, meant she could legally drink wine in Scotland when Catherine and Lys took her out for a celebration dinner that evening.

Tonight had been Casey's culinary debut, and she had thoroughly triumphed. Catherine had taken her hunting the previous week and she'd bagged her first deer. With Catherine's help, she'd prepared Catherine's "special recipe" spicy venison stew for the whole synaxis.

As always, everyone in the synaxis loved the dish, and showered Casey with effusive compliments. Casey's self-esteem was flying high.

Everyone had eaten 'till they could eat no more, then retreated to the living area and spent close to an hour in relaxed conversation, sipping their favorite wines. Everyone seemed to be enjoying the evening except Jamie. Jamie sat in silence, feeling like an intruder at someone else's party. She was still struggling to process Roger's death.

Noticing that Erin's glass was empty, Michael fetched two wine bottles from the kitchen and drained the last of the Sangiovese into her glass before refilling his with a French Syrah. Seeing that the Syrah bottle was still half-full, Lys extended her glass to Michael, who promptly poured a generous portion.

"I never thought I'd want to leave Machair Cottage," Lys said thoughtfully, swirling the wine in her glass, then taking a sip, "but living here in Iona House with all of you is better than anything I could have ever imagined."

Suddenly, there was a knock on the door.

"I'll get it," Jamie said.

Jamie walked slowly to the door, turned the knob and gave a gentle tug.

As the door swung open, Jamie Thatcher's eyes widened. For a full minute she stood frozen, unmoving, in total silence. Jamie couldn't comprehend what she was seeing, and had no idea how to respond. Slowly her body began to tremble. Her mouth dropped open. Tears were welling in her eyes. Her mouth struggled to speak one word—a hoarse whisper, barely audible... *"Roger?"*

The man standing in the open doorway smiled warmly, "Hi, Thatcher."

Watch for the third and final book of the Synaxis Chronicles.

IONA RISING!

NOTES

"Deep Peace" really is an ancient Gaelic lullaby, and most of "Columba's Prophecy" is taken from actual prophecies recorded by Columba in the sixth century.

The incident of the man injured in a motorcycle accident, (described by Roger in chapter nine) actually happened, though it took place in a city near Dallas rather than Boston. The author knew the people involved, and was present when it happened.

ABOUT THE AUTHOR

Robert David MacNeil is an author, wine-lover, and investigator of things supernatural. Over the last twenty years he's traveled to more than 31 nations researching, writing, and teaching on angels, demons, and supernatural encounters. His travels have taken him from the steppes of Mongolia to the jungles of Thailand, and from the Eskimo villages of Northwest Alaska to *le fin del mundo*, the "end of the world," at the tip of South America.

Long a fan of sci-fi and suspense thrillers, Robert also has a love for history–especially ancient Greece, Rome and medieval Europe. He's particularly fascinated with Patrick, Columba, and the ancient Celts of Ireland and Scotland. The Celtic monks had a special relationship with the angels. They also loved beer and invented whiskey. The Irish really did save civilization!

Robert and his wife, Linda, live near Dallas, Texas. He has authored seven non-fiction books under a different pen-name. Robert's novels include Iona Portal and Iona Stronghold. He is currently working on the third novel in the Synaxis Chronicles trilogy, IONA RISING.

You can visit Robert on the web at **ionaportal.com**

Follow him on Twitter at **@RDavidMacNeil**

Or email him at **Robertdavidmacneil@gmail.com**

PLEASE HELP SPREAD THE WORD

If you've enjoyed reading IONA STRONGHOLD, please tell please your friends. Independently published books depend on "word of mouth" publicity.

If you'd like to help even more, you can drop by Amazon.com and leave a nice review!

Made in the USA
Middletown, DE
20 August 2020